EVEN IF I FALL

Books by Abigail Johnson

If I Fix You
The First to Know
Even If I Fall

EVEN IF I FALL

WITHDRAWN

ABIGAIL JOHNSON

ink
yard
press

Recycling programs
for this product may
not exist in your area.

ISBN-13: 978-1-335-54155-0

Even If I Fall

This edition published by arrangement with Harlequin Books S.A.

For questions and comments about the quality of this book, please contact us
at CustomerService@Harlequin.com.

InkyardPress.com

Printed in U.S.A.

To Sam Johnson, the best big brother I could ever ask for.

CHAPTER 1

The car jolts back and forth, rocking Maggie and me along with it before stalling. Again. My nostrils flare and I dig my baby blue–painted nails into the steering wheel. Calm as you please, I pull the keys from the ignition, roll down the window and hurl them into the field of wild grass growing along the side of Boyer Road, less than a stone's throw from the base of my long dirt driveway.

"Feel better?" Maggie's mirrored sunglasses show me that the question is rhetorical. My left eye is twitching and the dimple in my chin has never been more prominent. I try to relax my jaw as I tuck the dark brown strands of my not-quite-shoulder-length hair behind my ears, but my reflection doesn't change much. With the window open and the A/C off, there is no ignoring the sauna-like June heat rolling in as the sun reaches the height of the day. It's the kind of hot and muggy that wrings every drop of moisture—and optimism—from my body, leaving me limp and heavy in the steamy afternoon air.

"This is an evil car and it hates me."

"No, not Daphne." My friend and self-appointed driving instructor gives the dash a little pat.

"Why did I give her such a cute name?" I eye Daphne, aka the navy Camaro from hell. I've owned my first car for three days and have barely driven her as many miles. "I should start calling her Jezebel."

"Call her whatever you like but you still have to learn to drive stick."

"I'm trying." I lean forward to yell directly into the air vent. "I will be so good to you if you just stop stalling every two seconds!"

"You're lifting your foot off the clutch too soon."

"I know." I collapse back against my seat.

"So stop it."

I can hear the grin in Maggie's voice before I turn my head to look at her. Yeah, she's enjoying this. "You said learning to drive stick would be fun, that I'd have it down in an hour. We've been at this all morning and I'm pretty sure I'm getting worse."

"You're not going to get any better without the keys, Brooke."

With a sigh, I push open my door and cross the single lane dirt road. The thigh-high grass skims the hem of my faded blue sundress as I search the open field. Fortunately, the keys have a ridiculously large fuzzy keychain in the shape of an ice skate on them—my new-car present from Maggie—so they aren't hard to find.

"Who has a stupid keychain now?"

Turning back, I see she's crawled over the console and is resting her forearms on the driver's side open window. "I never said stupid, I said interesting."

Maggie bursts out laughing. "You're always so polite. Is that a West Texas thing or a Covington thing?"

"Worried it's catching?" I ask with a faux scowl.

Maggie pulls the collar of her sleeveless watermelon-print shirt up to her chin and hunches her shoulders. "It better not be. If I start calling anybody ma'am, I'm moving back to LA."

"It's not my home or my family. I just don't see the sense in being rude for no reason." I let my gaze travel back to Daphne. "But that's with people, not cars." A smile alights on my face. "Hey, you think there's something wrong with her and not me?"

Maggie raises an eyebrow—well, I think she raises an eyebrow. Her aviators cover half her rather small face, so it's hard to tell. She plucks the keys from my hand while fully moving into the driver's seat. A second later I'm left choking on a dust cloud as she speeds a few hundred yards down the dirt road, executes an action-movie-worthy U-turn, and drives back. She's grinning as she slows next to me.

"Guess it's not the car."

"Not fair. Didn't you tell me your dad is a professional stunt driver?"

"Professional stunt driver, professional cheater and liar." She lifts one hand then the other as though she's weighing the two options. "He is a man of many talents."

"Sorry," I say. I feel like I've known Maggie my whole

life instead of just a couple weeks, so I keep forgetting that there's still a lot she hasn't shared with me.

Maggie dismisses my apology with a wave of her hand then lifts her sunglasses into her pink-tinted hair, which exactly matches the double-winged liner on her eyes. She's definitely raising her eyebrows now. "If we're talking about fair, ask me how I feel watching you do quintuple silk-cow jumps around me when I can barely skate backward."

"*Salchow* jumps, and they were only doubles. Plus, you're getting so much better."

"Says the girl my mom literally offered to pay to be my friend."

"She offered to pay me for ice-skating lessons." While I needed the money—we live on the outskirts of town and gas to and from anywhere isn't cheap—it turned out what I really needed was someone whose eyes wouldn't shade with pity or scorn whenever they looked at me. "Besides, I think we can both agree you're the one paying now." I eye the hand rubbing her neck. I've been jerking us around for hours trying to tame Daphne.

Maggie tries not to smile. "You know my mom would have paid you twice what she offered. She's convinced I'm turning into some kind of recluse who only talks to the camera when I'm filming YouTube tutorials. She only really likes the Korean beauty videos I make, but I'm half American too. Anyway, I'm just glad the first person I met turned out to be as amazing off the ice as she is on it. One less thing she can nag me about, right?"

"Yeah," I say, ignoring the queasy flip in my stomach

as she opens the door for me and slides back into the passenger seat.

"All right, enough stalling." She mimes a rim shot to go along with her pun. "Everybody does it when learning to drive stick. Suck it up and get back in the car."

I try, I really do, but before my butt even hits the seat, I'm grabbing the gearshift like it's a bull ready to buck me off. Not that I've ever ridden a bull—we may live in cattle country but the empty acres around my family's farmhouse are purely ornamental—but the idea is starting to look a lot less daunting in comparison.

"Do you remember the most important rule of driving stick?"

I nod, buckling my seat belt. "Don't confuse the clutch for the brake pedal."

"No—cars can sense fear."

I slide my gaze toward my friend and watch her grin at me.

"Are you thinking about punching me in the boob?"

She knows I would never admit to something like that out loud, but the reluctant smile inching onto my face gives me away.

"Joke's on you." Grinning wider, Maggie twists to face me and pushes her chest out. "Flat as a board, baby. Who's laughing now, besides every boy ever?"

Both of us, apparently. It takes way too long for my composure to return enough to start the car again. I don't even mind that it stalls the first time. Or the second. I manage not to stall on my third try, but Daphne is jerking us around so much that it's a hollow victory.

You can drive from one end of town to the other in ten minutes, but I'm not ready to face even those few stoplights and intersections, so we stick to the back roads on the outskirts of town near my house, where traffic is practically nonexistent. The only other vehicle we've encountered is a truck pulled onto the side of Pecan Road, its driver nowhere to be seen. Not that I'm paying much attention to anything but the gearshift growing sweaty in my palm and the stop sign looming ahead. I could roll through it, except I know I won't. So I downshift and come to a full and legal stop. Beside me, Maggie says nothing. I know what to do; it's the execution that keeps tripping me up. I still don't understand how I can be so good with my feet in one area and so awful in another.

Slowly...slowly... I lift my left foot off the clutch as I press down on the gas with my right. I'm not even breathing at this point. Daphne starts to rock a little, but I give her more gas until... Air escapes me in a laugh. "I did it!" More of the happy sound bubbles up inside me as we roll smoothly forward. I didn't know it was possible to be this happy off the ice.

Maggie is hooting beside me, which only makes me laugh harder as I slow to make a turn toward town, knowing I won't stall.

And then I see him walking along the side of the road. He turns toward the car as we get close and our eyes lock. My laughter dies a second before Daphne's. An invisible fist slams into my stomach, and the last of my laughter chokes out. Guilt slithers up my legs and torso, tethering me to my seat so that I can't look away from him.

"No worries," Maggie says, still bouncing her shoulders in celebration. "Start her up again and…" She leans forward just as Heath Gaines's eyes narrow at me before he turns away. "More of that famous Southern charm I've seen so much of since moving here. And my mom wonders why I'm happier online. Seriously, who even is that?"

Considering Maggie and her mom just moved to Telford, she might be the only person in our entire town who'd have to ask that question, which is one of the many reasons I don't tell her the truth. If I did, I'd have to tell her about Jason. She knows I have an older brother, but to hear my mom talk about him, you'd think he was away at college instead of where he really is. I hate lying to Maggie, even indirectly, but I'd hate even more for the truth to drive her away.

"No one I know." That isn't technically a lie, but it's so far from the truth that I can't look at Maggie when I say it. I add something about not wanting to push my newfound understanding with Daphne too far in one day, and since I still need to go by the rink to pick up my paycheck, we end up at her house just as thick gray clouds start rolling across the sky.

"Yuck," Maggie says, looking at the approaching storm. "That's gonna hit before you can get home. Why don't I come and drive you home afterward, in case it gets ugly?" She brightens. "Then I can drive the Zamboni while you grab your check."

I nod, looking at the clouds with my own frown and absently saying, "Sure, if you want me to lose my job."

Maggie makes a show of wrestling with indecision before sighing in defeat. Normally, I'd laugh at her, but I'm still looking at the sky and the last thing I want to do is laugh. "I'll be fine. Besides, your mom would have to pick you up after."

Maggie's scowl is fierce but fleeting as she gets out. "Promise me you won't total Daphne by backing into another car. Trust me when I tell you how demoralizing it is to rely on your mom for rides when you're seventeen."

"I'll be fine," I repeat. My hands tightening on the steering wheel hides a tremor that has nothing to do with driving, but Maggie doesn't know that.

"Hey." Maggie's put-upon tone is gone.

I bring my gaze to hers.

"You drove Daphne, stop and start, all of it, the whole way here without stalling once. This is my impressed face."

My smile probably doesn't touch my eyes. "I learned from the best."

She grins. "Shut up, baby, I know it. And besides, that's my line." With one last pat of Daphne's hood, she heads inside.

I'm halfway to the rink when the first lightning bolt forks in the distance, constricting the band of guilt in my chest. I look in my rearview mirror. In my mind, I see the familiar brick red truck on the side of the road—a truck I can't believe I drove past without cold recognition icing over me—and the guy in a sweat-drenched white T-shirt having to walk miles back to town during a thunderstorm.

And I was laughing when he saw me.

Daphne doesn't stall once as I turn around.

CHAPTER 2

I backtrack along the same road Maggie and I took into town, and all too soon a form takes shape ahead of me. It's been nearly a year since I saw him, and yet I remember his features perfectly—the gray eyes, the strong jaw, the too-long brown hair only a few shades darker than his tanned skin.

We went to the same high school for two years, a high school whose entire student population topped out at about four hundred people. Even though I was a still a junior when he graduated this past year and I must have seen him more times than I can count, I can't recall exchanging a single word with him. I don't know what he looks like smiling with a group of friends, any more than he does me. I know him only as looking tense and stoic through my silent tears.

The haunting memory threatens to overtake me as the thunder continues to roll, loud and angry around me—

through me. The air is growing heavier with the promised deluge as I slow Daphne while my pulse does the opposite.

He knows my car this time, and my gaze is so trained on him that I see the exact moment recognition hits him. *Hits* is the right word. He flinches back even before he sees my face. I pull over into the opposite lane beside him. We're closer this time when I stop just feet away, inches really. His eyes, even narrowed, are as startling now as they were that last day in court. Hard. Cold. Full of something I didn't want to look at then any more than I do now.

I swallow. "Do you need a ride?"

A bead of sweat forms and trickles down my temple, and I feel his gaze trace it. Despite the storm clouds unfurling overhead, there's no breeze to cut through the thick, humid heat. He's still staring at me, silent, when the sky cracks open.

The rain pours down in fat, stinging drops, slapping against Daphne's hood like bullets. In seconds, he's soaked through. In minutes there'll be water streaming along both sides of the road. Within an hour, whole stretches will be submerged if the rain holds. The crack of lightning bursting brilliantly in the sky promises at least that long.

"It's just a ride," I say, but it's not. Beyond the fact that he's looking at me as though I'm roadkill, my family would be horrified that I'm asking, and I can't even imagine what his family would think of us riding in a car together. And suddenly I'm not sure I want him to accept. We're inches away from each other, and I don't know what his voice sounds like. I don't think I've ever heard it, never even officially met him.

"You want me to get in your car?" he yells over the din of rain, like I'm asking him to eat the roadkill in addition to looking at it. "Why?"

I draw back farther against my seat, wishing I could crawl behind it and never see anyone look at me this way again, however much I understand it. There's so much I can't say to him, so much I don't know how to say to him, so I say the simplest and most honest thing I can. "I don't want you to have to walk in the rain."

There's a flash, quick as the lightning, where the wariness in his eyes changes to something that causes my breath to catch in my throat. He gazes at me a moment longer, then he's moving, crossing around the front of the car. There's no point in dashing anymore—he's as wet as he'll ever be. I don't have a towel or anything to protect my seat, and I don't care. He lets himself in through the passenger door and closes it with enough force that I don't even try to hide my flinch. It's not for the door though.

Heath Gaines is in my car.

I start driving again, smooth, no stalling. Once I learn something, I never forget it.

"You can drop me at the garage on Main." His voice is low, and I hear the drawl that the rain muted before, the one that says we've both lived in Texas our whole lives. I tell myself that the raspy quality is from disuse rather than distaste at having to talk to me, but he's not looking at me, and I can see him only from the corner of my eye. "They're used to towing Cal's truck."

"I remember it breaking down a lot," I say before I can think better of it. And then Heath is looking at nothing but me. My guilt is a straitjacket strapped tight. That's not new—but the pain that twists deep at my tiny admission is.

If I didn't know Heath, I knew his older brother even less. Cal and Jason had been wary rivals in high school and didn't become friends until they were assigned as room-mates at the University of Texas their freshman year. They made the six-hour road trip home from Austin together a few times along with Jason's girlfriend. Calvin seemed nice the few times I met him. Always called my mom *ma'am* and my dad *sir.* Made a fuss over my little sister Laura's cocka-tiel and ensured her eternal devotion, beyond that which he inherently had as Jason's friend. He even let me drive his truck the day I got my driver's permit, when Jason had been reluctant to hand over his keys. Calvin had told me not to worry about anything, that I could drive into a tree if I wanted and the damage would just add character to an already beat-to-hell truck. He let me drive all the way to the ice rink before my shift so that I could get in some skating time.

I didn't hit any trees, then or now.

Omitting any mention of Jason, I tell Heath the story. The more I talk, the more my eyes begin to prick, until the road ahead of me blurs despite the rapidly moving wind-shield wipers. I come to a stop sign with no other cars in sight. The garage is just ahead. Once Heath gets out, I might never see him again. I move through the inter-section and into the parking lot. With tear-filled eyes, I turn to him. "I'm so, so sorry about your brother." It's the first time I've said that, aloud or to myself. Everything that happened to Calvin is connected to Jason, and until that moment, that memory, I hadn't known I could feel for one without taking away from the other. I hadn't let myself try.

Heath's gaze is slow to meet mine, and when it does, I see pain so staggering that a tear spills free from my eye. I leave it.

He turns away from me and looks out the windshield before lowering his head and locking his jaw. I resist another urge to press back against my door. Not because I'm physically afraid of Heath, but because I am afraid of what he might say and how his words could shred me if he wants them to.

He glances back at me, just his head turning. The pain and everything else is gone, shuttered behind an expression as flat and impenetrable as mine must be naked and raw. "Thanks for the ride."

Then he opens his door and steps into the rain.

CHAPTER 3

I drive to Polar Ice Rink on autopilot. Jeff, my manager, gives me a funny look when he sees me coming through the door.

"You're not scheduled today," he says, accusation causing his still-boyish voice to rise a few octaves even though his thinning red hair and pallid lined face put him somewhere in his early forties.

The handful of people waiting in line to buy wristbands turn to look at me too. I keep my head down pretty much everywhere but especially at work, where I'm forced to wear a nametag. Not everyone recognizes me by sight anymore, but add a name to a vaguely familiar face and whispers start tearing through the rink faster than a brush fire. Small towns—and with a population of less than ten thousand, Telford, Texas, definitely qualifies—are wonderful, until they aren't. I hold my breath as so many gazes settle

on me, but today people only frown at my seemingly in-
nocuous appearance and dismiss me.

"I know," I say, exhaling and raising my skates for Jeff to
see. The funny look doesn't vanish. And calling it *funny* is
easier than calling it what it really is. "I'm just here to pick
up my check and skate a little." He can't stop me, much
as he'd clearly like to. I do my job and I do it well—the
spotless floor and the smooth-as-glass ice I left the night
before are proof of that. Normally, I'm here early or late,
a schedule that everyone prefers, but as it is for all employees, the ice is always open to me.

I move through the door before he can make another
pitch for directly depositing my checks so that I come in
less often—as if I would. I take every excuse I can to be
on the ice, despite what it costs me personally. I can't help
my involuntary pause, no more than a heartbeat in length,
when I see Elena behind the register. I used to call the
slightly rounded, salt-and-pepper-haired woman my fairy
godmother because she used to let me stay late and skate
whenever she closed instead of Jeff. Now I don't call her
anything at all if I can help it. It took her a little longer than
most to stop interacting with me, and I tell myself that I'm
glad her gaze lowers quickly as I pass her.

I pass a few other coworkers, some more or less obvious
in their discomfort with my presence than Jeff, and none
give me the smile I would have gladly returned a year ago.
Not even the newer people I don't know well.

I do my best to ignore the pang of loss and my still-damp
eyes as I lace up my skates then gather my dark brown
hair—as many of the short strands as I can—into a stubby

ponytail. Beyond the hoodie I grabbed from my trunk along with the skates I never leave home without, I'm not dressed for skating and I've never cared less. Everything in my chest is tight and twisted until I step onto the ice. Instantly, the air feels crisp and bracing, and the sound of the blade hitting the ice—not quite a scrape, not quite a hiss—reaches my ears. I'm smiling before I'm halfway across the rink, reversing and gathering speed for a single lutz jump. My heart lifts before my skates leave the ice. There is nothing like that weightless, soaring feeling. I land and wind up for an upright spin, leaning with my arms extended before raising my left leg high and then pulling my foot in toward my right knee. I slide it down as I draw my arms to my chest, spinning faster and faster, watching the world around me blur. In my happiest dreams, I never stop.

When I get home, Laura is setting the table for dinner and acknowledges my entrance with only the briefest of glances. Upstairs in her room, her cockatiel, Ducky, is squawking loudly to be let out of his cage, something she never does anymore. She has earbuds in and bobs her head to some song I can't hear. She never used to be allowed to wear them at the table during meals; it was a technology-free zone where we had to look at and listen to each other. Sometimes we'd grumble—Laura, Jason and me—but I think we all secretly liked the break. More than that, we liked each other. Jason is three years older than me and Laura is three years my junior, but when we were together, those six years felt like nothing. It isn't like that for everyone; I know that, which used to make our bond all the more precious. Wordlessly, I take two plates from her to help. My high from being on the ice fades the longer we move in silence.

Laura looks like a female copy of Jason when he was fourteen. She has the same long legs, gangly arms and narrow face. Fortunately, for my sister, they also share the same mane of gorgeous honey-brown hair that naturally waves in a way mine can only begin to imitate after a good hour with a curling wand. Her jawline is softer than his though, and even though she still has a baby-like fullness to her cheeks, it's clear that she inherited the same stunning bone structure and olive-toned skin from our Castilian grandmother on Dad's side. I take after Mom's side, which means that my features are less defined and I burn if I so much as think about the sun. Laura's wide, deep-set eyes—brown like Dad's whereas Jason and I have Mom's blue eyes—are trained on nothing as she drifts from place setting to place setting, and I'm struck anew by the way she's changed during this past year.

She used to bounce around this same table when she set it, brimming with inexhaustible energy that inevitably led to squawking birds, broken dishes and Mom threatening to ground her if she didn't calm down. Grounding used to be a fate worse than death for Laura, who would have lived outdoors if our parents let her and who could be bribed into doing any chore if it meant she was allowed to spend the night in our old tree house. That Laura is a far cry from the wan figure in front of me. She's lost so much of the tan she always had, and her hair hangs limp down her back, still bent from a ponytail she had it in days ago. She moves like she's half-asleep.

"Brooke, is that you?" Mom calls from the kitchen.

"I'm home."

"Help your sister set the table, please."

I throw a smile toward Laura, because I'm already helping, but she doesn't look up, doesn't stop bobbing her head. My smile fades. "Yes, ma'am," I call back.

Mom comes through the swinging kitchen door carrying a steaming bowl of pasta and tells me and Laura to get the salad and spaghetti sauce while she darts back for the bread. Unlike Laura, Mom never lost her nonstop energy; she's set to high speed whether she's getting food on the table or sprinting to shave seconds off her mile time for an upcoming marathon. If we didn't eat dinner as a family every night, I don't think she'd sit down. She passes back and forth between the kitchen and dining room half a dozen more times, bringing butter on one trip and a pitcher of sweetened sun tea the next only to start back for salad dressing the second she sets down the tea. She thrives on her own brand of manic energy, and I'm exhausted just watching.

At last she pauses in the doorway, her chocolate-brown curls threatening to slip free from her hastily piled bun as she looks from kitchen to dining room, triple checking that she didn't forget anything. She didn't, but that won't stop her from leaping out of her chair the second she sits down, just in case.

At her call, Dad comes up from the basement, turning sideways to fit his shoulders through the narrow doorway and leaving a trail of sawdust and wood chips in his wake despite his attempts to beat his clothes free. His safety glasses are pushed up on his bald head. His hair started thinning in his twenties, and Dad, practical to a fault, has been shaving his head ever since rather than fight the inevitable. It looks good on him. And what hair he lacks on his head he more than makes up for on his face. His full beard rests just above his collarbones and hides the dimpled chin that I can't cover on my own face.

The sweet scent of sap and hickory clinging to him blends well with the garlic spaghetti sauce and oven-fresh bread on the table. As he sits, Mom is still flitting from room to room, and it's only when Dad says her name in his deep but soft tone that she stops.

"Carol. It smells good." He's always been that remedy for her, that soothing presence she can't seem to unwind without, but this past year, even he has had trouble fully reaching her.

She nods and casts one last longing look at the kitchen before taking her seat, as though all the problems in the universe would be solved if she could make one last trip. "Right."

Laura removes her earbuds for a quick prayer but replaces them the second Dad says "Amen" and we start eating.

Beside me, Laura picks at her food while Dad has nearly emptied his plate and Mom is eating like she'll win an award if she finishes first. No one looks at anyone else. No one speaks. The only sounds are the occasional scrape of a fork or the clunk from a lowered glass. The meal is such a stark contrast from the boisterous conversations we used to have when Jason was here. I glance across the table, to the empty spot where his chair used to be before Dad removed it. The table, a present Dad made Mom for their first wedding anniversary, is round, but Laura and I still bump elbows sometimes from sitting too close rather than reclaiming the space.

I feel the wrongness of it all wrapping around me and seeping into my lungs. It's like trying to draw a full breath of steam.

Talking about Jason, acknowledging that he's gone and trying to make sense of how that could have happened only makes them shut down further. At best I get a *Not right now, Brooke* from Mom or a *Let it be* from Dad. The most I get from Laura is nothing at all—sometimes she'll just turn up the volume on whatever she's listening to and break what's left of my heart.

Mostly, I've stopped trying. But seeing Heath today, talking with him for those few minutes and somehow not destroying either of us in the process, gives me a courage I'd thought had long since abandoned me.

"I saw Heath Gaines today." Three forks freeze as three sets of eyes lift to mine. "I was driving with Maggie and he was just walking along the side of the road out past Hackman's Pond."

The only part of Mom to move is her lips. "Did you stop?"

"No," I say. I didn't, not then.

Thinking that is the extent of the encounter, Mom's shoulders relax infinitesimally. "Laura, honey, that plate won't stay warm forever." She starts eating again, and without looking at me says, "Brooke, finish your dinner please."

I fill my fork, wondering at my own sanity when I keep talking. "But I did go back and offer him a ride when it started to rain."

This time Mom's fork clatters to the table, sending spaghetti sauce splattering like drops of blood on her white tablecloth.

"We talked, a little," I tell her, tell all of them, my gaze bouncing from one person to the next, looking for a face that hasn't gone pale. "It wasn't horrible, not like it could have been." *Not like it is with everyone else,* I add silently, thinking of the coworkers I once considered friends. I know it's not just me who gets the looks, the whispers, the so-called friends whose parents won't let them come over anymore. It's been arguably the worst for Laura. Her peers don't even feign politeness the way some of mine do. I'd probably want to hide behind earbuds too. I pause, listening for her music, but she has it turned down so low—possibly even off—that I'm sure she can hear me. Which means she wants to, so I keep going. This time I'm not looking for answers; I just want to talk about my brother with the only people on the planet who don't recoil at the sound of his name.

"I told him that story about me getting my permit and how when Jason wouldn't let me drive his car, Cal tossed me his keys. Jason was always so protective of his—"

Dad's fist slams down on the table, nearly toppling Laura's full glass of iced tea. The impact is so sudden that my teeth clatter together, but I'm not cowed. My heart races. This is the most emotion I've seen from Dad since the night Jason was arrested. I don't want his anger, but I'll take it over the indifference he's cloaked himself in the past year. I'll take *anything* over that. I'm waiting for his head to lift and his gaze to once again meet mine, for him to yell or shout, so long as he speaks, but he doesn't. Instead, he pushes back from the table and disappears into his workshop in the basement. As I turn my head to follow his exit, I see Laura hunched over her plate and the single tear that drops onto her untouched spaghetti. My hand reaches out to her as my heart clenches, but Mom is faster.

"Go on upstairs, Laura. I'll bring you a plate later."

Laura bolts the second Mom finishes speaking. Then Mom is gathering up Laura's plate along with her own. Unlike her hands, Mom's voice is steady when she addresses me.

"Brooklyn Grace."

That choking feeling squeezes me again. I just wanted us to talk, to be able to say Jason's name without everyone fleeing in a rage or tears, without seeing Mom struggle to hold on to her composure by her eyelashes.

"Don't you do that again, do you understand me?"

"Yes, ma'am," I say, quiet as a whisper, because it feels like a lie.

The plates are shaking so much that she has to rest them on the edge of the table. "Promise me you won't mention that boy or his family ever again."

I don't know if the boy she means is Heath or Calvin—not that it matters. Both make it harder to deny where Jason is and why. I can't find the words to explain myself or to tell her that just because I'm not slamming things or crying doesn't mean I'm hurting any less; that I *need* us to talk about Jason just as much as they seemingly don't. I stop searching for words, because Mom is pulled so tightly between Dad and Laura and Jason that I'm afraid she'll snap if I try to tug her in another direction. And I don't want to make any of them suffer more than they already are.

"I promise," I say, and then I help her clear the table. We don't mention Jason again, or Heath. Or Calvin...the boy my brother confessed to killing last year.

CHAPTER 4

In the morning, no one mentions a thing about what I said last night. It's like it didn't happen.

Mom is darting around the house with a phone cradled between her ear and shoulder, talking with people on the other side of the country who care only about how quickly their custom furniture pieces will be finished. Her skin is glistening with sweat, which means she's already run who knows how many miles this morning and it's barely 8:00 a.m. Dad is in the basement, the whirring sounds from his lathe the only noise I'll hear from him until dinner. It doesn't make sense that I miss him almost as much as I miss Jason—I see Dad more, even if it's a fraction of the time we used to spend together.

Mom may be the runner, but Dad was the one behind my skating from the very start. He's the one who used to make the three-hour round-trip to Odessa with me five days a week so that I could skate with a top coach. He never once complained, even when I sometimes did. We had a routine; we'd hit the same gas station, buy the jumbo-size peanut butter M&M's to share, and listen to the same Blackfoot album over and over again, laughing at the looks from passing drivers when we air-guitared the solo during "Highway Song."

Skating used to be my life, but right now, if I had to choose one thing to have back the way it was, I'd rather spend three hours in a car with a spotty A/C, tossing M&M's in the air for Dad to catch, than compete for one more medal.

Laura is outside on the porch, bending her head over her phone instead of looking at the green and glorious world waking up in front of her. Still in the T-shirt and shorts I slept in, I push open the screen door and pad barefoot to the empty rocking chair beside Laura. She doesn't look up when I sit, not even when I say her name. She's too busy reading a forum thread about whether Jack Kirby or Stan Lee created Marvel Comics. I'm tempted to tread into the debate since I know which side she holds even if I don't really understand why it matters. I'll get a response from her, I know, but arguing over comics never earns me more than a brief flare of anger, quickly snuffed out by the apathy she wraps around herself. Instead I tap her knee with my free hand. Her gaze lifts in my direction, but not her head. She makes no move to lower the volume of whatever she's listening to. I return her stare, waiting. Finally, she removes an earbud. One. I ignore the heaviness in my chest.

"Where's Ducky?"

"In his cage."

As if he heard his name through the open window of Laura's room, he calls out, "I'm Batman."

I close my eyes slowly, letting a smile lift my lips. It took Laura a year to get him to say that. For a while she tried to teach him to say *Hulk smash* when she shifted from being DC obsessed to a Marvel fanatic, but Jason started playing a recording in her room while she was at school that repeated *Jason's so cool*, and the poor bird got confused. Laura caught on when Ducky started saying *Jason smash*. My smile grows. Jason had to clean Ducky's cage for a month after that. Ducky still says it sometimes. *Jason smash.* Though no one finds it funny anymore.

Before she can replace her earbud, I switch topics. "I didn't get to tell you but I finally tamed Daphne yesterday."

"Who?"

I frown, the movement slight in comparison to the ache from Laura's single-word response. "My car." I gesture with my chin toward the Camaro parked in the carport. "Come on, Laur. You were here when I brought her home last week." It was possible she'd been in the exact same spot. She rarely went anywhere besides the porch and her room these days.

"Oh."

Oh. Her eyes are already drifting back to her phone, but I halt her hand before she can lift her earbud again. I wasn't expecting the same house-shaking shriek from her that heralded Jason's first car, nor did I think she'd wrap herself around my legs like a monkey until I promised her the first ride, but something more than *Oh.* "I named her Daphne, you know, after Jack Lemon's character in *Some*

Like It Hot." It was one of the few movies we both loved.
The summer before Jason's arrest, we watched it together
almost every night. Watching a lot of movies is one of the
side effects of living in a town where cattle outnumber people and me not being old enough to drive anywhere. I'd
wanted to watch *The Cutting Edge* for the millionth time,
and she'd wanted to watch the latest superhero flick. I'm
still not sure how *Some Like It Hot* became a compromise
between the two, but it did. It got to the point where neither of us could fall asleep unless it was on. I've suggested
watching it a few times this summer, but she has yet to take
me up on the offer. Her closed-off demeanor this morning
means I know better than to ask again.

"Anyway, I can drive her now," I say. "I was thinking
about going to Walmart. Wanna come?" Apparently, there
are lots of Walmarts in Texas, but like Bigfoot and good
gluten-free pizza, I have to take that on faith, because the
only one I know of is an hour away down in Midland. It's
kind of a big deal to go to Walmart, so I dangle the prospect in front of my sister like the proverbial carrot I hope
it is. It's almost embarrassing how badly I want her to say
yes. I don't even try to hide the eagerness in my voice. It
hurts all the more when she frees her hand from mine.

"I'm good." She puts her earbud back in place. I might
not be there anymore for all the attention she pays me.

My gaze bounces between her eyes. She's *not* good—
neither of us is. I hate this lifelessness between us when we
used to have so much more. I don't want to watch my sister
withering away in a prison of her own making when Jason

is the one truly locked up. I have to keep trying with her. I'm afraid of what might happen if I stop.

"Then forget Walmart." I scoot to the edge of my seat. "Let's do something. Anything, you pick." I glance at the superhero forum on her phone. "Find a Comic-Con within a hundred miles and we'll go." I am not about comic anything, but Laura is. I once told her I'd rather skate over my own fingers than go with her to a comic book convention— emphasis on the comics. I'd been only slightly exaggerating. That had always been her and Jason's thing, not ours.

I realize my mistake. I can see Laura's thoughts following a similar path to mine—to Jason. I shift gears. "Or we can watch a movie or go skating or swimming or we can just drive. I'll rob a bank with you right now if that's what it takes to get you off this porch." I try to laugh a little, a weak attempt to hide how scared I am for her, for us. How much I miss her.

It's too late though. Her eyes have settled on my azure T-shirt and the now-chipped blue polish on my nails. She's gone again, even before she heads back inside.

I still go to Walmart. It would have been better with Laura, but just because she passed doesn't mean I can. Knowing it'll be another couple weeks or even a month before I can justify the gas to get there again, I spend way too long at the superstore. I wander the aisles and revel in the luxury of meeting a stranger's gaze without bracing for the excruciating moment of recognition. These people simply smile—or not—and move on.

It's afternoon by the time I leave, and I don't rush the

drive home. After crossing the Telford city line, I detour toward the garage on Main Street without stopping to consider why. I'm only going to pass by, assure myself that he's not there. I almost believe myself until the garage comes into view. Cal's red truck—Heath's truck—is still there. I pull in and get out automatically, not needing a closer look to confirm it's the same truck but taking one anyway.

"Can I help you with something?"

I turn and see a man in gray coveralls wiping his hands on a paisley-print orange handkerchief. His pleasant smile falters when he sees my face, and my stomach flutters uncomfortably. I don't get recognized everywhere anymore, but I wouldn't be surprised if this mechanic knows who I am considering how frequently Heath said Cal had his truck fixed here. Still, it's possible there's another reason for his flat expression. Straightening my back, I force a smile onto my face. "Yes, sir. I was just curious what's wrong with this truck?"

"That truck's not for sale," he says without a hint of his initial smile.

I swallow down the splash of bile in my stomach. He knows exactly who I am. "No, sir, I'm not looking to buy it. I was only wondering why the owner hasn't picked it up yet."

The mechanic takes a step toward me. "Not sure as how that's any of your business." His demeanor isn't openly hostile, but it's as far from welcoming as it can get. It isn't wholly unexpected so instead of slinking away, I close my eyes and draw in a steadying breath before opening them again.

"I dropped the owner off here yesterday. Are you waiting for a part to come in or something?"

His expression goes blank, and I think I stunned him into answering. "It's fixed. I agreed to hold it for a few days until he could pay for the repair."

I have a flash of Heath walking in heat and rain when he doesn't have to do either, when he shouldn't. "How much is it?"

The mechanic hesitates, gaze flicking to my Camaro as if to confirm it was the car Heath got out of yesterday. I don't know how well this guy knew Cal or knows Heath, but I can guess that he's struggling to understand why Heath would have anything to do with me. Staring at Daphne, he tells me the repair cost. It's slightly more than half of the paycheck I picked up the day before. More than I can comfortably part with, if I'm being honest.

The mechanic is beyond words at this point, but he takes my money if not my guilt.

CHAPTER 5

I park the Zamboni—Bertha, as I call her—in the garage after my last pass on the ice for the night. The skaters are all gone, and apart from Jeff, the manager, I'm the only employee still working. It's just after ten and even though weariness is tugging on my limbs, I stop and stare at the ice, now smooth and luminous as a moonlit lake. A smile lifts my mouth and my heart as I breathe in the clean, chilled air. Someone thought it'd be funny to flood the boys' bathroom and pee everywhere except in the urinals, so the only ice time I got that day was driving Bertha back and forth across the rink every hour. She's slow and lumbering and older than I am, but anything is preferable to scrubbing pee stains from grout. My knees are aching as I duck my head in the office to see Jeff.

"I bleached every inch of the boys' bathroom and the ice is ready for the morning. I was going to head out unless you need anything else."

"I need all the trash cans empt—" He cuts off when I heft up one of the two colossal trash bags I'm lugging for him to see.

"Last ones," I tell him. "I'll drop them in the Dumpster on my way out."

Jeff leans back in his chair, considering. He has no idea how the bald spot on his crown catches the overhead light when he does that. My attempt to smother a laugh makes his eyes narrow on me. "That bathroom was a mess."

I refrain from saying that after the hours I spent in there, no one knows that better than me. I smell like I doused myself in eau de urinal cake. "Well, it's clean enough to eat off now," I say, knowing that my assurance means less than nothing.

With a sigh, Jeff pushes himself up. "I better just give it a quick look-see."

I'm too tired to muster up more than a passing annoyance. I follow him to the bathroom and stand in the doorway watching him inspect every inch of the visibly gleaming bathroom as if the Pope is planning an imminent visit to the Polar Ice Rink.

Jeff's "quick look-see" takes ten minutes, after which he agrees—begrudgingly—that the bathroom'll do before letting me leave. I'm halfway to the front door, lugging the trash bags in my wake, when his clucking tongue draws my attention to the wastebasket from the office, which he's holding. There are two tiny pieces of paper inside. I raise my gaze from the wastebasket to meet his eyes, silently asking him if he's serious. In response, he swings the basket slightly from side to side like a pendulum.

"We don't cut corners here, Brooke. Every trash receptacle, every night, regardless of how full. I don't want to have to keep checking your work. It's a waste of my time and, frankly, you shouldn't need supervising after all this time."

I know he's considering making me show him every emptied trash can in the building, and honestly, I don't trust myself not to lose my temper if he does. I'd gain a moment of satisfaction but at the cost of getting fired. Not to mention how ashamed of me my parents would be. They raised me better than that.

"I'm sorry," I say. "I promise it won't happen again."

He makes me wait several long seconds before bestowing the most condescending of nods on me. My teeth grind so hard that I'm afraid they'll crack as I empty the basket and even return it to its spot beside the desk, but I hold my tongue and gather up the two trash bags, which are bigger than I am. I can feel Jeff watching as I head toward the double-door exit with my unwieldy load. He's not about to offer to get the door, and I'd rather clean the bathroom again with my toothbrush than ask him. If being petty and double—sometimes triple—checking my work is the best he can do to try to get me to quit, I'll outlast him. If this were any other job, I'd have been long gone, but until Telford opens up another ice rink, I need this one.

I tie my jacket around my waist before shouldering my way outside. The muggy night air feels good on my refrigerated skin for about thirty seconds before stickiness sets in. This is one of those nights when it feels like I'm living inside a giant mouth, as though the earth itself were covered in a still, steaming breath from the recent rain. It's as gross as it sounds and does nothing to improve my mood as I pile the trash bags I can barely see over into my arms and trace the path to the Dumpsters that I know by heart. I pass Jeff's pristine red midlife crisis, and the temptation to leave the bags on his hood is a pleasant one. I'm not genuinely considering it, but thinking about it makes me feel better.

My thoughts are a little too distracting, and my sneakered toe catches on a crack in the asphalt. I'm stumbling, trying to regain my balance, when one of the bags is lifted from my arms. I'm ready to utter a genuine if surprised thanks to Jeff for deciding to help me when I look up not into my manager's face but into Heath's.

My brain can't conceive of a reason for him to be there, so I gape at him for a good few seconds, taking in the height and breadth of him. He's not huge or scrawny, but somewhere in between. Standing before him, I don't feel dwarfed—which I often do at five foot four—or lumbering, which I also sometimes do since skating has added muscle to my otherwise petite frame. If I had my skates on we'd be nearly eye to eye; without them I have to look up just enough that it makes a flutter shiver through me despite the still, sultry night air. Until I take in his expression. His gray eyes are hard and there's a tightness to his jaw that pulls all his features into harsh relief, like he's both angry and trying not be at the same time. The effect is somewhat lost considering he just rescued me from face-planting into a trash bag.

His gaze moves to the remaining bag I'm still holding. He doesn't say anything but, unlike Jeff, he doesn't hesitate before taking the other trash bag from my unprotesting arms. I'm suddenly struck by the conviction that Heath's the type to open doors and pull out chairs, and I'll bet he says *ma'am* and *sir* as easily as his brother did.

He rounds the shadowy corner of the building and pitches both bags into the Dumpster a few yards away. He doesn't immediately return or even look in my direction. And that's when I start to sweat.

If it was earlier and the rink was still open, I could try to convince myself that it's pure happenstance, us running into each other again. But not when we're closed and it's this late, not when I remember how angry he'd been last time we saw each other. That last thought is the one that keeps me from taking more than a few steps after him so as to remain in illumination of the overhead parking lot lights.

"How did you know I'd be here?" As soon as the question leaves my mouth, I know the answer. The story I told him about his brother letting me drive his truck to work at this rink. It would have taken only a small gamble on his part to assume I still did. The question I should be asking is why he waited until after closing when I'm alone in a deserted parking lot to approach me.

When he at last meets my gaze, I know from the renewed set to his jaw that he's not here to thank me for his truck repairs—not that I expected him to. My pulse kicks up as he walks toward me, stalks really, and stops just shy of the parking lot light that feels less and less like it can protect me. He pulls something from his pocket and holds it out in a tight fist.

Cash.

CHAPTER 6

"It's all there," Heath says, cool as the rink I just left. "Count it."

I swallow before responding, and my voice isn't half so chilly. "You don't need to pay me back."

Heath's voice drops in volume but seems to double in intensity as he leans toward me, his dark brown hair skimming his cheekbones. His gray eyes catch the reflection of the lights and seem to flash. "I don't need you to pay for my truck."

My skin ripples, chilled by the animosity rolling off him and rendering me mute. I've gotten used to hostility from people I know and even complete strangers. I welcomed it at first—what else could I do when people started saying horrible and vicious things about my brother and vile things about my parents and my then barely thirteen-year-old sister? My first instinct had been to vehemently defend all of us against every insidious—and at the time, I thought, wholly unfounded—speculation bandied about by people who used to smile at us when we passed in town. I didn't let even the softer, sadder questions and concerns from my then friends penetrate my resolve, my infallible faith in my brother and his innocence. In a single month, from the night Jason was arrested through his first court appearance and later his arraignment, I stood tall, daring anyone to imply let alone say a bad word about my brother. His arrest was a mistake; the evidence was flawed or flat-out wrong. My brother wasn't a murderer. I'd gladly make an enemy of every friend I'd ever had rather than believe for one second that my brother was capable of taking someone's life.

And I did.

When my boyfriend at the time tried to get me to "face the truth" by reading some article he'd found online that supposedly contained leaked info from the police report, I snapped and it was the closest I'd ever come to hitting someone. The story of that incident quickly spread through our circle of friends, lending credence to the theory that homicidal violence ran in my family.

When Jason pleaded guilty, the crushing reality hit me. I'd been immobile in the courtroom that day, watching Jason's final look at our sobbing mother before he was hauled away by the upper arm through doors where I couldn't follow. I'd turned then, not wanting my brother to see the tears I could no longer hold back. While almost everyone around us rejoiced at seeing a killer brought to justice, I watched someone I loved more than my own life taken away in handcuffs after admitting to a crime I couldn't conceive of, even as I had to accept that he was guilty.

It didn't matter that I had friends who might have tried to console me afterward if I'd let them. I *didn't* let them. I let the wary glances and the sad eyes roll off me without distinction until I no longer noticed any difference.

But I recognize the sharp distinction between Heath and everyone else. I'm not a story to him; I'm a nightmare, a personal one that neither of us can escape by crossing to the other side of the road. He doesn't feel sorry for me, and he's not afraid. I have no defense against what I see in his expression. He batters through without even trying.

He raises a hand to his head and half turns before facing me again, his strong jaw locks. "What made you think I'd want anything from you? That I wouldn't rather walk for the rest of my life than drive a truck that you paid to fix?"

Pain blossoms in my chest, but I blink away the sting in my eyes. I'm not about to cry in front of him again. That was before, when I hoped he was capable of doing what seemingly no one else in our town could: look at me and not see my brother. "I was only trying to help."

"*You,*" he says, forcing the word through barely moving lips, "don't get to feel bad for me. And you sure as hell don't get to use me to make yourself feel better." He flings the money at my feet and turns to leave.

I almost turn away myself, ready to flee to where Daphne is parked a few dozen yards away, but I make the mistake of glancing beyond Heath to his truck. And I think of his brother and the fraction of pain I must feel compared to his.

"You can't make me feel better," I call after him, and it

comes out in a voice much stronger than I'm expecting. I sound confident and strong when I couldn't feel more opposite.

Heath halts and turns but doesn't take a single step toward me.

I don't blame Heath or his family for anything. They have every reason to despise everything associated with my brother, including me. I have to visit my brother within the confines of a prison, where ever-present guards close in if I try to so much as hold his hand. But the only place Heath can visit his brother is at a cemetery, where the closest he can get to touching Calvin is a headstone.

There is no comparison.

"There is no 'better,'" I say, careful not to draw in too deep a breath lest it come out shaky. "I would never use you like that even if there were."

Heath's expression goes flat, and he looks so much like his brother in that moment that I feel as if I've got a broken bird trapped in my chest, fluttering desperately to free itself. "You saw me laughing yesterday," I say. "I'd just learned how to drive stick, and that was the first time I didn't stall. You saw that one moment, and I didn't want you to think I don't care, that life is just fine now. It's not." The bird is frantic now. If I look down, I might see my ribs shaking from the impact of its little body. "I think about my brother and your brother, and I know it will never be better."

He stands there, looking a little ghostly in the light from the parking lot while emotions I can't begin to decipher flit across his face. I can't move my feet while he's staring at me. Instead, I bend down and start gathering the money scattered on the ground. I'm moving slowly, grabbing one bill at a time. "I shouldn't have paid for your truck repairs," I say. I don't know why I ever thought he wouldn't react this way, thinking I was trying to absolve some of my own guilt or even Jason's.

He doesn't hesitate at all when replying. "No, you shouldn't have." He pauses then says, "I didn't notice you were laughing yesterday."

My gaze lifts and my heart considers following suit. "You didn't?"

He shakes his head and I frown.

"But you looked so angry."

"The last time I saw you was in a courtroom." He doesn't have to say more than that. My reaction, though different, was just as automatic when I saw him.

"You know you could have just had the garage refund my money. You didn't have to track me down in person."

"I know."

"Did you want to yell at me that badly?" I ask, already knowing the answer.

Again, there's no hesitation. "Yes."

I'm still in the process of reaching for the last bill. The bird in my chest makes one last attempt at freedom before collapsing into a motionless ball right below my heart.

A door bangs open behind me, and Jeff's voice fills the nearly empty parking lot. "That's what you said last time. Come on, Angel. One drink. It's not that late." The whiny/pleading tone in his voice cuts off when he sees me. "Brooke? What are you still doing here?"

My gaze shoots to Heath, but his truck hides him from

Jeff's view. Jeff was obsessed with Cal's murder. He'd know who Heath is immediately. At the thought of his finding me and Heath together, nausea flares then subsides just as quickly. "I had an issue with the trash bags," I say to Jeff as I gather up the last bill and stand. "But it's fine. I'm leaving now."

"Brooke." Jeff says my name using the same tone you'd use if you were facing someone holding a loaded gun—a mix of fear and accusation. "What's in your hand?" His gaze moves almost comically to the building then back to me. "Did you—did you steal that money from the register?"

CHAPTER 7

"*What?*" Incredulity forces the word out harsher than I've ever dared with Jeff. "No, I—" I start to say this is my money from my last paycheck, but technically it's Heath's.

Jeff's eyes are so wide that I know he's already convicted me in his mind. "How much did you take, Brooke?"

He could have slapped me and I wouldn't have felt more dumbstruck. I glance at the money I'm holding then back at Jeff. "Are you accusing me of stealing and then waiting outside so you could catch me counting it?" I'm trying to inject as much disbelief as possible into my voice, but Jeff's opinion of my intelligence is apparently as low as it is of my morals, because he doesn't even blink.

"Jeff." I wait a few seconds to make sure he's listening and not lost in some fantasy where he fires me and gets a special commendation from the police department for catching a thief. "You emptied the register. You counted the drawer, I even watched you do it." I make the mistake of laughing. It's a single sound, the kind meant to disarm and invite him to reassess, but instead Jeff's eyebrows shoot up his forehead as if I confessed.

In the back of my mind, a note of panic starts to sound that makes me forget that Jeff and I aren't alone in the parking lot.

"You left the door open." My arm shoots out, pointing. "I could see into the office while I was resurfacing the ice. I wasn't—" I fumble for the right word, but in my increasing agitation I can't find it. "I have never stolen anything in my life."

Jeff doesn't say anything to me, instead directing his response to whomever he has on the phone, eyeing me like I might try to flee. "I'm not going to be able to meet you tonight after all. I've got a theft situation with one of my employees that I have to deal with."

My breath exhales in a high-pitched, disbelieving huff. The real surprise isn't Jeff accusing me of stealing—an offense he'd finally be able to fire me over—it's that he hasn't done something like this before.

He's unbelievable. I have been an exemplary employee since the day I started working here, and he continues to make me feel like he's doing me a favor by letting me clean toilets and take out the trash. He's not. It's a job I do because after all Jason's legal bills, I can't afford to pay for ice time without it, and I do it despite him treating me like the only difference between me and my incarcerated brother is time.

I think even my parents would understand me losing my temper in this situation, but I don't. It wouldn't do any good. If he wants to have a power trip in order to show off for whomever he's got on his phone, me yelling will only make it worse.

"I didn't take anything and I'd like to go home now."

His entire body goes rigid. "And I'm just supposed to take your word for it because you come from such a law-abiding family?"

I see spots. Blacks and reds bursting in my vision until Jeff and the parking lot are almost entirely gone. "I'm not a thief," I say, but so quietly I might be the only one who hears.

He starts to pocket his phone then stops, glancing from it to me before puffing out his chest and placing his free hand on his hip. "You have two choices here, Brooke. We can go back inside while I recount what's in the safe or I can call the police and let them deal with you. I'm guessing they aren't going to be overly sympathetic once they hear that your last name is Covington. They might just decide to take you in and sort this out at the station." Jeff makes a show of unlocking the door and opening it wide. "What's it gonna be?"

It's no choice at all, and Jeff knows it, but that doesn't stop him from sighing audibly every few steps as I precede him back inside. The heavy metal door closes behind us and for a moment the darkness is so thick that it seems to sluice down my throat and into my lungs, but then the light comes on and I squint away from the brightness. We have to stop while he unlocks the door to the office.

"This is not how I planned to end my night, Brooke." But he's reveling in it. He opens the office door. "Inside. Now."

I go willingly. There is no money missing. He can posture all he wants. I've done nothing wrong.

Knowing that and proving it to Jeff is easier said than done. He makes me watch as he painstakingly counts every bill from the day, laying them out in neat stacks on the desk. His hands start to shake when he nears the end. When he finishes and looks up to meet my gaze, my expression is stone-faced. Rather than offer me an apology, Jeff gathers up the money and begins to count again, licking his finger between each bill.

"I told you I didn't take anything."

He doesn't even acknowledge I've spoken; instead he finishes his second recount and starts a third. It takes twenty minutes for Jeff to accept that I didn't somehow pilfer the register he himself emptied and counted earlier. I'm convinced the only reason he relents is that he realizes how inept it would make him look if that were true rather than any actual belief in my innocence.

I deserve an apology. What I get is a shift cut.

"You can't do that!" I say. The rink isn't exactly close to my house. The three shifts a week he plans to drop me to will barely cover gas and car insurance, and that's assuming I don't come in to skate on my days off.

Jeff raises both eyebrows at me from the other side of his desk. "Excuse me?"

"José and I are the only ones who can drive Bertha—the Zamboni—and he's not coming back after his hip surgery next week." The words leave my mouth and relief floods me. José had been working at the Polar Ice Rink since it opened in 1965, and he was the only employee who refused to let me ice him out. He's the one who taught me to drive Bertha, and for the first time since he told me about the surgery and him moving to Tampa to live with his daughter, I feel something besides sadness.

The smile Jeff returns causes mine to falter. "No, that just means I'll be hiring another driver and maintenance worker." His smile grows. "Of course, if you'd rather seek employment elsewhere, I won't bring up the theft situation."

"But I didn't steal anything!"

Jeff purses his fat, baby lips in response. I'm not a violent person, but I know in that moment I could slap that look off Jeff's face and feel nothing but satisfaction pulsing through me.

"I guess you have another choice here, Brooke. What's it gonna be?"

CHAPTER 8

I'm brushing away an angry tear with the heel of my hand when I step into the muggy night air once again. Three shifts a week, less than thirty hours. It's a forty-five minute round-trip to the rink. Assuming I don't drive anywhere else or spend money on anything but gas and car insurance, how many days can I afford to come here? I'm throwing numbers around in my head when Heath walks around the front of his truck.

I slow for a second, then resume my pace. He could have said something to Jeff; a few words in my defense to explain the money and Jeff would have had to let me go. But he didn't. He watched Jeff accuse and insult me, and he stayed silent.

I keep walking even when I see Heath moving in my direction. I shouldn't care what he thinks of me. I shouldn't care what anyone thinks of me, yet my eyes are stinging and the closer he comes the harder it is to keep them from doing more than sting. I reach Daphne a few steps ahead of him. I can't make it any clearer that I don't want to talk to him as I fit the key into the lock and turn it. Heath stops barely two feet to my left, watching but saying nothing. He's not leaving.

"What?" I say, letting him hear the barely leashed anger in my voice. I shake my head a little before looking at him. *"What?"*

"Did you lose your job?"

I scoff and open the door so it's between us. The last two times we saw each other, he couldn't wait to get away from me. Now he's standing there like I'll have to hit him with my car to get him to move. I curl my fingers around the doorframe. "Is that what you want to hear? That I got fired?" I abandon my indifference, turning fully to face him. "Why are you still here? Do you need to yell at me more? Do you want to follow me home so you can yell at my family? What? Tell me!" My gaze flicks back and forth between his eyes, almost frantic where his is steady. "What do you want from me, Heath?"

He takes a breath, one so deep it stretches the cotton of his T-shirt. "I don't want anything from you."

"No?" I glance down at the hand he has on my door-frame. I don't think he was aware of putting it there, but he doesn't remove it. "I didn't get fired," I say, watching his face and wondering if it can possibly be relief that crosses it. My stomach twists. I don't even know why; I know only that I want to get away from the feeling.

"I don't get you," I say. "Before you acted like you were in physical pain just from sharing the same air as me. You don't need a ride, and you've already thrown my money back at me. Looking at me makes you mad, and that's the best-case scenario. Why are you still here? What else do you want? Just tell me, because this hasn't been a great day for me and I really don't want to be here when my boss comes back out." I exhale the remaining air in my lungs, waiting, but all Heath does is stare at me with a frown that he can't seem to fully hold. "Fine," I say, starting to get into my car.

"Wait, damn it."

I freeze in a half crouch, only this time I don't think his clipped tone is directed at me. When I stand again, I see that his eyes are squeezed shut. I lower my gaze to the hand still resting my doorframe—no, not resting on it, holding it open.

"I should have said something to your boss. Earlier. I'm sorry."

I'm afraid to breath. Heath Gaines just apologized to me, Jason Covington's sister. It feels wrong on so many levels. I force myself to hold Heath's gaze when he opens his eyes, and I say something that feels every bit as wrong as his apology. "Thank you."

Heath tries to hide his flinch, but I see it. I feel it. After another moment, he lowers his hand from my door and takes a step back. "Did you say anything to your family about talking to me the other day?"

"Yes," I say, remembering with a twinge of guilt the promise I gave my mom that I'm currently breaking. "Did you?"

"No."

Smart. Or maybe he's just kinder than I know how to be. "I shouldn't have. My family doesn't talk about...anything."

"Mine does," Heath says. "Not the way it is now, just..." He stops for so long that I don't think he's going to finish. With a swallow that looks painful, he does. "About before. Like Cal's not gone."

"With mine it's like Jason never was." My throat constricts painfully at the admission.

Everything about this interaction is strange. My reaction to Heath, and definitely his to me. We're both still standing there, just a few feet from each other when anyone else in our situation would have already left. I have that desire inside me, the one that longs to throw myself behind Daphne's wheel and speed as fast and as far away from him as I can. But I also want to stay. I can't reconcile the two impulses, and yet the one to stay is winning. The only thing that makes me say anything is the knowledge that Jeff could come out at any moment, and I wasn't kidding about wanting to avoid that.

"I need to go—"

"Where my truck broke down near Hackman's Pond," Heath says. "There's this big live oak just off from the road, down by—"

"—I know the one," I finish quietly. His gaze is locked with mine, and it almost feels like he's daring me to let him keep talking and begging me not to at the same time. I swallow. "It's nice there in the afternoons, when it's not too hot." Heath's stare doesn't leave my face, and it's all I can do not to squirm.

"Like the day after it rains," he says.

I nod, knowing I shouldn't. All I can do is wonder with a pang if it will ever not hurt to look at him.

I'm still wondering when he walks back to his truck and I slide behind Daphne's wheel.

CHAPTER 9

"I'll do it!"

I can't help but laugh, a weary sound, as I roll my head toward where Maggie is expertly applying eyeliner at the vanity in front of her bedroom window the next morning. I'm lying on her bed while she films a voice-over makeup tutorial for her YouTube channel, *Pretty Well Read*, where she posts beauty and book review videos. Her current creation is an interpretation of the cover of *Everything, Everything* by Nicola Yoon. It looks like colorful wildflowers are bursting out of the skin all around her eyes. The effect is arrestingly beautiful.

"It's not a glamorous job," I tell her.

She eyes me through her mirror, pausing in the process of adding teeny tiny lines to the minuscule purple butterfly she's drawn on her cheekbone. "Zamboni. Driver."

Maggie has a thing for cars, or really anything with a steering wheel. Fast, slow, big, small, she doesn't discriminate. The first time she saw me driving Bertha she practically drooled. Handing over Bertha's keys is probably safer than letting her behind Daphne's wheel, considering she's already totaled two cars in the year that she's had her license—she claims she has trouble staying focused, whereas I'm more inclined to think it's due to her resentment toward her dad given his profession as a stunt driver. Either way, the only trick Bertha can do is occasionally leak hydraulic fluid on the ice.

"I don't care if I have to be a minimum-wage toilet cleaner," she continues, "if it means I finally get to drive Bertha. Want one?" When she points to her butterfly, I nod. She stops her camera and scoots down on her bench to make room for me to join her, then positions my face the way she wants it. In minutes, I have the twin to her butterfly on my cheek, though mine is blue instead of purple. I didn't even have to ask for the color change, that's how awesome my friend is. "And speaking of turds, you won't have to deal with Jeff—" Maggie's nostrils flare when she says his name. Not even mentioning Bertha was enough to cool her temper after I relayed Jeff's accusations from the night before. "—on your own anymore once I'm working there too."

I don't respond right away. It would be so much better having Maggie at work, assuming Jeff doesn't go out of his way to schedule us for different shifts. He'll probably just put me on permanent bathroom duty. But she's likely to hear from a coworker exactly why they all give me such a wide berth.

She'll find out about Jason.

"You're not wearing that bronzer I gave you, are you? I swear you just went like five shades of pale." She plucks a giant fluffy brush from a glass jar on her vanity and starts buffing "life" back into the perimeter of my face. "There," she says, with a satisfied nod. "You no longer look like someone outlawed figure skating."

"Bronzer is magic," I say, echoing her oft-repeated phrase while I will actual color back into my face. I don't want to think about what I'll do if Maggie learns the truth about my brother and I lose the one remaining good thing in my life. "But driving Bertha is the smallest part of the job. It's ten minutes every hour—the other fifty it's a straight janitorial job."

"Says the girl who gets paid to drive her." Maggie holds up two lip glosses for me choose between. I tap the peach one and then try not to move my lips as she swipes it on me.

"Did I mention that Bertha's top speed is a whopping nine miles per hour and typically I don't go half that? Try turning above four and you'll nick the ice. It's seriously not as awesome as you're thinking. You have to be perfectly precise with your laps to avoid overlapping but not allow any gaps. You have to grease and sharpen the blades regularly. You have to constantly monitor the hydraulic and water lines, and even when you do everything right there's still a chance that the ice could start crawling— literally buckle in on itself—if the temperature is too low. And then there's the fact that Bertha is a million years old and sometimes she just goes down, which means you'll be out on the ice with a squeegee and buckets of water."

I roll my shoulders, remembering the ache from last time that happened.

"If I didn't know better, I'd think you didn't want us to work together." She says this without suspicion or wounded feelings. She has no reason to know how true her statement is. Maggie closes the lip gloss and lowers it to her lap, her head tilted in a half puzzled, half concerned manner. "Why am I having to convince you that this is a good idea? You'd get your favorite person in the world at your favorite place in the world and I could help you finally film your audition for your favorite job in the world. What part of that isn't awesome?"

A year ago, I'd have said no part. Now, hearing them all together is like trying to breathe while a thick, scratchy blanket smothers me. *Stories on Ice* is THE national touring ice show. It may not be the Olympics, but it's still a big deal, especially to me. Skaters from all over the country submit audition videos every year, and at seventeen I'm finally old enough to send in my own.

I try to grin with her, but it feels more like a grimace. "I still haven't decided if I'm going to audition." We've had versions of this *Stories on Ice* conversation dozens of times since she found the website bookmarked on my laptop, and they all end with the same evasive responses from me. She never gets mad; she just retreats and attacks again later. And she'll keep on attacking until she wins. That relentlessness served her well while building her YouTube channel and learning to skate, and serves me less well when it comes to things I'm not ready to tell her.

"That's officially the dumbest thing you've ever said."

Maggie swings a leg over her bench, straddling it so she fully faces me. "We can totally do this. You can do the skating, and I will make you look like a dazzling princess." She nods to her filming equipment and computer. "They won't be able to say no. After you graduate next year you could be touring the country as part of a national ice show! I mean, you'll get paid to live on the ice. Tell me that's not the best thing you've ever heard?"

It is, yet I have to feign a smile and hold it while Maggie goes on about how close I am to the dream job that can't ever be mine.

From the first moment I stepped onto the ice, I knew I belonged there. I can't remember a time in my life when I wasn't skating, when I couldn't make myself happy just by thinking about it.

Although Dad and I used to make that three-hour round-trip to Odessa five days a week, we hit a wall when I was thirteen and my coach said we needed to decide what my goals were—because if I had serious aspirations, five days a week wasn't going to cut it, not even close. The schedule she proposed and the accompanying cost kept my dad silent the whole drive home. I remember hearing my parents discussing it that night. Dad talked about getting a second job and Mom mentioned taking out a second mortgage on the house. I still believe they would have found a way for me to do it if I'd wanted, but the idea of putting this huge financial burden on my family and essentially moving in with my coach so that I could dedicate every waking moment of my life to ice-skating was terrifying.

I loved the ice, but I loved my family more. I always would.

So we said no, and instead of a three-hour round-trip to Odessa to train with a world-class coach at a private rink, my journey turned into forty-five minute round-trips to Polar Ice Rink in town to learn however and from whomever I could. I let the bigger dream go—the one I wasn't sure I'd ever really wanted—and replaced it with one that promised to let both parts of my heart, my family and the ice, beat together. That was when we started focusing on *Stories on Ice* and my hopes to join it after high school and make it my career.

I pored over skaters' audition videos online and spent countless nights planning for the one I could film when I turned seventeen. But my birthday came and went, and I put it off. Because by the time I turned seventeen, everything was different.

Jason was gone.

My family was shattered.

And dreams no longer fit into the nightmare we lived in.

I'm not ready is the only excuse I can give Maggie. And I become less ready every time I visit my brother in prison, every time Mom sneaks away to cry when we come home, every time Dad disappears into his shop for hours on end without touching a single tool, every time Laura goes more than a day without speaking unless I make her.

Every time I try to hold us together and tear myself apart more.

Thunder booms outside, startling us both. Maggie peers out the window and scowls at the clouds rolling across the

, sky. "Seriously, Texas? I was kind of using the sun to film right now." She slumps beside me as the light in her room grows dim. "Think it'll pass before my face starts to melt so I can finish this look?" She misinterprets my slightly nauseous expression and sighs. "It's fine. We'll talk about the audition later." She reaches for a makeup remover wipe and scrutinizes her now shadowed face. "My left eye looks kind of cluttered anyway."

Normally, I'm transfixed watching her take off her more elaborate makeup looks. But today, I'm watching the window and the bilious gray clouds sweeping across the sky. In the distance I can already see threads of rain beginning to fall.

Tomorrow, Heath will be at the tree by Hackman's Pond. And I won't.

I'll be with my brother.

CHAPTER 10

A single knock on my bedroom door is my wake-up call on Saturday. My eyes snap open at the soft sound, my whole body alert as though an entire marching band has encircled my bed rather than Mom's quiet footsteps moving past Laura's door so as not to wake her. Careful as she is, the stairs creak as she tiptoes down to the kitchen.

For a moment, I think I won't get up. I didn't draw my curtains fully closed the night before, so the cheery morning sunshine—bright and clear after yesterday's rain—is dappling through the windows on either side of my bed and glinting off the shelves Dad built for me, which are full of old, slightly dusty figure skating medals and trophies. It's going to be a beautiful day, and already I want it to be over.

It's the same every Saturday, that mingled sense of dread weighing my limbs and longing tugging my heart. I get to see my brother today. After endless security checks, drug-sniffing dogs and invasive pat downs, I'll get to sit with him at a table in the visitation room inside a prison for exactly two hours—two for every one hundred and sixty-eight that he spends there each week. I'll get to pretend we aren't surrounded by other inmates with their own visitors and prison guards who bark out warnings if we get too close. I'll have to smile the whole time and convince us that we're going to be okay, that the next thirty years of once-a-week visits will be over before we know it, that watching the guards take him away afterward isn't like having a piece of heart ripped from my chest.

It's more of a battle than usual to get out of bed that Saturday and I know it's because of Heath. It's hard enough seeing my brother behind bars; today's visit is going to be harder still because I'm bringing unwanted thoughts of Calvin and his family along with me.

I slip out from under my too-warm covers and turn to make the bed the moment my feet hit the ground. The bedspread is old and faded, patched together with remnants from old clothes and blankets. My grandmother made it when Mom was a little girl, but Mom had to earn it each day by doing chores and having good behavior otherwise she shivered at night. I never met my grandmother—after some of the stories I've heard about her I'm not sure I could've stomached the sight of her—and the quilt used to be locked away in a trunk in the attic, but I started using it a few months after Jason went away, feeling like I earned something that I couldn't get anywhere else. Every morning I fold it away and keep it under my bed in case Mom comes into my room.

Once the bed is made and the quilt hidden from sight,

I move to my closet. I dress automatically, eschewing the sundresses I normally live in during the summer in favor of items that meet the prison dress code for visitors: jeans and a long-sleeve crewneck T-shirt. I remove the tiny stud earrings I always wear and slip into my sneakers instead of flip-flops. I take a little time putting on makeup and add soft waves to my hair with a curling wand. I even repaint my nails. The goal is to look nice but not overly happy. It's a balance I've honed to perfection over the past year.

Mom is similarly dressed when I find her downstairs. Laura is still in her room and Dad is nowhere to be seen. They always make themselves scarce on Saturday mornings, knowing Mom will invite them to come. They always refuse, adding to the pallor of an already melancholy event. For once, I'm glad they're not there.

Seeing me, Mom smiles. It's more an expression of relief than anything else. One of her many fears is that I'll start disappearing on Saturdays too, leaving her to visit Jason alone. The everything-is-fine act she puts on is for her own benefit as much as everyone else's. If she had to make this trip on her own she'd have only this long-denied reality to keep her company.

I return her smile. "Want me to drive?"

She gathers up her purse and keys. "Maybe on the way back, okay?"

"Sure," I say, following her to the car. She doesn't ever let me drive. I think it's one of a million tiny distractions that she needs, on visitation days more than ever.

As soon as the car starts, talk radio blares from the speakers. Mom turns up the volume.

★ ★ ★

My knee bounces under the round table in the visitation room. There are a dozen other people in the nondescript space, including a toddler whose mother is trying to keep the child entertained while they wait.

"Daddy's going to come right through that door." The mother points to the entrance flanked on either side by guards. "Can you show me how you're going to clap when you see Daddy?"

My knee bounces faster as I look away. Beside me, Mom is watching the now clapping child, her expression strained in the same way mine feels. Anywhere else, it'd be impossible not to smile at the sweet little face, but not here, not when *Daddy* is in this place.

There is nowhere else to look for distraction. The cinder block walls are white, and there aren't any windows. Even the air feels sterile and so artificially chilled that goose bumps pebble my skin despite the long-sleeve shirt I'm wearing. I force my gaze upward to the fine cracks in the ceiling. I've traced the familiar pattern twice through when the door opens and the first inmate is led inside.

I'm on my feet in an instant, trying not to look at the inmates' faces as they see their loved ones waiting for them. Most of them remain outwardly stoic, but there's usually a flash of naked emotion—relief, despair, shame—that bleeds through. I don't know these men or what they've done, who they are to my brother, friend or not. He's never once mentioned his fellow prisoners, not even the name of his cellmate.

Jason is the fourth one in, and even though I've steeled

myself in preparation for his appearance—one so altered from how he looked a year ago—I can't keep from sucking in a breath I hope Mom doesn't hear. It's not any one thing that forms the lump in my throat; it's everything together.

He was always lean, like Mom, but now he's borderline gaunt in his orange jumpsuit, with high cheekbones that look ready to split through his too-pale skin. The shadows under his always-darting flat blue eyes have deepened, and his hair, once a sun-kissed brown, is a dark stubble shorn so close to his head that no hint of the natural wave shows. What I do see is the puncture mark scars from when he was ten and he fought off a stray dog that had attacked a neighbor's cat in our yard.

That's the brother I know, not this.

The smile Jason offers is as tight as the fist around my heart.

We're allowed one quick hug each while a guard stands nearby in case Mom or I try to pass him drugs. His whip-lean arms barely close around me before they drop and he shuffles back a step, glancing at the guard for approval before sitting. The lump rises higher. *He's like a dog*, I think, *and not a loved one.*

Mom's smile is bright to the point of looking painful. "How are you doing? Good week?"

"Yeah, Mom," he says, but his voice is so raspy that even Mom's smile falters the second he glances at me. "Hey. Dad and Laura?"

"They're good," I tell him, before adding what I always say. "They couldn't make it."

I hate that they don't come. Laura is still so young and

Jason was always one step down from a superhero to her, so a part of me understands that it might be too hard for her to see him here like this, knowing what he did. But I don't understand Dad's refusal to visit. Jason is his son. No crime, however awful, can change that. And Jason isn't that person; I *know* he's not. Whatever happened that night, whatever drove him to act out in that brief burst of violence, that's not the person sitting across from me.

That's not the person who pleaded guilty rather than put his family through a long and painful trial in the hopes of getting a lighter sentence.

That's not the person who asks about his dad and sister every week even though they refuse to visit him.

That's not my brother.

"Dad's so busy," Mom hurries to add with an exaggerated eye roll. "Did I tell you about the order he's been working on? The buyer wants him to replicate a ten-chaired Russian dining set that belonged to his great-grandparents. All he had was a faded photograph, so it's a lot of design work and research for me before he can even start."

"Sounds like a lot."

"It is, but I think it'll be really beautiful once it's done. And Laura is good. I can't believe she's already fourteen. I can still remember your fourteenth birthday," she says to Jason. "And yours." She reaches for my hand and squeezes it. "Time goes by so fast."

Jason lowers his gaze to the twitching hands he's resting on the table. Only last week he'd let slip how long the days feel here, how sometimes he'll watch a clock and swear the hands are turning backward. He normally doesn't say things like that, about what it's like for him. He normally doesn't say much at all, preferring to let Mom talk with my occasional interjections, which is why I don't answer right away when he asks me a question.

"So what happened with the Camaro? Guy wouldn't budge on his price, would he?"

"Actually, he did," I say, warming to the subject change. "I brought my friend Maggie with me and we kind of bullied/charmed him into the price I wanted. It helped that I had cash, but yeah. I bought a car." I start to reach for my keys to show him the ridiculous fuzzy keychain, but abort the gesture midway when I remember that I had to surrender them along with all my other belongings at security. Jason's gaze is sharp, following my movements, and I know without a doubt he guessed my intentions and it's another unwelcome reminder of his situation. "Anyway, I named her Daphne."

Jason shakes his head a little at my propensity for naming inanimate objects, but it's accompanied by an exhale that's at least partially a laugh. "That's a terrible name for a muscle car."

Lightened by the once-familiar teasing from him, I smile. "Trust me, I regretted it after about the hundredth time she stalled on me."

"What'd you expect buying a stick when you've never driven one?" He glances at Mom. "You guys shouldn't have let her buy that car. I wouldn't have."

I still think he's teasing me, so I laugh. "Right, like you could have stopped me, besides—"

Jason sneers, and it's such an alien expression on his face

that I don't even try to finish telling him that I'm now completely comfortable driving stick. I don't know what switch I hit, but I try to throw it back. "You always told me Camaros were your favorite cars," I say, tucking my hands into my lap. "She's even blue."

Jason's eye twitches. "So you get to own it for me? That's great, Brooke. I'll be sure to think about you stalling it all over town next time I'm walking around the yard." He pushes back into his chair so forcefully that it skids, screeching across the floor and causing the guards to move in. Mom and Jason and I have to repeatedly assure them everything is fine before they retreat.

I can see Jason struggling to control his breathing even after they move away and Mom steers the conversation toward more neutral territory. I'm barely listening. The car was supposed to make him happy. Sure, I liked the car, and now that I can drive stick, I prefer it to automatic. But the reason I found that Camaro in the first place was for Jason. I never for a moment considered he would resent me owning a car he wouldn't get to see, much less drive, for decades, if then. Sitting across from him, I feel so foolish for not realizing how much it would bother him. I'm still stewing in self-recrimination when Jason says my name and I lift my gaze to meet his.

"I'm sorry. I don't know why I got upset."

His apology makes me feel worse. "No, it's my fault. I wasn't thinking. I thought of you as soon as I saw the Camaro and I knew you'd love her."

"I would. I do."

"Yeah, but for yourself."

His eye twitches a little again. "Maybe, but that's not an option. If it can't be mine, then yeah, why shouldn't it be yours?"

Because you shouldn't be here, I think. *Because you belong outside with us, driving a car you'd love and enjoying everything else that would have been yours if you'd made one different choice.*

Unbidden, Heath's face tangles in my thoughts, and it's all I can do to push it away and focus on my brother for the too-little time I have left with him that day.

"Do me a favor though, okay?"

I'd do anything for my brother and he knows it, so he doesn't even wait for my assent before asking.

"Don't go on any main roads until you can handle the back ones without stalling. This would be easier in the car, but basically, what you need to do is—"

I open my mouth to tell him Maggie already taught me, but I feel Mom's hand squeeze my knee beneath the table and I close it while Jason goes on to explain the process.

He rarely says more than a sentence or two together, but now he's talking and animated as he gestures and mimes the movements I need to make next time I drive Daphne. He does this sometimes, comes alive in a way the prison seldom lets him. It's bittersweet, seeing him like this, because it never lasts. A single wrong word or a sound or even just a random thought, and he'll go quiet as sudden as a candle snuffing out. I'm watching him intently so I see it happen, like a flinch, and I have no idea why. One second he's smiling and shaking his head about my car, and the next his shoulders are rolling in as his head drops down, the transformation happening before my eyes in the most heartbreaking way possible. He's gone for the rest of the visit, lost in himself no matter what Mom or I try to do or say to draw him back out.

After Mom hugs Jason goodbye she moves away to give my brother and me the semblance of privacy for a few seconds. I wrap my arms around his waist and try not to think about how much less of him there is to hold.

"You're really okay?" he asks, his words muffled by my hair, softening the rasp.

I want to return the question to him, only I know I won't like the honest answer any more than he'll like mine. So I sigh audibly. "I spent all my money on a car that hates me. Why wouldn't I be okay?"

I feel his slight laugh and it's like sunshine finding its way into this windowless room. I want more of it. "Maybe when you call this week you can go over shifting gears again with me?"

"Sure, Brooke."

A cleared throat from the guard makes me let him go, but his expression doesn't dim when he looks at me.

"But you gotta practice on your own too. Why don't you drive out on the dirt road by Hackman's Pond? You know we're pretty much the only ones who go out that way since they paved Williams Field Road. You can stall and start without anyone around to notice."

I lower my eyes and, when I answer him, mine is the voice that sounds hoarse. "Maybe," is all I can say, because I know that today at least one other person will be there.

"No maybe," he says, looking and sounding more like

my bossy brother. "You gotta leave me knowing you're gonna do right by that car."

Looking up at him, I nod.

CHAPTER 11

Mom and I don't say much after leaving the prison. I keep waiting for it to get easier, for it to feel normal seeing him in that environment, but it never does. If anything, it gets harder to have to leave him in a place he doesn't belong any more than Heath's brother belongs in a grave.

I glance at Mom once the prison is well behind us, but if her thoughts are similar to mine, no part of her shows it. Her hands on the wheel stay loose and relaxed while mine tighten around the hem of my shirt. Blue, Jason's favorite color. Mom's blouse is the same hue.

Closing my eyes, I will my heartbeat to steady.

"Headache?" Mom asks, switching off the radio and briefly turning to me.

"No," I say. "Just thinking." But she's already reaching for her purse, and I take the aspirin she gives me without protest.

"He looked better today, don't you think?"

I resist closing my eyes again. I don't want to remember Jason as we left him. There's always something desperate lurking below the surface in his face when they take him away, a fear and longing that he knows better than to voice. Some visits, I have to pry my fingers from the edge of the table, not because I want to stay but because I can't bear to leave without him.

And yet...he took a life.

I glance out the window and the few trees we pass, they aren't live oaks, but they're enough to remind me of the boy who might have been waiting for me, and the boy whose life was taken.

Two hours later we hit the dirt roads that signal we're a few miles from home. Apart from the warm breeze and the cicadas' timbal clicking, the afternoon is as quiet as the road is empty. I lean back at the odd slowing of my heart, wondering if even now there's a red truck parked by Hackman's Pond.

I hesitate by our car when we get home, and my unwillingness to go in is more than the usual reluctance I feel whenever Mom and I return from visiting Jason. It doesn't even help that I see Uncle Mike's truck parked out front, and Uncle Mike usually makes everything better.

Uncle Mike isn't technically my uncle. He was my dad's best friend growing up and is the closest thing to a brother he has now, and to hear him tell it, the owner of a still-broken heart from when Mom chose Dad over him. Mom always reminds him that they barely dated and that he was the one to introduce her to Dad.

Uncle Mike is still single though. Back when he used

to drink and would end up crashing on our couch some nights when we had to take away his keys, he'd sometimes say stuff about how he should have fought for Mom instead of watching his best friend steal her heart. He always laughed it off though, made some joke to me, Jason and Laura about any prospective single moms we might know.

Uncle Mike is trudging up from the basement when Mom and I push open the screen door. His gaze alights on Mom's face first, but the smile he gives me is almost as good. Uncle Mike isn't as tall as my dad, or as broad. He still has all his hair, blond and a little curly, though he keeps it short, and he's constantly lamenting his inability to grow a full beard. He's a nice-looking guy, Uncle Mike; he's just never going to catch the eye of the one woman he wants to catch.

He hurries over to hold the door for us.

"Thanks, Mike," Mom says on her way to the stairs. "Can you stay for dinner?"

"What kind of fool would say no to that?" He cranes his neck to watch her ascend the stairs. Then his gaze falls on me. "Hey, kid. How's the ice treating you these days?"

"Cold," I say.

"No kidding. When are you heading off to the Olympics to win me all those gold medals?"

I offer a tight-lipped smile. "Any day now."

"Yeah? 'Cause I figured out this move that I think you should do. It's got gold written all over it. It's kinda like a cross between *The Karate Kid* crane kick and a hula."

I've never seen *The Karate Kid*, and watching Uncle Mike do…whatever he proceeds to do in my living room, I have my doubts about his ever having seen it either. He almost crashes into the coffee table as he balances on one foot before striking a pose so ludicrous that I have to laugh, a loud one that comes right from the belly.

"Right?" he says, straightening and then wincing as he rubs his knee. "I'll teach you after dinner, 'cause it's not as easy as it looks."

Another laugh erupts from me. This is what Uncle Mike does. He makes the near two-hour drive up from San Angelo every Saturday that he can while Mom and I visit Jason. He distracts Dad and Laura if they let him, and always, *always* finds a way to make me laugh when I get home, even if he has to nearly break a bone to do it.

He lets me help him limp to the couch, and then hits me with a real question while I'm still off guard.

"How's J?"

I meet his gaze, mine instantly sobering, and claim the chair opposite him. "The same?"

"Kid."

I draw my knees up, wanting to squirm under his stare. Next to Laura, our parents and me, nobody loved Jason more than Uncle Mike. After fourteen years of sobriety, he fell off the wagon hard when Jason went to prison. He's the only one who has any idea what it's like being behind bars, having spent two years in a minimum-security prison after his third drunk-driving strike almost fifteen years ago.

"He's hanging in there. I know it helps seeing us. I think it'd help more if Dad and Laura came." I don't mention Uncle Mike visiting. It eats him up that his request was denied due to his past felony conviction and the fact that he's not technically family.

Uncle Mike hangs his head. "I'm working on your dad."

"I know. Thanks."

After a moment he says, "You tell him I love him?"

Jason, he means. I nod.

When the silence stretches on, I start to stand.

"What about the skating thing? The real one. What's it called again?"

"Stories on Ice."

"Stories on Ice," he says, smiling. I don't smile back. He scoots forward on the couch. "You know I was kidding about the Olympics. This ice show is a big deal. I'd be real proud of you."

The clouds outside shift, letting a beam of dying sunlight through the windows, bathing us in a warm glow, and for a heartbeat, I feel better.

"Proud of her for what?" Mom asks, unwinding her earbuds as she comes downstairs dressed for another run. This on top of the predawn one she already took. There aren't any marathons coming up, none that she plans to run in anymore, but she trains like she'll be running one in a week. If she could time it, she'd probably run all the way to the prison and back each week in an effort to exhaust her mind as much as her body.

"Storybook on Ice."

"Stories on Ice," I correct in a much less enthusiastic voice.

Mom halts on the second to last step. "What?"

I understand her surprise even as I'd hoped—at least a part of me had hoped—not to see it.

"That's the plan, isn't it?" Uncle Mike asks, eyes wide and as innocent as he's capable of making them—which isn't very. "You agreed she could set college aside if she made the show. When is the audition deadline?" He looks from me to Mom, and it's anyone's guess to say who looks more ill at the question.

I know the answer just as surely as Mom does, but neither of us is inclined to give it. We used to talk about it all the time, but that was before. How can I leave, or even think about leaving? If I made the show, I'd be touring the country for most of the year. Laura wouldn't talk to anyone besides a bird she keeps caged for fear he'll fly away. Dad would take up permanent residence in his workshop, sanding away at himself more than the wood he shaped. Mom would be left running away from it all, literally.

And Jason. He'll be fifty when he gets out of prison, older than Mom and Dad and Uncle Mike.

I don't know that any of us will make it that long.

My hand flies out to the nearest wall to hold me up when it feels like nothing else ever will. I can't do it. "Howard College," I say, almost like a gasp. "I'm going to enroll in community college when I graduate. Being far from home doesn't really appeal to me anymore."

Jolting back into motion, Mom nods. "People don't give community colleges enough credit these days. And she can always transfer somewhere else later if she wants."

Uncle Mike frowns at me. "Yeah, but what about skating? We're not just gonna let you give that up." He turns to Mom to pull her to his side, but she's already halfway out of the room and doesn't look at either of us.

"I think I forgot to preheat the oven. Mike, do you mind? 350?"

Uncle Mike is on his feet before the request is out. He'll do anything for her, even drop a conversation cold simply because she's not ready to have it. She won't meet my gaze, but Uncle Mike does. I try to smile at the apologetic look he gives me, and I manage enough of one that he moves past me into the kitchen without saying anything.

"Mom?" I call when she bends to retie her running shoe. "I think I'm going to head out for a bit. Maybe see if Maggie wants to go with me to the rink." The words turn bitter on my tongue. I don't like lying to her, but neither do I want to hurt her by revealing where I actually intend to go. She might decide to veer from her normal run south along the Wilcox River to watch me.

She hesitates, but if she can convince herself that Jason's cadaverous form "looks better," then my lingering pallor from Uncle Mike's question should be nothing. She nods before turning toward the back door. "Be home in time for dinner."

I leave through the front, hating that I feel better as soon as our house and the people in it fade from the rear-view mirror.

CHAPTER 12

I don't stall even once as I drive down our long drive-way and turn up Boyer Road. I like that all the roads back here are dirt, especially on the days after a light rain when the ground is packed down and still a little red. It makes them feel alive to me. It's a few miles before I see any other houses, but the earthy smell of cattle and manure reach me long before I see the McClintocks' ranch. A few cows look up as I pass, and I let my gaze travel fondly over the soft brown bodies until they shrink out of sight in my rearview mirror. I turn west on Pecan Road, which leads me far-ther away from town rather than toward it, and the road becomes less defined, with tufts of wild grass sprouting up between faded tire tracks. Jason was right about how little used these roads are these days.

A stranger might not even see the faint impression that marks the turnoff for Hackman's Road, but I'd know it in my sleep. Soon I'm driving up the hill above the pond and wondering at the erratic beating of my heart. Heath's not waiting for me by the massive live oak tree, and I tell myself he never was. It seems ridiculous to think we had a conversation, however vaguely, about meeting here, much less either of us actually showing up. Yet here I am, and I can't say that a part of me isn't disappointed that he's not here too.

As I pull off the road at the top of the hill and lower my hands to my lap as the engine idles, I force my gaze to roam beyond the tree. This stretch of road doesn't even have a name anymore. There's a rusted pole several miles back, but if there ever was an actual sign on it, no one remembers what it was. It's the road by Hackman's Pond, and how the pond got that name is as big a mystery as the unnamed road. There isn't a house or structure for miles. The verdant grasses grow high and wild and so thick on either side of the road that when the wind blows it looks like waves on a sea splashed with sprays of golden yellow wildflowers.

The sun is still high in the sky, making the smooth surface of the pond glow amber and gold. The sun-bleached white dock jutting from the pond's edge is empty, but I know how smooth the worn planks would feel beneath my feet. This is exactly the kind of summer afternoon that would have seen me and Jason and Laura here, leaping off our bikes and kicking off our shoes—when we bothered to wear them—as we raced to see who would reach the end of the dock first. No matter how big our head start was, Jason always beat us. He usually had time to spin backward so that he could grin in triumph at us as he cannonballed into the water, drenching Laura and me before we even left the dock.

We didn't come here as much once Jason turned sixteen and got his license, but there were always a few days each summer—the sweltering sticky ones—when Jason would look at Laura or me and without a word we'd all just know. We'd drive to the pond instead of biking, but still race like little kids to see who could reach the water first. My heart clenches tighter and tighter as I look at the empty dock, imagining the three of us running across it. It hurts to hold on to the memory, but I'll never let go.

There's nothing feigned about the relief I feel at being alone. It's different than the kind of alone I feel surrounded by other people, even my family. I can cry here if I want, or scream, or both. I can think about the dreams I had for my life, the ones a tiny part of me still hopes will come true, and how not even my mom wants them for me anymore.

I can think about my brother and feel however I want to about the fact that he's not with me and that we'll never again be the kids who leap laughing off the dock at Hackman's Pond. If I wasn't alone, there'd still be no one I could talk to about Jason anyway, least of all Heath.

A few dozen yards from the road is the massive tree Heath mentioned, with its gnarled, tentacle-like branches that rise and dip like they truly were once moving. Even from this distance I can see lighter patches against the gray bark, the names and initials carved by people in this town going back generations, back when this road was the only road. I watched Mark Keller, the first and last boy I ever kissed, immortalize our initials onto the trunk some twenty feet above the heart Jason painstakingly carved around his and Allison's—the girl he'd openly talked about marrying after college.

Jason claimed he broke up with Allison in the wake of his arrest and wouldn't let her come to the courthouse or visit him in prison. He said he didn't want to ruin her life any more than he already had, but that never sat well with me. I know Cal was her friend in addition to Jason's, but Jason was supposed to be her soul mate. If she loved him a fraction as much as he loved her, she'd have been there even if it hurt, even if it was only to say goodbye. But she wasn't. The girl who was at our house so often that Dad made her her own chair vanished, practically overnight. She didn't come to the arraignment or show up at our house to cry with Mom. She never once sought solace from the only people who understood what she was supposedly losing. As far as I know, she still hasn't said a word to him. I don't know if Jason would have told her what drove him to… do what he did that night, but I do know that she made it impossible for him to even try.

Daphne's engine dies before I'm conscious of turning the key. A warm breeze ripples across the tall grasses lining the road and surrounding the pond. I shade my eyes from the sun and keep the loose strands of my hair from blowing into my face as I scan the ground for a rock sharp enough to suit my needs. A few more steps take me under the canopy shade of the tree, and instantly the temperature feels a good twenty degrees cooler on top of the sudden ice in my veins. Someone has already beaten me to the task of severing Allison's initials from my brother's. Where Jason's initials used to be, there's a jagged hole as deep as my fist, as though someone took an ax to that one part of the tree and made sure not a single line remained. It was such a violent assault that not even Allison's initials escaped the attack. My fingers reach for the gouge and press against the splintered wood as I bite the inside of my cheek to hold back the tears building in my eyes.

I turn my back to the tree and to the memories that have grown more bitter than they ever were sweet, and that's when I see what the pounding in my ears didn't let me hear: a red truck pulling up behind Daphne.

CHAPTER 13

I take a step to slide in front of the hacked part of the tree only to stop when the realization hits me that Heath might have been the one who did it. The entire town down to the smallest child would like nothing more than to see the blighted memory of my brother cut out of this tree and every other thing that proves he was ever here, possibly none more so than the guy staring at me through his windshield. Something sharper than the rock I scooped up slices at my heart, and I let the stone tumble from my fingers. Understanding how Heath could hate my brother doesn't dull the bleeding pain I feel when confronted by it; if anything the pain feels magnified, because reality no longer makes sense. It's like there are two different people—my brother, and the person who killed Cal.

I shouldn't be here. I shouldn't have given him any indication that I would be. The whisper of disappointment I felt earlier when I thought he hadn't come is shouted down by the dread locking my joints. It feels like the time I let Laura and Jason talk me into jumping off the train tracks over the Wilcox River.

Kids in Telford had been jumping off the tracks for decades despite the warning signs. It didn't look very high from the ground, and even I could admit it wasn't dangerously high. The worst thing I'd heard happened to a jumper was a split lip, and that was because a couple had tried to jump together midkiss. My siblings had both made the jump before and were relentless in taunting me about being a coward. So one day I caved. I followed them to the middle of the bridge when the morning sun was bright and warm on my skin, watched my then fearless eleven-year-old sister step backward off the edge like she'd done it a million times and had to swallow back a scream as she fell. Not even Laura's smiling wave from the water below could quell the tremors racking my body. Jason tried to give me a pep talk, pointing out that the drop wasn't high enough to hurt anything even if I belly flopped. But it was too late. My toes were curled around the rail as I looked down from the dizzying height—in reality no more than forty feet but it felt like forty miles.

"I can't do it," I told Jason.

"You can," he said. "I'll even jump with you."

I tore my gaze away from the river to the hand my brother offered me, but only shook my head. I was up too high and the water was down too far. My heart was jackhammering in my chest, fear flooding my mouth with saliva that forced me to swallow endlessly.

"Don't be such a baby, Brooke!" Laura shouted up.

"Give her a sec!" Jason called back, and then met my wild, frightened gaze with his steady one. He inclined his head in Laura's direction. "She's gonna hold it over your head for a really long time. I've seen you get more height at the rink than this, and water is a lot more forgiving than ice." He smiled at me, but my lips stayed thin and pressed taut. He sighed. "You can't do one jump? You can say it wasn't fun or whatever and you won't ever have to do it again. Come on, let's go on three?"

My answer was a violent *no* that shook my whole body. I was so petrified by then I was sure I'd have to crawl off the tracks.

"Okay, okay," Jason had said, wrapping me in a hug I needed more than my next breath. "You don't have to jump—"

I'd instantly calmed when my brother rested his chin on my forehead.

"—all you have to do is hold on." His hands had locked around my back as he flung himself over the edge, taking me with him.

One second, two? That's how long I was airborne. Fear has a way of freezing time, spinning it into an eternity that the body remembers long after the fact. I remember the endless scream ripping from my throat, the wind trying to tear my hair from my scalp, the air punching against my skin. I remember my brother's arms, once strong and protective, turning hard and binding as I fought to free myself. I want to shake the memory away, but it just burrows deeper.

I barely remember hitting the water or Jason's grinning

face when I finally surfaced. He'd tried to pump me up, tried to get me to admit that it hadn't been that bad, but it had. I didn't talk to him for a week, during which time I tried to convince myself that Jason made me jump only because he thought he was helping me face a fear that he didn't understand and had therefore minimized. Once he saw how very real that fear had been—and still was—he'd been the picture of contrition. He'd even offered to jump off one of the bridges in Lufkin that was easily five times as high so he could understand what I'd felt if that's what it took to earn my forgiveness.

So I forgave him. But I didn't forget.

Heath turns off his engine, and countless little eternities fade away before he gets out and walks around the front of his truck. He stops at the edge of the road, standing in the bright sun and squinting at me through eyes he doesn't bother shading. We're far enough away from each other that I can't be sure if I see his mouth moving, saying words he doesn't mean for me to hear. He starts walking toward me, each step kicking my pulse higher. I tell myself I'm not standing on the train tracks above the Wilcox River, that no one is lying in wait to force me over the edge the moment I lower my guard, but the vertigo ringing in my ears is louder.

He stops a few yards away, just inches from the shade, seemingly incapable of moving closer.

"I wasn't sure you were going to come," he says.

"I was sure you weren't."

He might have narrowed his eyes at that; it's hard to tell when he's still squinting from the sun.

Minutes ago I was grateful for the solitude I'd found here and the emotional freedom it afforded me. I can feel my eyes shining and still so perilously close to overflowing, and I want it back now more than ever. I don't know what Heath would do if I did cry in front of him, true tears, not just the promise of them that he's seen before. Maybe it would harden him enough that'd he'd be able to walk away for good. Maybe they'd fuel yet another accusation that I'm trying to manipulate him. Worse, maybe they'd rouse his pity. That last thought is so abhorrent to me that my eyes dry and the dizziness along with all memory from the train tracks vanishes in a single shaky breath.

I take a step toward Heath only to prove to myself that I can, that I'm not that same fearful, shaking girl I used to be, but I slow when he tenses. For some reason, I'm relieved to see that he's as unsettled as I am.

When I make no further move, he exhales. "Is that why you came? To make sure I didn't?" There's the barest hint of a taunt in his tone, and it makes my chin lift.

"Does it matter? I'm here, you're here, exactly where neither of us should be."

Heath shifts his weight. The slight movement triggers an impulse to back up, only the tree is behind me, blocking any real retreat. "Why'd you come, Brooke?"

I feel a flash of hatred for my own name when he says it. "Why did you?"

His expression makes it clear he's not going to answer first.

"I don't know," I say, and it's only a slight lie. I came because I told my brother I would, and because there was a tiny nagging scrap of doubt in my mind that said if Heath did come, I'd feel worse for standing him up than I would confirming he was a no-show. Only now, with the bark behind me digging into my back and memories I don't want mingling with the ones I do, I stiffen. If the reason he wanted me here was so I could see what was done to Jason's name—by his hand or another's—then I was dead wrong.

"I'm surprised you even know about this place. I'm not used to seeing anyone else out here anymore."

"I only live on the end of Mulberry, and I used to fish here with my granddad before his hip started acting up. I guess it's been a while though."

"Was this you?" I ask, reaching behind me to place my hand over the hacked part of the tree.

His stare follows my hand and I lower it, exposing the gouge marks. Heath doesn't say anything for a long, long time. Whether he knows Jason's name was once there or not, it's obvious now. At last his gaze returns to my face. There's no triumph at seeing the pain I'm not trying to hide, but neither is there true compassion.

"No," he says, the word followed by an audible click of his jaw. Forcing it open again, he adds, "I wouldn't have picked this place if I had." Which isn't the same as saying he wouldn't have done it.

The sound of the cicadas clicking swells in the ensuing silence. All I can think is *Why did you pick any place? Why put us together when you know it feels like this? What can we possibly gain from each other besides more of this?* I can't blame anyone else for what Jason did, but that doesn't stop that pain of what I've lost from surfacing when Heath is near any more than my presence rouses more for him. The only thing left is for him to go. He doesn't have to say anything else; I know I won't.

His gaze sweeps over me. The movement is swift and seemingly involuntary, based on the way he jerks his gaze back to my face.

My cheeks flush. That isn't the kind of scrutiny I expect from him or anyone anymore. I find myself frowning at him, like he betrayed some unspoken rule by looking at me.

"You're wearing blue again."

I blink at the random comment.

"You wear it a lot."

I nod, wondering if he's asking a question or stating a fact, and then deciding it doesn't matter. I do wear blue a lot. Maggie thinks it's my favorite color.

It's on my nails, my shirt, even my car.

My brother isn't perfect. He can be overbearing and judgmental, and he always thinks he's right even when he's not. Forcing me to jump off those train tracks wasn't the first less-than-perfect thing he's done and it wasn't the last either. There were times growing up when I hated him and he hated me. I used to try to block out those memories, push them to the background of my mind and let only the good ones rise to the front. That's what I did when Jason was first arrested. I acted like people do at funerals, making saints out of even the most wretched people as though the involuntary act of death erased all the bad things they'd ever done. That's harder to do when the person isn't dead but in prison. Jason killed someone, yet I still surround myself with his favorite color because he's my brother and I miss him. But that isn't fair to confess to Heath. My brother is alive, but gone; his brother is dead, but everywhere.

Because of Jason.

I can't look away from Heath, even as my staring approaches an uncomfortable line and then barrels past it. I'm thinking about Jason and Laura and whether or not I'd be able to stand here with him if our situations were reversed and his brother was responsible for either of their deaths. The answer is swift and sure. *No.* I'd have gouged *his* name from the tree. I'd have chosen the rain over a ride. I'd have done more than yell when I threw Heath's money back at him. I wouldn't have been able to hold on to my composure in front of him, not for a single second. It bothers me that he can stay calm, even though I can see that the effort is costing him.

"I don't hate you." Heath's face is as expressionless as his voice. "I thought I would, that the sight of you, any of you, would be like seeing *him*." Jason. Heath's weight shifts forward as though he's considering taking another step, one that would bring him under the shade with me. "It hurts, but it's not hate." After a moment he nods like we've just settled something, only I can't begin to fathom what it is. He turns toward his truck.

But then he stops. He doesn't look at me when he says, "I'll be here again after it rains."

CHAPTER 14

The murder of Calvin Gaines was the worst crime to ever hit our town. It briefly made national news and locally it was broadcast around the clock for months. TV crews lived in our yard, shoving cameras and microphones into our faces the second we stepped outside. They followed me and Laura to school, chased Mom down at the library where she worked and bombarded Dad at every possible opportunity. One even pretended to be a nurse at my doctor's office. And it was always different versions of the same questions:

"Did your brother ever display homicidal tendencies before he killed Calvin Gaines?"

"Did your brother torture animals?"

"Your uncle is a convicted felon. Did he play a role in the murder?"

"Did your brother talk about planning to murder his friend?"

"Were you ever afraid your brother might harm you or your sister?"

"What do you say to those who are demanding the death penalty for your brother?"

Once Jason confessed, that was it. There was no safe place, no safe person. Too many of our so-called friends were suddenly all too eager to give interviews revealing that they always secretly knew how unhinged Jason was. Not unhinged enough for them to say anything to anyone, but just enough to cash in on their fifteen minutes of fame afterward.

Mom never said she was asked to leave her job at the library, but Dad had some choice words for the branch manager when she called to say that Mom didn't need to put in her two weeks.

We didn't stop going to our church all at once. Heath's family were members of the massive Southern Baptist church while my family attended the smaller United Methodist church. Otherwise we would have stopped right away. Our church numbers swelled in the weeks following Jason's arrest; the new attendees ranged from gawkers to gossips to reporters waiting for us in the parking lot. The brazen ones even sidled up next to us during Communion. Mom actually kept going for a full month after Dad, Laura and I stopped, but even she couldn't hold out forever. I think most of the congregation was relieved. They tried not to be, but what do you say to someone when their child is a murderer?

At our old church, Pastor Hamilton used to preach about forgiveness and the grace of God being greater than all our sins, but Telford was still small enough that most of the people outside the walls of our church were either unwilling or uncertain how to extend kindness to my family without spitting on the Gaineses. The ones who didn't keep their distance on their own weren't given a choice.

And I know they were relieved.

Now we drive an hour and a half south to Odessa once or twice a month to attend Uncle Mike's mega church, which is so big I've never seen the same face twice, and where the rotating pastoral staff preach sermons with titles like God Wants You to Win the Lottery.

Slowly but surely we all withdrew from everything and everyone in Telford. It was almost too easy. I'd been home-schooled briefly before due to my ice-skating training, so it was simple enough to transfer Laura and me to an online school. We don't live in town, and once Dad took an ax to our mailbox, it became a lot harder for reporters to find us. He picks up our mail—and the groceries Mom now orders online—from the post office once a week. Apart from Dad handling that unavoidable task, I'm the only one who still ventures beyond our property on a regular basis.

I wouldn't even do that if it weren't for the ice rink.

And now Maggie.

Which is why I'm riding shotgun while she drives Daphne to Keller's Creamery for frozen custard on an early Monday afternoon. Keller's fresh frozen custard is so rich and so creamy, I didn't put up a protest when she called earlier begging me to make a run with her. She thinks I have a mild form of agoraphobia. She hasn't forced the issue with me, since she openly prefers the online world to the real one herself, but she's not wrong about Keller's frozen custard being worth a little potential discomfort.

I'm hoping it won't be too busy. It's barely noon and the people who grew up in this town know to wait until after one, when Ann Keller herself comes in. She's seventy-eight years old and almost as revered as Willie Nelson around these parts. Whatever she does when she serves the custard makes it infinitely more decadent than it already is.

I have my excuse ready for why I'll need to stay in the car while Maggie goes inside, but I can't speak when we pull into the half-empty parking lot.

A silver SUV is parked not three spaces from us and Mark Keller, grandson of the beloved Ann and Mitch Keller and the guy I gave my first and last kiss to—the guy who even now has his initials carved next to mine near the top of Hackman's tree—is making his way to his vehicle. He stops when he sees me, but whereas I try to slink down to hide, he only pauses to swallow before heading straight for me.

"No, no, no, no, no…" I mutter as he approaches. Maggie is too busy shimmying while singing the frozen custard song she made up as she digs through her massive purse for cash to notice until he raps on my window.

"Oh, sweet, they do curbside now?" Maggie asks. "Tell him I just need one minute." She then proceeds to empty half the contents of her purse into her lap.

I don't answer her; instead I take a fortifying breath and open my door. Mark steps back to let me stand, but not nearly enough to be polite. As I shut the door behind me I'm praying Maggie stays in the car long enough for me to get rid of him.

"I just came to get a custard," I say, keeping my gaze

on a spot just over his shoulder. "I didn't know you were going to be here."

Hands in his pockets, he leans forward. "Hi, Brooke. It's nice to see you too. Me? I'm good, thanks for asking."

I shift to meet his eyes. I used to think they were the perfect shade of chocolate against his lightly tanned skin, warm and flecked so slightly with gold that you had to be only inches away to notice it. Seeing them now, I feel nothing save for a desire not to. I try to move to the side but his hand shoots out to block me. A second later I hear Maggie's door open and then she's bending down to retrieve some of the items that spilled from her purse.

"Don't say anything," I whisper, clutching his wrist.

Mark flicks his gaze to Maggie before returning it to me. "What am I not supposed to say?" he asks, not bothering to lower his voice. "'Cause it's always what *you* want, right?"

"If you ever cared about me, you'll leave now. Please." I have to force the last word through my teeth.

"If I cared about you? *If?* You're the one who ended things, not me."

My hand flinches at my side, the urge to slap him almost overwhelming me. "What you did to me was unforgivable."

"But I thought you were big on forgiveness—or is that only for certain people?"

I blanch, and he drops his hand and softens his voice.

"I said I was sorry, Brooke." His hand shifts to brush my forearm. "When is it gonna be enough for you, huh?"

I yank my arm away from his touch, my eyes boring into his, and lean into his space. "I trusted you. I won't make that mistake again."

"You know what, whatever." He pushes off from the side of the car and stalks to his SUV.

I'm still shaking when Maggie appears at my side.

"You okay?"

I nod. He's gone, so I am. "He's—he was my boyfriend a while ago. We had a bad breakup."

"No kidding," Maggie says, flinching along with me when his tires squeal as he tears out of the parking lot.

"What's wrong with him?" Maggie asks.

"A lot," I say, hoping Maggie won't press me for details. He did care about me, I know that. Otherwise seeing me wouldn't affect him the way it just did. He did his best, at first, to support me when everything happened with Jason. I should have ended things after he tried to show me that leaked crime scene report, but he was so convincing when he said he didn't care about Jason's crime as long as I still loved him.

I can't believe how stupid I was.

"It's a small town," I tell Maggie, swallowing a bit of guilt for the half story I give her. "And people tend to hold grudges when you break the heart of Ann Keller's grandson."

"Ann Keller as in…" She points to the Keller's Creamery sign.

I nod. "It's fine though." Through the window I see a small group of girls. I recognize a couple from my chemistry class last year, including my former best friend, Tara Hudson. They all look harmless, the type to introduce themselves to, say, a stranger their own age if they happened to spot them alone. I know Tara would. I glance at

Maggie and shift in front of her, blocking her view of the girls and, more important, their view of her. "You know, I'm suddenly not in the mood for custard at all. What if we just go back to your house and make Coke floats. You have vanilla ice cream, right?"

Maggie gives a longing look at the store, but then notices the girls I spotted, and her expression softens. "You know, I've seen people looking at you kind of weird. I didn't understand it." She shakes her head. "I don't have to ask if you did anything cruel to your ex-boyfriend. I know you didn't, so why should you be the one to hide? If people want to suck, then I'll be right there next you. Maybe a few'll even surprise you and not suck a little. My mom would be happy if I made a few more friends—not best friends, that's all you, but just, you know, people I could sit with at lunch when school starts, since you won't be there. We could try…"

But I had tried. After Jason confessed, I made the mistake of trying to reconcile with Mark, mostly because I'd never felt so alone in my life. I let him in through my window one night just to hold me while I cried.

The next day, cell phone pictures of pages from my diary showed up on an online news site.

My chest feels tight and panicky at the memory, the private, broken words I'd let pour out of the deepest recesses of my heart that were stolen from me and dissected for the whole world to see. Maggie feels like the only person who hasn't seen them, who doesn't know.

"Brooke?"

I whirl around at the voice, not incredulous like Mark's

had been, but no less surprised. Tara is standing less than twenty feet from me, her hand holding open the creamery's door for the other girls to spill out into the parking lot with her. My face warms when two of the girls see me and start whispering.

"Wow, I feel like I haven't seen you in forever. Not since—" She cuts herself off and her cheeks flush.

Tara's dad is the sheriff and one of the elders at our old church. He helped my parents find a lawyer for Jason. He also stopped letting Tara come to my house, and limited our other interactions so much that there was very little friendship left to lose once that awful summer ended and I didn't return to Telford High.

I know she only did what her parents made her do, and I'm certain that she felt really bad about it. Looking at her now, with the added color still flushing her pale face, I can tell she still does. It doesn't fix anything between us though, and it hurts to see her and feel like we're strangers.

"—and Mark was just out here with her," one of the girls with Tara whispers none too quietly. "I hope he's okay."

Tara steps toward me just as I back away from her. She rocks to a halt. "I'm really sorry about everything, but—"

The girl who mentioned Mark—I think her name is Shannon—pulls at Tara's arm. "We're gonna miss the movie. Let's go." She looks askance at me and then transfers that same disapproval to Maggie.

"We have to wait for Emily," another girl says, pointing back inside. With jolt I recognize Dawn Beckmann, another former friend I went to school with since kindergarten. She used to have the biggest crush on my brother, and when the news first broke about Cal's death, she was my staunchest supporter in believing Jason was innocent. Now she can't even bring herself to look at me. I don't know whether that's from guilt over deserting me, or if she's still freaked out because he was guilty.

I don't care. Tara looks like she's considering doing something awful, like inviting me and Maggie to go with them, and the other girls look like they're trying to psych themselves up to start interrogating me about having a felon for a brother.

"Please," I say, to Maggie. "Can we just go?"

We leave, because Maggie isn't as selfish as I am.

The sky opens up as we drive back to her house, pouring enough rain down on us to wash the earth clean.

CHAPTER 15

My unease chases me home, up the steps of my porch and through my front door. It snaps at my heels when I hear the muffled sobs coming from the closed pantry. My footsteps slow, but I forget to step over the one creaky floorboard in the hall. The crying cuts off midsob.

A moment passes.

Another. I have to lift my foot again to move, but the second I do the floor creaks again.

"Brooke?"

I force my voice to be light. "It's me, Mom."

She clears her throat before speaking again, but it doesn't disguise the fact that she was crying and has been for a good long while. "I was looking to see if we had any of those canned tomatoes left, but I'm suddenly not feeling very well. Would you heat up the leftover lasagna for you, Laura and Dad?"

"Yes, ma'am."

"Brooke?"

"Yes, ma'am?"

"There's fixings for a salad in the fridge too."

"Yes, ma'am."

Mom slips out of the pantry and upstairs while I'm getting the food ready. When I call that dinner is ready, Dad and Laura come, but not Mom. The shower is running upstairs and it will keep running until long after the hot water is gone.

"Jason called?" I ask no one in particular once our silent meal has begun. It's not that Mom cries *only* on days that he calls, but she always cries when he does.

Dad swallows the bite he's chewing and fills his fork with another. "Yes."

One word, no more.

I glance at him, the mere effort of holding my fork up suddenly beyond me. I let my arm lower to the table. Had Mom been with us, her hawk eyes would have immediately noticed that I'd stopped eating and she'd give me a gentle admonishment to finish my dinner, her gaze never moving from me until I complied.

Dinners—really all meals—were a big deal for her, always had been. Growing up dirt-poor in a house with more bellies than food to fill them meant that gnawing hunger was a near daily reality for her as a child. I never knew that getting sent to bed without dinner was even a thing as a kid, because Mom would have sooner driven bamboo skewers under her nails than let her children know the sensation of an empty belly.

How many splintered meals had we shared since Jason

went away? Breakfast, lunch and dinner for a year...a thousand maybe? Would we ever all sit at this table again? I glance at Mom's empty chair then at the space where Jason's used to be. It was empty sometimes before he left for college. Not often, but it happened.

Once, right after Jason turned sixteen, he'd gotten into a fight with Dad over wanting to spend the summer with Uncle Mike instead of helping to replace the roof. As soon as we all sat down to dinner, Dad started talking about the material they'd need to pick up for the project. Jason swallowed a single bite before announcing that he was driving up to visit Uncle Mike after we ate.

"Can I come?" Laura asked. Jason rarely denied her anything, so she was already half out of her seat on her way to pack when his *no* stopped her.

"We'll get started on the roof as soon as you get back then," Dad said, slicing into his steak and making a noise that had Mom blushing.

"It's a good cut," she said, trying to dismiss the wordless compliment.

"It's never just the cut," he replied, holding her gaze.

"Why can't I come?" Laura plopped back into her chair. "Uncle Mike'll let me, and Ducky loves driving." She made kissy noises at the cockatiel on her shoulder before offering him a piece of broccoli to nibble.

"Leave Ducky," Mom said, adding more broccoli to Laura's plate and giving her an excuse-me face until Laura stopped scowling at the growing pile of vegetables. "Brooke'll take care of him."

"Sure," I said, distracted by the largely untouched steak

on Jason's plate. Normally he inhaled his food. Mom noticed too and frowned at him.

"You can't come, because I'm not just going for a few
days." I watched his Adam's apple bob as he swallowed.
"I'm going for the whole summer."

"No," Dad said, without looking up from his plate. "I
need you here. That roof isn't going to survive another
winter."

Mom and Laura weren't paying attention as they argued
over whether or not Laura could bring Ducky to Uncle
Mike's, but there was something beyond his full plate that
kept my attention tethered to my brother.

"Mike's got a job lined up for me at the rig," he said.
"I'll make more money in two months than I have the past
two years at Tom McClintock's ranch. And before you say
anything, I already talked to Tom about it and told him I
won't be working for him."

Dad resumed eating. "You're not going off to work an
oil rig at sixteen. I'll call Mike after dinner and—"

"I'm going, and you can't stop me."

"Jason smash," Ducky squawked.

Dad's gaze slid to the bird on his youngest daughter's
shoulder before catching Mom's eye. She gave her head a
slight shake—this was the first she was hearing about this
too.

Dad leaned back in his chair, giving his son his full attention. That alone should have been reason enough for
Jason to backpedal. It always was in the past when he and
Dad clashed over something, an occurrence that was be-
coming more and more frequent of late.

"I'm sorry about the roof, but there are plenty of guys you can hire to help or—" He glanced at Laura and me and cut himself off. I was skating religiously at that time, and Laura was only ten—a small ten at that.

"No," Laura said. "You can't go all summer. We're supposed to go swimming every day and to the movies and stay up all night and—"

Jason looked pained. "You and Brooke can—"

"All she does is skate, and you promised!"

Skating wasn't *all* I did, and my mouth was open to defend myself—because Mom, Dad and Jason had all started talking over themselves at that point—when Dad's raised voice drowned us all out.

"I'm not hiring anybody to do a job when I have you to help me."

"You *don't* have me, not this summer. I've got my own car and my own money. This is my decision. I would have tried talking to you about it, but you wouldn't have listened."

"Jason, honey—" Mom started.

"You have money," Dad said, lowering his voice so that the hairs on my arms stood on end, "because I convinced Tom to take you on at fourteen even though you could barely lift a sack of feed by yourself, and now that you can, now that you're strong enough to help out like a man, you're telling me you've decided not to be one."

Jason lost some color in his face, but nothing else. "I'm being a man by making my own decisions."

At that declaration Mom slowly closed her eyes and all but shook her head at the stupidity of her oldest child. At least, that's what it seemed like to me.

"Being a man means taking care of your family and putting their needs before your own, you understand me?" Dad's voice dropped to a normal volume, one that was infinitely more unnerving than the yelling of a moment ago. The tendons in his neck looked ready to snap. "The roof that your mom and sisters sleep under needs replacing, so you're staying until it's fixed." He stabbed a piece of steak with his fork.

I was looking at my brother and willing him to say *Yes, sir* with every fiber of my being. Not just because I thought staying to help fix the roof was the right thing to do but because I knew this moment would forever change things between Dad and Jason if he didn't.

"The roof will still be here to replace in two months," Jason said. "The job on the rig won't."

Dad stared at Jason so long that I started to squirm. Jason didn't move.

"I have the right to make my own decisions."

I don't think Dad blinked for a full minute. "Maybe. But what you don't have is the right to sit at my table and eat the food your mother made and—"

"Then I won't eat it." Jason pushed back from the table and stood. "And I'll leave right now."

"Sit down and eat." Dad jerked his gaze down to the seat Jason had left even before the small sound of protest left Mom's mouth.

"No. Fix the roof with someone else or wait for me to come back after the summer, but I'm going." He moved around to Mom's chair and kissed her cheek. "I promise I'll eat something on the way and I'll call when I get to

Mike's." He tried to catch Laura's eye, but she wouldn't meet his and instead ran upstairs. He found mine though, and silently tried to make me understand something that I never would.

When Jason went upstairs to grab his bag, Mom reached out to squeeze Dad's hand. "Go talk to him, please?"

But when Dad left the table, he went downstairs instead of up.

After Jason left, I thought that would be it. But two hours later I heard his car pulling up outside, and when I looked out the window I saw Laura sitting in the passenger seat. She'd snuck into the back seat of his car, and he'd made it halfway to San Angelo before she revealed herself. She'd used the drive back to try to cajole, bribe and plead with him to stay—tactics that had worked well for her in the past, only that time, they fell on deaf ears.

He didn't even get out of the car as he let Laura out.

It took Dad twice as long to do the job with only my unskilled help. He had to overcompensate for my lack of strength and ended up straining his back so badly that we did have to hire people to finish it. Dad's back still bothers him when he lifts anything much heavier than Laura.

In Jason's mind, everything worked out fine. He spent a summer hanging out with Uncle Mike and making real money for the first time in his life, and the roof got replaced before any real damage was done.

After dinner, I clear the table and load the dishwasher. I don't ask Laura to help me, and she doesn't offer. I hear Dad's heavy footsteps upstairs, and a moment later the shower turns off. I hear his low voice saying something soft and indistinct, then Mom's attempted response before she dissolves into further tears. I listen for the sounds that tell me he's wrapping her shivering body in a towel and carrying her to bed even though I know it hurts his back.

I go to sleep that night loving my dad.

And hating my brother just a little bit.

CHAPTER 16

"Hi," I say, smiling at the unexpected sight of my sister sitting on my bed when I come back from the shower the next morning. My clothes used to steadily migrate to her closet—or more accurately the floor of her closet—and Laura herself used to spend so much time in my room that I started keeping an extra pillow and sleeping bag for her under my bed. But it's been so long since she's been in here. I'd rather she be waiting to ambush me into going swimming with her or trying to convince me that the mustard stain on my favorite tank top was there before she borrowed it, but the sight of her here for any reason is enough to make me the best kind of nostalgic.

"Whatcha doing?" I dressed in the bathroom but I'm still rubbing a towel through my wet hair as I draw closer to her. "Hey, I'm going to pick up Maggie to hang out if you want—" I break off with a swallow, seeing our grandmother's quilt bunched up next to her. I know I tucked it away before heading to the bathroom.

Laura fingers one corner of the quilt. "Why do you have this?" Her face contorts a little. "Why would you want to?"

I take another step, my hand already reaching out to take the quilt, but Laura pulls it closer to her. "Why were *you* digging under my bed?"

She doesn't flinch, which means she knows that in this case, my defensive question is just that. "I needed my other pillow."

"Just give it back, okay?" I turn my outstretched hand up. "And don't say anything to Mom."

Laura gazes down at the quilt. "Mom hates this," she says softly. "It's the only thing she has from her childhood, otherwise she'd have let Dad burn it when he asked." Mom's much estranged older sister had sent her the quilt a few years ago along with a note that said she couldn't keep it in her house anymore and that Mom could do whatever she wanted with it. It was remanded to the attic that very day, and no one had touched it since. Or they hadn't until I brought it down.

I can feel Laura's bewilderment, but more than that I can see censure in the tightness of her mouth. I drop the towel from my hair. "I've been looking at it, okay?" But I dodge her gaze when I say this.

"You could have looked at it in the attic. If Mom knew you had it in your—"

I whirl on her. "But she doesn't. And I'm pretty sure Mom has enough problems worrying about—" I'd been going to say *worrying about Jason*, but I bite back the words at the look of panic that darts across her face. I soften my voice. "She's not going to find out, okay?" Laura's left eyelid twitches, but she doesn't resist when I pull the quilt from her fingers. She stands and watches as I fold it and tuck it back underneath my bed.

"It's not the same," she whispers. Her arms wrap around her middle. Her lip trembles, and even though her eyes have barely moved, I can tell she's not looking at me anymore. "What you're doing and what I'm doing."

Still kneeling by my bed, I press down the lump in my throat. "What are we doing?"

There's an old touch of defiance in the lift of her chin when her eyes refocus on me. "You're trying to hurt her, and I'm trying not to."

Laura's lip is still trembling and mine is far from steady. What does she think I do every Saturday when she's up here hiding behind her closed door? If anyone is hurting Mom, intentionally or otherwise, it's not me. But I can't say that, not when this is the most she's opened up to me in a year. "You know there's one thing you could do that would make her truly happy…"

She backs away a step, blood rushing to her cheeks.

"You could start small, maybe just write him a lett—"

"Hey, so my mom— Oh. Hi." Maggie swings into my room only to draw up short when she spots Laura and takes in her blotchy face. "I passed your mom running when I came up the driveway and she told me to just let myself in." She glances back and forth between Laura and me. "Should I maybe wait for you downstairs?"

"Just for a minute," I say, at the same time Laura shakes her head.

"No, we're done." She turns to slip past Maggie out into the hall.

"Laura, wait." I catch Maggie on the arm as I hurry after my sister. "I'll be right back."

"Yeah, go. I'll just snoop around in your room while I wait."

I come to a halt in my hallway, halfway between my room and Maggie and halfway between Laura and her room. I want to go after my sister so badly, but I can't leave Maggie alone in my room. There are way too many things she might see and too many questions she might ask. I don't even like having her in the house if I can help it, which usually I can. My face scrunches as Laura slams her door a second later.

"Pissy much," Maggie says from behind me.

"Um," I say, still staring at Laura's closed door with a heart so heavy that it feels impossible for it to still beat.

"Hey, sorry about just showing up. My mom wanted to drop me off at the last minute so she could meet your mom. Guess I should have called first."

"Our moms are outside talking?" My leaden heart tries to explode in my chest and I spin to face her. "Right now?"

Maggie frowns. "Well, no. They basically just said hi, nice to meet you, that kind of thing. My mom didn't want to hold up yours in the middle of a run." Her frown deepens. "Why?"

My lungs exhale in relief. "It's just that she doesn't like it when I spring people on her."

Maggie's eyebrows lift instead of narrowing. "Ohhh. Is that where you get it from—I mean, is your mom the same about people and places like you?"

My heart rate is still much too high, so I only nod and head back into my room, stopping to pick up the towel I dropped.

"She did seem a little—" Maggie shrugs. "Not rude or anything, but five minutes with my mom and you know her entire life history. Yours was more on the reserved side. I just thought she was out of breath, but this makes more sense. Anyway, my mom didn't notice anything— Oh wow. This is beautiful!" She heads straight for my wild-flower inlaid sleigh bed.

"My dad made it for me. Everything that's wood in here is him."

Maggie does a full spin, her eyes going wider with every second. "So he's like the Michelangelo of furniture. I mean look at these nightstands. They look like actual giant sun-flowers. Does he hand carve everything?"

"Those he did, but he uses power tools mostly. Didn't you hear him down in the basement when you came in?"

She nods absently, still looking at my nightstands. "I'm glad you didn't paint them."

My half shudder in response is automatic. "My dad would sooner put a nail through his hand than paint good wood."

Her mouth lifts on one side and she plops onto the bed beside me. "Well, it's amazing." She gestures around my room. "Are your brother's and sister's rooms like this too?"

I hesitate at the reference to Jason, and because I don't

want to widen the already massive gulf between our two fathers. "Not the same, but he made everything."

She stands. "Can I see? I know you and your sister were having a moment, but what about your brother's room?"

I stay sitting. "Um, maybe later. I don't want to push with Laura right now, and I don't really think Jason would love me bringing people into his room when he's not here."

"People?" Maggie asks with mock effrontery. "Since when am I people?"

"I just meant—"

She waves me off and moves toward my dresser. "So is this him?" She picks up the framed photo of Jason, Laura and me from his last birthday—his last free birthday.

As casually as I can, I join her and take the photo from her, as though I'm looking at it closer myself instead of because I'm uncomfortable with her touching it. "Yep, that's my brother."

"He's really cute."

"Thanks?" I say, setting the frame back down.

She laughs and bends down to see his face again, though thankfully she doesn't touch this time. "Look, I wasn't going to say anything, but I know he's not at college."

All the air in my lungs turns to ice, but Maggie is still looking at Jason and doesn't see me freeze from the inside out.

She sighs and straightens. "My mom asked yours which college your brother was at and your mom—" she turns to face me "—yeah, she looked about like that."

Even though I know I need to snap back to life and

contradict her, I can't. I couldn't move in that moment if I wanted to.

"We do that too, my mom and me, when people ask about my dad. It's okay," she adds seeing the tension pulling at all the muscles in my face. "You don't have to tell me unless you want to, I just wanted you to know that I know. You don't have to lie about him, okay?"

"Maggie, I—" I never said he was at college, but that's what I let her believe.

"I know it's nothing like what my dad did." She nods her chin at the frame on my dresser. "I mean, you don't see any pictures of him in my room, so… I know your brother's not a philandering dirtbag who tried to steal all your money."

The money bit is news to me, but she doesn't give me a chance to open my mouth before she goes on, and when she does, it locks shut.

"I supposed he could be a murderer or something, but I'm guessing that would ixnay the photo too, so…" With another big sigh her brows draw together in concern. "I'm thinking it's drugs."

My eyes are focused on my brother's laughing face and the small bit of icing left on his chin from when he let Laura and Allison smash his face into his birthday cake.

"Yeah," I say. "It's drugs."

I dream about the murder again that night. I see Jason and Cal meeting in the woods near the high school, the same area that is full of kids after Friday night football games during the season. It would have been deserted that night, empty save for the charred remains of the bonfire pit that could blaze taller than me at its zenith. The ground was damp, still sodden from the rainfall earlier so that it captured footprints in the mud—Cal's and Jason's—and skids and handprints. Fingers clawing into the earth, pulling, dragging. The imprint of Cal's body and Jason's knees.

In my dream I imagine the fight they had, the reasons that slip like water through my fingers when I try to grasp them. They're shouting, shoving hard enough for Cal to skid backward in the mud then regain his balance enough to push Jason. There's more yelling, more words I can't get close enough to hear. And then Cal is saying something so horrible that Jason's face goes white as Cal's contorts in rage. Cal turns, looking for something—the dream blurs, and he's not looking anymore; it's something he already has with him, something that will hurt Jason. Fear flickers over Jason's face. The expression is alien on him, because he's always so brave.

He's shaking his head; his hands are raised, and he tries to talk Cal down. But he can't; Cal is going to hurt him. I can't see how, but he has to be trying to hurt Jason. That's the only reason for the knife that materializes in Jason's hand, the only reason he plunges it into Cal's back—

I wake up with a scream strangled in my throat and my body tangled in sweat-damp sheets. And then I'm thrashing, desperately kicking to free my arms and legs, almost knocking my lamp over as I panic to find the switch and the light that proves the sheets aren't damp with blood.

CHAPTER 17

I don't go to the tree the next day because of Heath. I don't. My shift doesn't start on Friday until six and Maggie is busy with her mom all morning. I know I'll go mad sitting at home with only Laura's closed bedroom door for company. I also don't have the gas money for a Walmart trip or anywhere else I might go.

That leaves the tree by Hackman's Pond. Even if it did rain the night before. Even if it means I might not be the only one there.

He's sitting on a low branch but he stands when I approach.

"Hi," I say.

"Hey."

It takes me a few seconds to realize that I'm looking at him and it's not pain I feel, or at least not only pain. I don't want to look too closely at what it is. I lower my head to gaze at the grass. My latest dream flickers back to me.

"I didn't know if you'd be here," I say. It didn't start raining until late the night before and kept raining almost until morning. The earth was still wet when I walked across it, my feet leaving shallow footprints in the ground.

"Yeah, me neither."

But we both came.

"I'm not working until tonight but I have to meet my friend Maggie in a little bit," I say, keeping the time vague in case I want an excuse to leave. We have plans to watch a few YA book-to-movie adaptations that she swears will turn me into a sobbing mess of feels—the good kind, but I still have hours until I'm supposed to be at her house.

A humid breeze toys with the hem of my sundress around my thighs, even slipping one thin strap down my shoulder. His gaze rests on me, following the movement and making my skin warm as I right it with one hand. His gaze skids past me to settle on the gently rippling surface of Hackman's Pond, swollen high from the rain.

"That's fine." He says it with such indifference that I'm almost bothered.

I hesitate and start second-guessing a million things.

He frowns before shifting his gaze back to me and the ten-plus feet still separating us. "Right. Sorry. I didn't mean that I couldn't care less if you were here or not." His frown deepens, then smooths with obvious effort. "I don't know how to talk to you yet. You're not—" he stares at me, his brows drawn together, perplexed this time rather than annoyed "—anybody else."

That was a vague statement, but I think I know what he means. There's no default for how to act around him. He's not some guy I can smile at and hope he smiles back. I'm not trying to impress or repel him, and I don't know if I can befriend him or if that's something I can even want. Making a joke would feel so wildly out of place, and yet I don't want to be somber and morose either. Plus we don't know each other, and the only shared experience we have is one that keeps us both up at night.

I decide to take the first step, literally, and even though he watches me somewhat warily, he doesn't tense up. I choose a section of the branch that's close enough to the ground that the tips of my toes graze the grass when I sit.

"What about you? Do you have a job?" I ask.

"Over at Porter's Grocery store, stock clerk, but mostly late at night."

I pluck one of the small, green leaves that seem to be dripping from above me and rub the smooth waxy surface between my thumbs. "Graveyard?"

"If I can get it."

I think about that, then nod, deciding I'd probably pull for the late shift too. Fewer people. I'm reaching for another leaf when the question spills out of me. "Can I ask you something?"

Heath reclaims his seat several feet away from me, his expression open and waiting.

I have rubbed the leaf I'm holding nearly clear through and I look down at the green residue on my thumb. "You said your family talks a lot about C—your brother—"

"Cal. You can say his name."

I don't look up, but the even tone in Heath's voice allows me to keep going. "You guys talk about Cal a lot."

"Yeah."

"Is it the same? Your family—are they sad but still the same, or is it like they're different people?"

Heath leans against the tree trunk. "Everyone tries to be the same, but it feels false a lot of the time, like they're pretending it's okay that he's gone because we have all these happy memories—'cause we can only remember the good ones. But then somebody'll slip and say the wrong thing, and it's like he just died all over again. The only thing we have then is the anger."

Leaves lay abandoned in a pile on my knee. "What about your sister?" He has a much older sister; I remember seeing her in the courtroom, stoic and unflinching even during the worst parts.

"Gwen will be angry for the rest of her life. If she found out I was talking to you, she'd come for me first, and she wouldn't feel bad about it afterward."

No wonder he didn't mention seeing me to his family.

"And your sister?"

"The opposite. Most of the time Laura acts like she feels nothing. She worshipped my brother, I don't think she knows how to cope with a reality where he's..." I still can't say it, so Heath does it for me.

"A convicted murderer."

It doesn't sound like he's relishing the words this time, so I nod. "The way my boss acted—we all get that reaction, but it's hardest for Laura. She's only fourteen, and people used to drive past her and throw things at her. My parents started homeschooling her last year after a bunch of kids rigged her locker with exploding blood bags."

Heath swears under his breath. "That's sick."

I nod.

After a moment, he asks, "What'd they do to you?"

"Nothing like that," I say, thinking of Mark being in my room while I slept. I hadn't wanted to let anyone chase me away from school, but at the time, I'd thought it might be easier for Laura if she wasn't the only one shifting to on-line school. If my going back to homeschooling has helped, she has yet to show it.

"I actually like doing school online. I get my work done in half the time and I get to do it all in my pj's if I want to. And it leaves me more time to skate when the rink is less busy."

"Do you compete or…?"

"I used to." I explained that skating on a truly competi-tive level required a full-time commitment, not just from the skater but from their family too. I found myself telling him about *Stories on Ice* and the audition video I no longer feel I can make.

"Because of your brother?"

I hesitate, then decide to tell him the truth as much as I understand it myself. "No, because of everyone he left bro-ken." And for the first time since Jason went away, I'm be-ginning to see what that brokenness looks like beyond my own family. I'm not sure I want to see any more. Looking at grass, I say, "If you felt bad for the other day or what-ever, you can stop. I didn't get fired, and I get why you were mad about the money. We can just leave it at that. You don't have to…to…" My gaze shifts to the scarred part of the tree where Jason's initials used to be, then back to

Heath. His anger from my just mentioning my brother is still right there in front of me, simmering under the surface. "You don't have to try."

Suddenly I'm so sad that I feel like I could just fall to the earth and never move again. It doesn't matter that I didn't personally do anything to him or that he had nothing to do with breaking down my family. It doesn't matter what we know; it's what we can't help but feel. I'm still who I am, however Heath phrases it out loud, and he's still who he is. "It's okay," I say.

He shakes his head, his movement agitated. "It was easier before."

I frown. Nothing has been easier. He knows that better than anyone.

"My brother is gone, and the person responsible is in prison. I don't get to ask for more in this life. It's the reason I can get out of bed each morning, the thing that keeps me moving each day, the reason I sleep instead of stare at darkness all night and think about his empty room down the hall from mine." He opens his mouth and then snaps it shut. He doesn't look at me when he says, "I didn't sleep last night."

"Why are you telling me this?" I ask, a tremor in my voice.

His voice is calm but his hands are braced on either side of his thighs and his fingers are digging into the bark and turning his knuckles white. "Because I don't think you slept either. Because I think you have to find a reason to get up every day and another to keep going once you do." Heath turns his head toward me. "Tell me I'm wrong."

But I can't. My fingers curl tight into the fabric of my sundress as his eyes lock with mine.

"I can't get it back," he says, and it's half a whisper, half a plea. "I can't just feel that one thing anymore."

I shift my weight, slowly, and then with more purpose until I'm mostly facing him on the branch. It's not the same for us. I saw my brother a few days ago. I see him every week. I get to talk to him and hear his voice. He's still here. And one day, my brother will come home. Heath's won't.

"No one expects your family to feel sorry for mine." My throat thickens just saying the words. "I don't. Be mad and hard. You get that. I don't want to take that away from you."

"You're not your brother," he says, and my eyes sting so suddenly and sharply that I have to squeeze them shut. "I'm getting that not a lot of people around here see that. I don't want to be one of them. I think…" He waits until I'm looking at him. "I think you want that too, or you wouldn't be here."

How can he know what I want? *I* don't even know what I want, or what I'm allowed to want anymore, what I'm supposed to feel or what I'm supposed to do when none of it seems to matter anymore.

"Your family didn't hurt my family," he says. "You didn't hurt me."

"No," I say, "but I'm hurting you now."

He doesn't deny it. Instead his gaze shifts to the road where our vehicles are parked, one behind the other. "I started driving Cal's truck after the funeral. My mom didn't want to sell it, so I sold mine instead. I used to feel sick just from picking up the keys. But I forced myself to drive it, to think of Cal until I could do it without wanting to run it off a cliff." I see his Adam's apple move as he swallows. "I want to be able to think about my brother and not just the fact that he's gone." His gaze shifts to me. "It's not as hard as it used to be, driving his truck. Sometimes it's even okay. Sometimes I'll go out and sit behind the wheel and it's like the only place on earth where it doesn't hurt."

I suck in a gulp of air, wanting to break away from his gaze but unable to. He's trying to equate entirely different things. I'm not a good memory buried beneath bad. I may not be my brother, but time and exposure will never soften the fact that Cal is dead because of Jason. Seeing me means remembering my brother, which means remembering Cal's murder, which means pain and rage and revulsion all corroded together.

I believe Heath means what he says; he wants to not blame or despise me. And I believe he knows that logically he shouldn't, but that doesn't mean his heart agrees. I know this because I feel it too.

When I find it, my voice is a whisper. "I'm not a truck." I wish I were, for my sake as much as his. "When you look at me like that, when I can tell that you have to force yourself to hold my gaze, all I can think is that I deserve it because of my brother. I can't hold my head up and walk past you like I don't make your skin crawl. It's not just you working through your pain and maybe finding something okay on the other side—it's my pain too. And I can't even say that to you, because how gross is that? Trying to equate our situations—" bile starts rising in my throat "—is so wrong. I'm not allowed to feel bad in front of you. I'm not allowed to feel bad in front of anyone, but *especially* not you, and I don't know how to stop." I suck in another breath so deep that it makes me dizzy. So dizzy that I think I see him stand and move until he's right in front of me. Close enough that I could touch him.

Close enough that he could touch me.

I want, for just a moment, to reach for his hand, if only to hold on to someone else's hurt so I don't have to feel my own.

His face in front of me isn't steady. He's letting me see just how hard this is for him. But he's not moving away.

"You don't have to—"

"I know."

My eyes sting when he sits right next to me. He holds himself very still, and so do I. After a moment he exhales and I feel the tension start to ease from his body.

"You can feel however you want in front of me, okay?" He's not looking at me when he says it, and I'm not entirely sure he won't surge to his feet to get away from me the second I answer him. Still watching him from the corner of my eye, I nod. "I'm not saying I'll be okay all the time, but I promise I'll try to remember who I'm really angry at, and it's not you," he says, sounding like he's talking to himself as much as me. "It was never you."

My phone is flashing when I open Daphne's door and slide behind the wheel. When I check the screen I see a ton of missed calls from Maggie, but no messages. I try her back right away but I go straight to voice mail. Frowning, I pull my door shut and try again.

"Hey, it's Maggie. If you're a recording then you can go straight to robot hell, otherwise leave me a message."

"It's me," I say, starting the car and pulling onto the road beside Heath's truck. "Sorry I didn't realize how late it's gotten. I was, um—" Heath and I make eye contact as he starts his engine, and that shaky, sick feeling I felt the first time we met by this tree is as faded as my dream; in its place is something surprisingly steady and safe. Or it feels that way to me. "—driving around with my phone off and well anyway, I'm guessing that's why you were calling. We still have time to watch a movie before my shift. I can be to your house in twenty minutes. Actually, make that thirty 'cause I still have to grab snacks. Okay. Call me back if anything's wrong." Still frowning, I end the call and check my phone again, but she didn't text me either. She just called a lot. My stomach clenches as possible explanations begin dropping like stones in my gut.

CHAPTER 18

Maggie's tearstained face meets mine when I enter her room armed with way too many boxes of Red Vines and enough Dr Pepper to fell a horse. I know instantly that her crying isn't because she got tired of waiting and started the movie without me.

"What happened? I'm so sorry I didn't get your calls. I didn't have my phone and—" I place the soda and candy on the nearest surface and climb onto the bed she's sitting on cross-legged.

She doesn't look at me, and the stones in my stomach start tumbling faster and faster.

"Do you remember what I said to you at your house yesterday?"

One of the stones leaps up into my throat. "Which part?"

"That my mom decided to drive me over so she could meet your mom? That's not why. I just had to get out of my house so I asked her to drop me off. I left my phone at home and I haven't looked at it in twenty-four hours be-cause…" She sniffs, trying to smile and limply gesturing toward the phone resting on her crossed ankles. "I know I shouldn't care, but…"

My gaze lowers to the phone. She doesn't stop me when I take it and look at screen.

"You know the dragon-look video I made based on that book series I love? Well the author shared it on all her so-cial media accounts. Her publisher too."

"Maggie, that's—" Except it's obviously not great based on her red, swollen eyes. "I don't understand why that's a bad thing."

"A lot of people saw that video." Her voice catches. "This time it's not just mean people from my old school commenting."

It's with a different kind of dread that I start scrolling through the comments on her phone. At first I still don't understand. People are praising Maggie's creativity and undeniable skill, but then I start seeing a few not so nice comments mixed in among the good. And a few more. My gut sinks the more I read.

Nice makeup, you need to fix your teeth before you make any more. Or don't smile.

Why are her eyes so puffy? Damn girl, you need to put some Preparation H on those things.

You'd look prettier if you lost weight. Your neck looks like a pack of hot dogs.

Chinese girls are so ugly. #notenoughmakeupintheworld.

The air punches out of my lungs and I have to stop reading. Because that's not even the worst one. I grip her phone so hard I'm surprised it doesn't shatter in my hands.

Memories come flooding back to me; memories from before I learned to avoid the internet because of what people said about my family and me.

I'm not surprised. I heard they homeschooled their kids, probably taught them all kinds of sick, twisted crap. The cops need to watch his sisters.

He needs to fry and they need to make his family watch.

The older sister wrote all about his temper in her diary. You can tell from her handwriting that she was afraid of him. Here's the link.

The uncle is a felon! Of course he helped plan the murder.

Somebody needs to set fire to that house while they're all asleep.

I don't trust myself to look at Maggie, and if I keep staring at vile, hate-filled words on the screen I'll start crying with her. I switch the phone off, wanting to hurl it through the window, but I lower it to the bed instead.

"I know what you're thinking," Maggie says, trying to hide a sniff. "I'm Korean, not Chinese. It's like, get your hate right, people."

My eyes lift to Maggie's and I don't smile at her attempted humor, weak as it is. "You are beautiful," I say. "And you're talented and funny and the fact that there are people out there who can't see that…" My chin trembles. "You are amazing. Those people—" I fiercely jab a finger toward the phone I've dropped on her bed, my one concession to how enraged I feel "—are nothing. Nothing."

She nods, but it's the nod she's supposed to give, not the one she actually feels. "It's not the first time and I know it won't be the last. People at my old school used to flood my videos with mean comments or leave notes in my locker. Every time, I tell myself I won't care." She lifts one hand to her face. "I want to not care but I can't help it."

I squeeze my eyes shut. She shouldn't have to.

"I do have neck rolls and my bottom teeth are crooked. Even if I lost weight, I wouldn't lose this. My mom is microscopic and she has hot dog–neck too." In a quiet, frighteningly unMaggie-like voice she says, "Maybe I should stop."

"No," I say, not caring that my voice shakes, because it captures her attention completely. "Don't let them get to you and make you think things about yourself that you know aren't true. Promise me." I lean over and wrap both my arms around my friend. "You are so good and you love this. Don't let a few awful people take this from you."

That's easier to say than to do. I still can't escape the anonymous things people said about my family and me online.

It's horrible, the way words can scar.

Maggie's arm lifts from my back to wipe her cheek and I let her go, moving to grab a pack of tissues from her vanity and bringing them back to her. She takes them with a small smile.

"These are blotting papers."

"So blot," I tell her.

She gets up and exchanges the blotting papers for an actual mini tissue pack from her desk drawer, holding them up to show me the difference.

"I thought you said you could use tissues for blotting."

"You can." She sits next to me again. "The papers are just better at keeping your makeup intact, but a tissue can work too. You can even use toilet paper in a pinch if you separate the ply." She starts to demonstrate with the tissue like she's blotting excess oil instead of drying tears, but her hands slow halfway through.

"See," I say, lifting another tissue to her cheek. "You're good at this. I thought toilet paper was only ever good for wiping your nose or your tush."

Maggie tries to smile at me; I know she does. "I thought it would be different here, you know? I'd leave all the mean people behind. I thought a smaller town meant smaller problems, nicer people, but it's not better. Look at you—half the town resents you for breaking up with the grandson of the custard queen."

Guilt smothers my anger toward the faceless trolls. Because of her friendship with me, we aren't much better than shut-ins. We almost never go out; it's always her house, or very rarely mine. I think about the friends she might have made at Keller's Creamery if not for me, Tara and Dawn at least, and how I've been persuading her not to apply for the job at Polar Ice Rink right away. Not because she'd hate it like I tried to convince her, but because I wasn't willing to risk that the people who work there would tell her the truth about my family and me.

When Maggie gets off the bed again, I pick up the phone, delete the last mean comment on Maggie's video and make a note to go back through her older videos to purge any others I find, and then I look up to where my friend is cuing up the movie. Because I'm so late we only have time to watch one, and of course she picked the one that features a figure skater, just for me.

She glances at her phone in my hand when she rejoins me at the head of her bed. With reluctance, she takes it from me and proceeds to set it on the far side, like almost-but-not-quite-falling-off-the-edge-of-her-nightstand far, before offering me a Red Vine. "Thanks, Brooke."

My throat tightens. Helping her tonight is so little compared to what I've taken from her.

The movie starts and the promised ice rink fills the screen. There's even a clear shot of a Zamboni in one of the early scenes. A shiny new resurfacer that's a far cry from Bertha's decrepit form, but I don't have to look at Maggie to know her eyes are looking at it instead of the meet-cute taking place in front of it.

"How badly do you want to drive Bertha?" I ask her. It's a rhetorical question, but Maggie pauses the movie and turns her whole body toward me, holding very still while answering.

"Right now it's up there with winning the NYX FACE Awards." Basically the Oscars of online makeup videos. She really, *really* wants to work at Polar Ice Rink.

"It's not a great job," I tell her, knowing I can't talk her out of it, but self-preservation making me try one last time all the same.

"But you'll be there."

"And Jeff is awful."

"But I'll get to drive Bertha."

"And clean toilets."

"We'll see." Maggie grins.

I suppress a tremor, truly afraid that my next words might lead to the end of our friendship. "My coworkers—" I stop, unsure how to even say what I need to say. I'm not worried she'll seek out Jeff any more than strictly necessary, but the others? Elena? My stomach is one giant block of ice and dread, because what can I say? *I'll help you get the job but you have to promise not to have a meaningful conversation with any of the other employees?* I try again, with no clearer idea how to end this sentence. "My coworkers—"

"Yeah, let's talk about them. There's Jeff the walking skid mark, Elena the shrew who hired you then turned you over to Jeff the walking skid mark, that other guy who drives Bertha when you aren't there and leaves her dented and smelling like Cheetos, the concession girls who I have personally witnessed use the bathroom without washing their hands. Am I missing anyone? No? Brooke, I'm not planning on wasting my time on any of them."

My relief would have buckled my knees had I been standing. I turn to my friend and take in the faint mascara smears on her cheeks as her eyes soften.

"Is that what this has been about? Do you honestly think I'd befriend the people who try day in and day out to ruin the thing you love most in the world? Well, besides me."

I want to cry with how much I love her and how little I deserve her, but there have been enough tears that night. My smile is a little shaky but my eyes are dry. "You're going to want to quit within a week."

She grins back. "I never quit anything." Simultaneously her best and worst quality. "Does this mean you're saying what I think you're saying?"

"Truth?" I ask her. She nods. "Driving Bertha is cool. It feels like controlling some huge, prehistoric beast."

"I knew it!"

"But you seriously can't go fast."

"I won't." She waits for me to go on, but I don't. I'm all out of excuses. Her smile gets bigger. "You're saying yes." I try to shake off my lingering misgivings. *Please God help me.*

"I'm saying yes."

Maggie kicks her heels into the bed like a little kid and squeals. "It's going to be so great. Just think about it, I'm going to be an official Zamboni driver! And...and..." She pats my knee in excitement. "Once we're working together at the rink we can start coming up with your audition routine for *Stories on Ice!*"

CHAPTER 19

I drift across the ice, trying not to glance at Jeff's office door every two seconds. Normally, I can forget everything when I'm skating, like the fact that Maggie's job interview has been going on for forty-five minutes so far, but today I'm struggling. I stop, lifting my hand to chew on a nail before I remember that I'm wearing gloves.

Realizing it doesn't matter if I look or not, I half spin so that I'm skating backward. The door is still closed. Gathering speed, I turn forward again, extend my arms out and raise my right foot behind me before springing up off the ice with my left. There's a single heartbeat where I'm in the air flying before I pull my arms in to rotate, spinning two and a half times before landing backward on my right foot. I rotated too early, I felt it, but I still manage to keep from falling, though my hand does kiss the ice when I land. My nostrils flare and I'm ready to try another axel—maybe even a triple—when Maggie emerges from the office with Jeff at her heels, smiling.

My next axel jump is possibly the most perfect one I've ever landed.

Jason is laughing—he's genuinely laughing a few days later—as I describe Jeff's sour expression when he gave me my shifts back. "He had no choice, since he had to fire David."

"And that guy just drove the Zamboni into the *wall*?"

I rest my forearms on the metal table in the visitation room. "David was supposed to be training Maggie, only nobody ever really trained him, so he wasn't using the guide mark José made on the top on Bertha's dump tank and he kept overlapping each pass on the ice by like a foot. And when Maggie, who's had like two days of training, pointed it out to him, he shifted to tell her to—" I eye Mom next to me and soften the actual words David used "—*be quiet* and pay attention. And that's when he drove into the wall."

Jason laughs again. "What an ass."

"Jason," Mom says with a slight reproof it her tone.

He's still smiling when he raises an eyebrow at her. "Really, Mom? I'm wearing an orange jumpsuit for the next thirty years and you're worried about me swearing?"

It's a guess who goes paler after he falls silent, Mom or Jason, but they both go white as milk and I don't feel far behind them. Finally, Jason leans back in his chair. "Well, I wish I could have seen it."

It takes me a second to pick the story back up, and my

words are a little jerky when I do. "David tried to claim she distracted him, but Jeff was watching, so..." I don't relay how David started yelling about Jeff hiring violent little girls, or how Maggie had reached her fill by then and walked away to check on Bertha before David could say more. "Anyway, David was gone, and Jeff was all sweaty and red-faced by the time I got there," I say, trying to bring the mood back to something lighter. "Bertha is still running and someone's coming out to make minor repairs on Monday, so I'm back to working every day with Maggie while I train her. It's been really fun having her there."

"That's good, Brooke, I'm happy it all worked out."

"Yes," Mom says. "We'll are very glad."

We don't laugh anymore after that. I listen to Mom talk about things Jason already knows or updates on family members who live too far away for us to know very well. I think this is it then; another visit that includes a brief spark of life but ends with us huddled around ashes and memories that have grown cold.

Mom is talking about some cousin in Tennessee when Jason cuts her off midsentence.

"Mom, I'm sorry, okay? I shouldn't have made a joke about being here. I won't do it again. But I need you to do something for me." Mom becomes statue-still beside me, ready to do anything. "Enough with the stories about people I don't know and never will know." He turns to me. "Do you care if cousin what's-his-face is building a cabin or a ranch house?"

"Um..." I say.

"No, you don't." Back to Mom. "I don't even think you

care. So tell me something else—something that I can hold on to when you leave. Tell me what's going on at the library. Tell me what Laura is teaching Ducky to say. Tell me that you're not just cleaning the ice at that rink, Brooke." He lets his eyes shut. "Tell me something so I can forget that I'm here, just for a little bit. Please."

Mom turns her panicked eyes on me, silently pleading. She can't tell him what's going on at the library, because she doesn't work there anymore, and Laura barely speaks to anyone let alone the bird he gave her. And me—I can't tell him that when I skate, I do it with the knowledge that I'll never skate anywhere else.

Because of him.

Because of what happened the night he killed Calvin Gaines.

Because of words and reasons only he knows and won't share. Saying they got into a fight falls so far short of explaining how his friend ended up dead by his hand.

So I can't tell him what he wants.

And he won't tell me what I need.

And I know I'll dream about the murder that night, just as I know I'll wake up heaving from sobs I can't sound.

Uncle Mike isn't there waiting to cheer us up when Mom and I get home. I'm already in bed for the night when I hear his voice mingling with Dad's downstairs, and even though it's been months and months, I can tell he's drunk. He would never again drive drunk, which means he brought a bottle with him and probably drank half of it before coming inside. He's not falling-down, pass-out-in-his-own-puke drunk—he has hasn't done that since Jason first went to prison—but he's drunk enough that he's saying things he never would sober.

He and Dad get into it, only it's the kind of fighting where they both maintain enough self-awareness to keep their voices down. Not that it matters. From up in my room I can hear their low yelling. When I slip into the hall I find Laura in her nightshirt clutching the banister at the top of the stairs. I don't say anything, and I'm careful to avoid the floorboard that creaks when I walk up beside her.

"Where's Mom?" I whisper, knowing she wouldn't be silent if she were downstairs with Dad and Uncle Mike.

"Running."

It's after ten and black as pitch outside, and she's running. I push that thought away.

"Then explain it to me!" Uncle Mike says, and there's a thud like something toppled over. "'Cause from where I'm standing—"

"Barely standing. You want Carol to see you like this?"

"I want Carol to see me however I can. I want—I want—"

"Mike, what are you doing?" Dad asks, the volume of his voice giving way to weariness.

"I'm trying to talk to you." Another thud followed by a muffled curse.

"Would you sit down before you break something I can't fix?" Shuffled footsteps and a grunt.

"Get your hands off me. I'm standing."

"Fine," Dad says. "You're standing. So talk."

"You need to go see Jason."

Beside me, Laura drops her hands from the banister and backs away from the stairs.

"Where are you going?" I mouth since it's fallen quiet downstairs and I don't want to risk a whisper. Laura doesn't risk even that much. She just shakes her head and hurries back to her room.

"That's not your business," Dad says, drawing my attention back downstairs.

"The hell it's not. I love him like he's mine and—"

"But he's not yours. None of my kids are yours, and neither is she."

I feel the word *she* hang ominously in the sudden silence. Now I'm the one clutching the banister. I've never heard Dad talk with Uncle Mike about Mom.

"If he were mine, I'd be there every week. I wouldn't send my wife and my daughter off alone to make excuses for me."

The floorboards downstairs shift, and I can imagine Dad drawing very close to Uncle Mike before he speaks. "I'm not going to see my son in that place."

"Then you're not going to see him! What if you don't live another thirty years? How old was your dad when he died, sixty? Don't you get it? You might not be here when he gets out, and you won't know him anymore if you are!"

"I don't know him now! How could he—" Dad cuts himself off before his voice can grow any more strangled. "I'm not having this conversation with you when you're drunk."

"What about your wife—you having this conversation with her?"

Dad's voice drops so low I almost miss it. "Watch it, Mike."

"Yeah, 'cause that's what I do. I stand back, I watch, I can't help and I never touch."

I hear more than a scuffle then, and it's punctuated by a hollow-sounding bang. I can't help it, I creep down the top few steps until I can crouch down and see into the living room. Dad has Uncle Mike pressed up against a wall but releases him as suddenly as he slammed him back, and I can see Dad taking deep, chest-filling breaths. Both of them are.

"Will, I—"

"Quit coming out here when you're drinking. Quit talking about my family like any part of them ever belonged to you. Quit acting like you know anything about being a father." He walks to the closet and pulls out the blankets and pillow Mom keeps on hand for Uncle Mike and tosses them on the couch. "Drunk or not, friend or not, you say *anything* like that about my wife again and I'll lay you out."

I have just enough time to retreat into my room before Dad heads upstairs.

CHAPTER 20

Days pass without rain. I drive past Hackman's Pond a few times anyway, but I never see Heath. Everywhere else things are okay. Not good, not awful, just okay.

I keep dreaming of Cal dying, of Jason killing him. Over and over again my subconscious projects the grisly scene in my mind, trying to fit the pieces together in a way that explains how my brother could have done what he did, but they never fit.

I wake up gasping one night, sure that I can hear Cal's blood dripping, only to find rain beating against my windowpane.

I'm not relieved exactly when Heath's truck finally pulls up behind Daphne at the tree the next day. My dream is too fresh in my mind. I'm worrying my bottom lip when he joins me under the shade.

"I thought I might have to leave for work before you got here."

"I couldn't get here sooner," is all he says while moving to the branch, to the spot I'm starting to think of as his.

We don't have an exact time for meeting up, and it's not like the rain is predictable. The smart thing would be for us to exchange numbers or set specific days and times to meet, but we haven't done that and I don't think we will. Keeping it vague and dependent on the whims of the weather helps it feel less premeditated. Less like I'm doing something I shouldn't.

"My work schedule changes basically every week," I say. "If I'm ever not here after it rains, that's why. Not, you know, for any other reason."

Heath nods. An awkward silence stretches in the few feet separating us. I don't know how to fill it. I've been sitting there for nearly an hour, trying and mostly failing to smother the guilt that surrounds me for wanting to see him. Last night, hearing the rain and knowing what it meant was the only thing that let me find sleep again after my dream.

I don't understand why, especially as I'm feeling worse and worse as the silent seconds tick by.

"So you visit him, right?" I startle hearing Heath's voice. "You go see him in prison?" He's squinting in the sunlight reflected of the pond. He doesn't sound angry, but I don't know how could he be anything else when talking about Jason so I nod rather than voice my answer.

"What do you even say to him?" A muscle in his jaw twitches. "Do you have normal conversations, like, do you tell him about your car breaking down or how the cat crapped in the living room again?"

"We don't have a cat," I say quietly.

Heath shifts his gaze to mine, forcing me to hold it as I perch on the branch a couple feet away.

"I don't know what you want me to say."

"Forget it."

But I know he can't. I move so that we're facing each other. "We talk about normal things. Never anything heavy or serious. My mom will change the subject if I even try."

"And your dad?"

"It's only my mom and me who visit him."

"Your dad and sister don't go?"

I shake my head. "Never."

"They say why?"

I think about the fight I overhead between Dad and Uncle Mike. "I think maybe my dad feels guilty, like he did something wrong raising Jason."

"And did he?"

My eyes flash to Heath's. "No."

He doesn't look away. "But somebody did, didn't they?"

My whole face goes hot. He's quoting me, my diary from the pages Mark photographed and sold. The questions I'd tormented myself with by writing them down, because I couldn't ask Jason.

Why did you do it? How could you kill him?

I don't understand.

I don't understand.

I don't understand. I loved you, we all loved you. Cal was your friend and you killed him. Why, Jason? We didn't do anything wrong, did we? Laura and me? Mom and Dad? But somebody did, didn't they? What did Cal do?

Heath leans toward me. "Did you ever ask him? Your brother ever tell you what mine did that he deserved to die?"

I recoil as though slapped. Heath doesn't look contrite in the slightest.

"We don't have to dance around, right? That's the whole point—I can say stuff like that, and you don't get to act wounded."

I'm not acting. I can feel my eyes stinging, but I blink the sensation away. "I didn't write that for anyone else to see—"

"Just the entire internet." Then he stills and looks at me as if realizing what I mean. "You didn't give anyone those pages to publish."

"I would *never* hurt my family like that, not for anything. They're barely hanging on now, and it was so much worse then."

"But it's better now?" That brief flicker of compassion snuffs out and he comes close to sneering. "My sister lost her job and had to move back home and my mom spends the majority of every day at Cal's grave, talking to him like he can still hear her. And my dad? Haven't seen or heard from him in six months. If it weren't for my job and my grandparents we would have already lost our house."

"I didn't know," I say quietly.

"But you're *sorry*, right? That's your line? It's what you say, but it's not what you believe or what you write when you don't think anyone will ever see it." Heath's face tightens like he's going to say something else, something that would hurt worse because he hurts worse. But his words don't come.

Mine do.

"I wrote that the night Jason confessed. I didn't want to believe that my brother was a—" I choke on the word "—murderer. I wanted to believe anything else. That there was a reason, some explanation that would make me understand what made him do it."

He nearly spits the question at me. "Did you ever find your reason?"

I can't answer him. I haven't found a reason, but that doesn't mean I've given up on there being one. I have to believe my brother isn't a monster, even though he did something monstrous.

"Whatever happened between them that night," I say, "my brother deserves to be in prison for what he did. I know that. I wake up every day knowing that." So, so slowly, Heath's features relax until he's just staring at me. Letting me see what *he* wakes up with every day. My heart squeezes too tight in my chest. "We're not supposed to think about each other, or care that ours isn't the only family affected by this, but I can't help that anymore."

"No," he says in a low voice, shaking his head at me. "You're not supposed to do that. I don't want you to be nice to me right now. Don't you get that?" He's breathing too fast and blinking too quickly. "I want you to get mad, to—" His chest heaves and I catch the sheen in his eyes before he lifts them skyward and locks his jaw. "Please, can't you just…"

When his voice breaks off I don't even think. I reach for

his hand and slide my fingers into his. He jerks but doesn't pull away. For me too the touch is jolting, both from how warm his skin is compared to mine and from how rough the texture is. Touching Heath's hand feels intimate in a way that should make me draw back, but instead makes me hold on. I find myself wishing that the ice had left its mark on me for him to touch, to feel that indelible part of me.

Heath eyes our hands and his chest rises as he inhales, but it's steadier this time. Then his thumb glides over the back of my hand, rough against soft. A single movement that he doesn't repeat, but the whispered touch ignites something in me that chills even as it burns.

Gently, I begin to draw my hand back, but at the slightest resistance from him, I stop. I close my eyes even as I feel his linger on me. I meant to comfort him, to remind him that he isn't alone and that even if we're not supposed to, I do care. More than I should. More than I realized until this moment.

A heartbeat later, the resistance is gone and our hands slide apart.

The hot, humid air feels cold in place of Heath's warmth. I feel him looking at me, and rather than meet his gaze I let mine sweep over the tree and the names carved into it, avoiding Jason's former spot and snagging here and there on names that I don't recognize.

"Where's yours?" If he spent any time here as a kid it has to be somewhere.

Heath moves to the far side of the tree and I follow, glad to leave the scarred remains of my brother's initials behind. He backs up and cranes his head. I follow his line of sight to a branch some thirty feet high. Normally, the higher the branch the less legible the name. The branches are bone thin toward the top, and anyone climbing that high risks a branch snapping rather than supporting much weight for longer than a hasty scrawl.

Heath's first name is both high and readable, even from the ground. It's more than readable, I realize, moving closer. His lines are straight and even and thick enough that the name hasn't faded like many of the ones surrounding it.

"Did you bring a router with you or something?" I ask, thinking of the power tool Dad uses to add decorative details to his furniture. I don't add that that's kind of cheating, but my tone implies it.

Heath shakes his head. "Pocketknife."

I'm frowning at him in disbelief before generations of ingrained politeness smooth my features. It would have taken him at least an hour to carve something that precise with nothing more than a pocketknife, which is about fifty-nine minutes longer than the branch he would have had to stand on would have supported his weight. "Hmmm," is all I say.

A small smile curves one side of his mouth. He pulls a knife from his back pocket, flipping it open in one move. He squats down and picks up a branch about as thick as my forearm that must have broken during the rainstorm the day before. He snaps it in half over his knee. The knife glints in the sunlight as he works on it for no more than a few minutes before slipping the knife back into his pocket and holding the branch out to me.

I step close enough to take it, and the rough wood slides

into my hand. Along the side, in letters so even and precise they look printed, is my first name.

Speechless, I look up at him.

"My grandfather taught me to carve. That's his name right there." Heath directs my attention to a certain branch, and I swallow when I recognize the same bold, clear lines spelling out a name I know well. "Cal was named after him."

I nod. "He taught you well." I'm not sure what to do with the branch I'm holding. Should I give it back? Does he mean for me to keep it? I end up half extending the branch back, but Heath shakes his head and returns his gaze to the tree.

I glance back up at Heath's name. "I still don't understand how the branch held you that long." He must have at least fifty pounds on me and, height aside, *I* would have snapped it.

"I was a tiny kid."

I widen my eyes at him. "How old were you when you carved it?"

Heath shrugs one shoulder. "Eight maybe."

I look up again and have this sudden vision of a little boy scurrying up the tree and swinging from branch to branch with a knife clamped between his teeth. My heart skitters a little. I grew up surrounded by saws and blades and all kinds of things that could amputate a finger as easily as cut a piece of wood. Dad instilled a healthy respect for them in all his children, and that included not climbing thirty feet in the air with a pocketknife.

"You didn't cut yourself?"

Another half shrug. "No. I finished the carving before I fell out of the tree."

I gasp.

Heath nods. "Broke my collarbone and one of my arms." For a reason I can't begin to fathom, he smiles at the memory. "Cal was with me, and when he saw that I wasn't bleeding—" Heath's smile grows wider "—he finished carving his own name before helping me."

"That's terrible," I say.

"Yeah." Heath moves to sit on the lower branch again, still smiling. "He was mad because I climbed higher than him. Plus he didn't actually see me fall, so he thought I was just being a baby. He cried when Mom showed him my X-rays, and then he carried my backpack to school for months afterward—wouldn't give it back even after I got my cast off." In a quieter voice he adds, "I'd forgotten about that."

I retake my spot a few feet away from him and set the branch he carved my name into beside me.

"I still feel guilty when I remember stuff like that, you know?"

"Stuff when he wasn't perfect?"

Heath exhales a laugh and nods.

I look down at the grass, the same kind that grows along the banks of the Wilcox River. "Yeah, I know."

It feels like I'm running away when I stand, but if I stay much longer I'll be late for my shift.

"You told me when you got here, remember?" Heath says when I fumble out an explanation. "I know."

I take a few steps, then stop and turn back to him. "I

am sorry about what your family is going through. I didn't know, but I should have."

He nods, his gaze unwavering. "That's on me too then." Then his voice hardens. "How'd that website get your diary?"

I pause, unsure if I should tell him. I gave my heart and my trust to someone who never loved me, and I can't help feeling like that says something about me. Heath is waiting for an answer though, and I don't want to lie to him. I can't help glancing up at the tree where my and Mark's initials are still linked. "My ex-boyfriend."

"What a scumbag."

I smile at him. "That's why he's my *ex*-boyfriend."

And he smiles back, and then turns to gaze up at the tree where I was looking. "His name is on there somewhere with yours, isn't it?"

"It's just initials," I say, glancing where Jason's used to be.

"Want me to cut it out?"

I shake my head. My brother would have obliterated Mark's name if I asked him. He wouldn't have even made me tell him why. "It's a good reminder."

"Of what?" he asks.

"That I don't get to change the past." I step to leave again, but something invisible tugs at me and I meet Heath's gaze again. Before the words are out I know I shouldn't say them, but I do. "What if…what if it doesn't rain again for a while?"

His eyes lower and I know I shouldn't have asked. "Brooke—"

"What am I saying?" My smile is falsely bright as I back

toward the road. "It's summer in Texas. I'll see you…when I see you."

I come just shy of sprinting to Daphne, grateful as I start her that she doesn't stall.

CHAPTER 21

Despite the heavy clouds rolling across the sky day and night, along with the occasional clap of thunder and lightning forking in the distance, it doesn't rain in Telford the rest of that week. I can't decide if I'm allowed to be disappointed by that or not. Either way, I am.

Martina McBride has been singing about Independence Day all week and thanks to Maggie and me, the entire rink is now finally draped in enough red, white and blue streamers to make Jeff declare us patriotic enough to match the rest of the town, which has exploded in excitement for today: the Fourth of July.

To Maggie's horror as a vegetarian, the grill masters have been smoking meat for days so that you can't set foot in town without salivating at the promise of the barbecue they'll finally be serving up at the firework show tonight. And even though I won't taste any this year, I'd put every dollar I have on Ann Keller's banana cream pie to take top honors at the bake off yet again.

The craft fair was already in full swing when I drove into work this morning, and the antebellum cannon will be firing in a few hours to announce the start of the parade, which passes right past Polar Ice Rink. Needless to say, Jeff graciously offered to let me off early today—not so that I can take part in any of the celebrations, but so that my presence won't hinder anyone from enjoying the ice after being out in the heat all day.

Wrinkling her nose as the door opens and the mouth-watering scent of pork spare ribs wafts in, Maggie eyes the clock for the fifth time and sighs.

I send a commiserating smile in her direction before returning to our task of scraping gum off the underside of the bleachers surrounding the rink. "Two more hours and we're done."

"But I can smell it from my house too! I wish your mom wasn't sick so we could go to your house tonight. I mean there's no way the smell reaches that far."

Sadly it doesn't, but even though Maggie has been to my house a few times, the lie about my mom came easily to my lips when she suggested it earlier. I never feel comfortable having her see my family, as though if she looked too long she'd figure out the truth I'm trying so desperately to keep from her.

"I guess if I'm wishing for anything it's to be home-schooled like you," Maggie says, jabbing with her scraper. "School starts the end of next month and I already know it's going to suck so hard. You're the only person in this whole town I want to talk to, and you're not going to be there. You do all your work on a computer in, like, a few hours, and you don't even have to put on pants." She scowls at her jeans. "I hate pants. Don't you hate pants?"

"Not usually, no," I say, not wanting to mentally jump that far into the future. Right now, Maggie and I exist in our own little bubble. I know I can't keep her to myself forever, but I don't want to think about losing her weeks from now either.

I want *now* to last just a little longer.

I'm bracing myself on my elbow for better reach under the bench I'm working on when I see something that makes me gag a little.

Maggie peers at me from the next bench up. "What?"

I show her *what* when I finally chisel it free, and she shrieks while crab walking to get away from it. *It* is a wad of gum and…other things wrapped around a Q-tip and covered in gray hair.

"What the actual hell? Is it dead?"

"It smells dead." Holding it as far from my body as I'm physically capable of, I drop it and the glove I'm wearing into the trash and knot it closed. Maggie runs over and starts jumping up and down on the mostly empty bag. She doesn't stop even when I give her a look.

"You want to take the chance that that thing crawls out of the trash bag and kills us in the bathroom?"

I start jumping on the bag with her. We pause after a minute, listening. Nothing, but we stomp on it a few more times just to be safe. I don't wait for her to say it. Even though it's less than half-full, I pick up the bag and head toward the exit. Maggie darts around me to get the door, flattening herself against it as I pass.

"Downside to being homeschooled—my shifts will always start earlier than yours, which means I'll be the one finding stuff like this." I raise the bag an inch and Maggie ducks away. "Still jealous?"

"Gross hairball gum monster or not having to wear pants..."

I pause halfway outside. "And?"

Maggie scrunches up her face as she eyes the trash bag. "I'm going to have nightmares about that thing, so I'm officially less jealous." She follows me to the Dumpster. Jeff watches us go but says nothing. Maggie gives him a wave and after a moment's hesitation, he returns it. Even with me standing right next to her.

Maggie was pretty much trained after the first week, even with Bertha, but she's somehow convinced Jeff that she still needs to shadow me everywhere in order to meet the "unimpeachably high standards he sets for himself and his employees." I'm actually learning a lot more from her than she is from me, especially how to couch even the most nonsensical request to Jeff in compliments so he can't say no.

"I swear I can hear it breathing in there," Maggie says, after the lid closes on the Dumpster.

"Then it can probably hear you." I tug her arm. "Come on." We round the corner back to the entrance and I stop.

Heath is standing in the parking lot by his truck.

Maggie does nothing more than glance in his direction, stopping only when she realizes that I'm standing still. Despite Maggie's presence, I can't tamp down the warmth that rushes through me when I see Heath. I take a single step toward him.

"Hi," I say.

"Hey." Heath takes a step of his own and a shy smile lifts the corners of my mouth.

"What are you doing here? Did you...come to skate?"

He breaks eye contact to look at the Polar Ice Rink sign then at Maggie. It takes all of three seconds for his gaze to return to me, and that's twice as long as I need for a chill to take up residence inside me. He can't be here with me, not with Jeff and my coworkers inside, and especially not with Maggie standing right there volleying her gaze back and forth between us. This interaction is nothing like the one she witnessed between Mark and me.

"Um, hi," Maggie says, her slightly recriminating but mostly excited eyes wide on me, before turning them toward Heath. "I feel like I'm supposed to know who you are, and yet I don't." Her words are reproachful, but she's doing a poor job of trying not to smile. I thaw infinitesimally, knowing she doesn't recognize Heath as the scowling boy we passed when she was teaching me how to drive stick. Then again, I might not have recognized him either. When Heath's features aren't twisted in animosity, he has the kind of face that would be easy to get caught staring at.

"I'm Maggie."

Heath eyes me quickly before replying with his name. I'm sure he's used to people around here knowing him on sight, especially once they hear his name, but with Maggie, there isn't even a hint of recognition. A knowing smile inches its way onto her face, but it's a normal my-friend-has-been-hiding-a-boy-from-me-and-I-can't-wait-to-torment-her-about-it smile and nothing more. Heath's gaze touches me again and I can practically see the question running through his mind: *She doesn't know?* I give him the tiniest of head shakes. He frowns for a split second, no doubt wondering how that's possible, but thankfully, Maggie doesn't see it and Heath doesn't say anything out loud.

"So how do you guys know each other?" Maggie asks.

Worried that Heath might say the wrong thing—namely the truth—I answer much too quickly. "Just from around."

"No kidding?" Maggie cocks her head at me. "'Cause, we're usually around together. How come I don't know Heath?"

I can feel the blood drain from my face. I can't think of a single explanation. Already I feel sweaty and tongue-tied and my brain is cotton, and every second I don't answer, Maggie's teasing smile shifts more into a confused frown.

"That's probably my fault," Heath says, drawing Maggie's increasingly penetrating stare to himself. "We haven't seen much of each other in, what is it, Brooke, a year?"

I nod, afraid of what might come out of my mouth if I try to speak.

"We ran into each other again last month and I thought I'd stop by and say hi again." He looks at me like we're completely alone. "Hi."

This time I do answer audibly; I can't not. "Hi."

Watching us, Maggie all but jumps up and down and claps her hands. I know her well enough to see past the semi-calm facade she's hanging on to for Heath's benefit—inwardly, she's definitely clapping. I can't blame her. In my wildest dreams, I could never be as disarming and charming as Heath is. He has me half believing that he's been waiting outside my work like some smitten boy, instead of the hurting one he feels he can only fully be with me.

"Well," Maggie says, "Brooke gets off work in a couple hours. We were supposed to hang out and hopefully start working on this ice-skating audition thing, but I suddenly feel way too tired for that." Her eyes are as bright and alert as a kid visiting Disneyland for the first time. "Maybe you guys can say more than hi to each other instead. Who knows, there might even be fireworks."

My face heats at her comment but because I can't presume on Maggie's prowess for keeping Jeff at bay for too long, I quickly nod when Heath glances at me for confirmation. "Yeah, I'll meet you when I leave." I don't say where, but Heath knows. That's more info than I want Maggie to have. I'm going to have to do plenty of damage control as it is, and I've already let her find out much more than I ever intended. One word about Heath to the wrong person—which is essentially everyone—and it's over. Everything.

We say bye to Heath, then I all but drag Maggie back inside.

"You are in *so* much trouble," she whispers in my ear, forcing a laugh I don't remotely feel from me with a well-aimed elbow into my ribs. "I want to hear everything!"

CHAPTER 22

Maggie practically drags me into the girls' bathroom when we get inside, stopping only long enough to snag the cleaning cart along with us for Jeff's benefit. As soon as the door shuts behind us, she crouches and checks to make sure all the stalls are empty before rounding on me.

"When were you going to tell me about him?" she asks, her voice echoing around the tiled bathroom.

"Heath?"

"No, the other cute guy you've been hiding from me." She swats my arm then draws back only to rethink it and swat me again.

"You heard him. There's nothing to tell."

"The fact that you said that with a straight face." She shakes her head at me then eyes the cleaning cart—more accurately, the plunger. I deliberately pull the cart behind me and Maggie sighs.

"You never look at guys."

"That's not true." I just make sure they're too far away to look back.

Maggie rolls her eyes. "You *almost* never look at guys."

"There's not usually a lot to look at." Jeff's voice reaches us as he walks past the closed bathroom door, effectively winning the argument for me.

"Well, you were looking at Heath and he was definitely looking back."

"Seriously with the fireworks line?"

"What?" She grins. "I meant in the sky. What kind of fireworks are you planning on tonight?"

I lower my head, not wanting her to see my cheeks flush. "Honestly, it's not like that."

"*Yet.*" Maggie points at me. "It's not like that yet."

I have no answer for her. It will never be like that, and yet nothing short of the truth will convince Maggie otherwise.

"All right, I want full details." She hops up on the sink with her back to the mirror. "How did you run into him? Where and what and all the questions. Go."

"He told you. There's no big story."

"Really?" she asks, hands on hips.

"Really," I tell her, putting every ounce of sincerity I can into the word.

"Really?" Her hands drop. "See, I hate this. I don't know what you're like with guys so I can't tell if you're telling me the truth or not. He's seriously cute though, like I can picture him on the back of a horse with a cowboy hat dipped low over his eyes. The sun would be setting behind him as he offered a hand to pull me up behind him and called me darling."

"Called *you* darling?" Too late I realize my mistake. Maggie's slow smile is pure evil.

"I thought it wasn't like that?"

"It's not."

"But you want it to be, and trust me when I tell you that you are not alone in the feeling. I swear he looked at you like...like...you look at the ice." She laughs. "Look at you blush!"

I can feel my face flushing, so I can hardly deny it. "Can we please drop this?"

"Uh-uh. Every time I try to talk to you about your audition lately, you shut me down. I'm not letting this one go too, not when you clearly like—"

"Then let's plan my audition," I say too loudly, my heart leaping into my throat over her unfinished sentence. I can't let her say it, because I can't for a moment let it be true.

Maggie's perfectly arched brows lift. "Are you serious?"

My heart rate barely slows when I answer her. "Yes."

The drive to Hackman's Pond gives me plenty of time to wonder why Heath showed up at my work the way he did, especially considering how many more people are in town today for the Fourth of July celebrations, and all of the reasons I come up with are bad. I'm trying to slow my panic-induced heartbeat as I hurry to join him in the shade.

Heath is frowning before I even get my breathless questions out.

"Are you okay? Did something happen?"

"No, it's fine. I just—"

Air whooshes out of my lungs and I hug him. Full-body hug him. My arms lock around his neck, pulling his somewhat resistant body to mine. It takes him a moment to respond, but when his arms encircle my back, it's the safest I've felt since before Jason went away.

The hug goes on too long, long enough for it to transition from a gesture of relief to one where I'm much too aware of his heart beating in tempo with mine and the hard muscles of his chest pressed against me. I loosen my grip and move away, and his arms slide around the small of my back until I physically step out of reach. Even then they linger for half a second before he lowers them to his sides.

"It didn't rain," I say, holding his gaze and thinking for the first time that Heath's eyes look like the blades of my skates before I sharpen them, a soft and muted silver. "I thought something must be wrong."

"I should have realized. Nothing is wrong." Heath drops his head and says something harsh under his breath, before lifting it a second later. "I just— I wanted to see you."

My heart twists a bit at that admission, and from the suddenly pained expression on Heath's face, I know he felt it too.

"I'm sorry about showing up at the rink. I wasn't thinking."

"It's okay."

He nods, and then his brows draw together. "Your friend, she really doesn't know?"

I shake my head, walking past him to sit on a branch. "She moved here at the beginning of summer."

"And nobody has said anything to her?"

"I don't think people go around talking about it randomly anymore." And I make sure she stays away from anyone who might.

Heath joins me on the branch, so that we're sitting side by side, closer than either of us have dared before. "Why haven't you told her?"

I glance at him. "Would you?"

He gives the question serious thought before answering. "No, I guess not."

"She's my best friend. Really she's my only friend." I look down at my crossed ankles swinging slightly above the grass. "I don't know that she'd still be the same with me if she knew." I give my head a hard shake, trying to dislodge the unpleasant thought. "Anyway, for now she doesn't know, and I'd like to keep it that way for as long as possible."

"And I just made that a lot harder for you."

"No," I say, extending my hand on the branch between us when he frowns. "She knows your first name but nothing else. She thinks—" I blush but I don't let myself look away "—she thinks I was keeping you a secret because I like you, not because of our brothers. I tried to explain it's not like that," I add quickly when his jaw locks. "Eventually she'll see that's all there is." I hope.

His eyes flick to my hand on the branch when I draw it back to my lap. After a minute he nods. "So the ice-skating audition thing. I thought you weren't doing it."

I sigh at the shift between one uncomfortable topic to another. At least this one doesn't involve Heath and me.

"I have to—film it anyway. I don't have to submit it,

and even then there's no guarantee that I'd get the letter in the mail inviting me to audition in person or that I'd have to accept a job offer if they made one." Even as I say this though, the idea of getting picked, of skating with a professional team has my heart nearly bursting in my chest. It swells warm and bright inside me for a minute before I let reality smother it.

"I still have a few things to figure out." When Heath keeps looking at me expectantly, I explain about securing rink time, figuring out choreography and, at Maggie's insistence, finding someone to work on lifts and partnering with. "Lifts aren't required, but showing even basic partnering work is a plus. I have a friend in Houston who should be able come for the actual audition if I ask him, but just for the day. I still need someone to practice with, and that's a big ask for Telford."

"Another skater?"

"Well, yeah, I mean—" I cut off, looking at Heath, remembering the strength in his arms when he hugged me. "Can you— Yeah, just stand up for a second." I hop down from the branch and he follows.

"I've never set foot on an ice rink."

"You don't have to." I position myself right in front of him and brace my hands on his forearms. "Can you lift me?"

"What, like—" his hands settle high on my rib cage and a breath later my feet are off the ground. My hands slide up to his shoulders as he raises me high above his head "—this?"

"Yeah," I say, a little breathless. "That's good. You can put me down now."

We both laugh a little, and there's so much uncertainty in that sound.

I tell myself this has to be a good idea even as my skin prickles with doubt. Not only will I have a partner to practice with but I can explain Heath to Maggie too, and since he'll be connected to my audition—which she'll understand me wanting to keep secret—that's all the reason I'll need to give her not to mention him to anyone. And Heath and I can still see each other whether there's a cloud in the sky or not. We'll have a reason that goes beyond our brothers.

We won't need the rain anymore.

"So you need somebody to practice with, off the ice?"

"The submission deadline for the audition is at the end of August," I say. "So it would only be for six weeks or so."

"I can probably do that," he says, though I can tell from the way he keeps shifting his feet that he's not sure this is a good idea.

So far we've spent an hour together here and there, usually with several feet of a tree branch between us, and they haven't all gone well. What I'm asking for now will bring us much, much closer. And practicing—working with and physically relying on each other—is intimate.

The first fireworks burst in the darkening sky. I'm suddenly afraid, and my feet have barely left the ground.

CHAPTER 23

I'm early to our first practice. Heath is late.

When he pulls up and gets out of his truck, I jump up from the branch and brush off the back of my black leggings like I've been caught doing something I shouldn't. That guilty feeling intensifies as he approaches, his hands shoved into his pockets and his shoulders hunched high like he's trying to ward off an icy wind.

Nothing about this afternoon is icy. We're both already sweating, and we haven't done anything yet.

"Sorry, I'm late," he says. I wait for him to offer an explanation, but he doesn't.

"It's fine," I say too brightly. "Gave me some time to mentally run through what I want us to work on. Thanks again for agreeing to help me."

Heath doesn't respond, but after a long moment he lifts his shoulders in an impatient gesture. "Is standing here part of what you want us to work on?"

I blink at him, the only response I allow myself to have to his curt words. They are way too reminiscent of our earlier interactions. I'd thought—hoped—we'd moved past that, or that we were at least trying to.

"Why are you even here?" I ask, softly but surely.

His response is just as calm. "I said I would help, so I'm here."

"Last time we talked you seemed okay with helping me. Now you don't." That is putting it mildly. He's practically vibrating with suppressed annoyance. I know I haven't done anything to account for the shift.

"It's freaking hot out here." Only he doesn't say *freaking*.

Yeah, it is hot, but it's always hot. Sometimes I forget what it feels like not to have sticky skin. He's not angry about the weather, so I don't say anything, but I keep looking at him. He's not a fan of that, because he starts to openly scowl at me.

"What do you want me to say?"

"Why are you mad?"

"'Cause I suddenly need a reason?"

"To be mad at me? Yeah."

He half snorts. "Same reason, different day."

I might have accepted that answer a couple weeks ago, but not anymore. His anger isn't about me, not directly, but digging for the reason will likely make it worse. I don't have to stand here and take it though.

"I don't want your help if this is how it comes. I can literally go anywhere else if I want to be treated badly."

His scowl slips. First a little, then a lot. In another minute, his features smooth completely. It's like watching a gun uncock. He swallows before speaking.

"I'm sorry." And it's nothing like the clipped apology he gave me for being late. The words don't come as easily, but this time he means them. "I had a bad day, but I don't need to take it out on you."

"Cal?"

Heath starts to shake his head. "No—I don't know. It's always about him." He shifts his gaze from me. "My mom asked me where I was going when I left, and I said work. I lied right to her face. She even kissed me on the cheek after I said it, since I help out with the bills. So I'm driving over here—" he points to where our vehicles are parked, one behind the other, and his voice picks up in volume "—in Cal's truck, and my mom thinks I'm sacrificing all my free time to make money for the family when in reality…in reality…" He falls quiet.

In reality he's meeting the sister of his brother's murderer. I can't help but cringe.

"No," Heath says. "Don't do that. It isn't about you. I just don't know how I can ever explain it to her. I'm stuck with lying to her, and I'll never feel good about that."

I understand that. I didn't have to lie to my mom about where I was going today, but that was only because she was still in bed with a headache from crying all night. Just because I didn't speak the lie aloud about who I was meeting didn't make it any less of a one.

"Look," I say, watching Heath walk over to the tree and lean against the trunk. "Maybe we should just stop—"

"No." He makes sure to hold my gaze when he repeats

the word. "No. That's not what I'm saying. I don't like lying to my mom because she wouldn't understand, not because I'm doing anything wrong with you. You aren't either. I just have to figure out how to not be a dick about it to you."

I exhale half a laugh. "Yeah, that'd be good."

"I am sorry."

"I'm sorry we have to lie to our families."

"Yeah." He pushes off from the tree and walks up to me, stopping maybe a foot away. "So how is this practice thing going to work?"

That is a very good question, and I'm grateful for the subject change even though I don't exactly have an answer.

"Well," I take a deep breath. "For my audition, I need to demonstrate certain skills, mostly solo stuff, but showing at least a little bit of partner work and a few lifts will give me a real advantage over some of the other people auditioning."

"Does that mean you're going to send it in?"

I look away. I haven't explained the mental gymnastics I've done to get to rationalize this stage let alone the rest. "It means I'm going to film the best audition video I can."

After a moment, Heath says, "All right."

Relieved that he's not going to press the issue, I keep talking. "Since I've always been a singles skater, this is going to be a lot of trial and error. I have some ideas of the kind of lifts I want to incorporate, but it'll really come down to the ones I can do with a reasonable level of proficiency before I have to film."

"And you have a friend to do that with you on the ice. I can stick to grass?"

"Right," I say. "But Anton, my friend who actually knows how to pair skate, lives in Houston. Between college and his own skating, he doesn't have time to drive out and rehearse with me. I need to be able to go over the parts of the routine I need him for and then pretty much film it right after. He can only give me a day, and I need to know what I'm doing before then."

"I guess that's the plan then."

I frown at Heath, but the expression is directed at myself. "Not really, no. I have to teach us both how to do something I've never done before, and I basically have a month and a half to do it."

Heath takes a slow step toward me, holding my gaze. "Then we better get started."

I decide to start easy and go with a simple half press lift. I reach for both of Heath's hands and step into him once they are clasped in mine. I make a point of staring directly ahead at his neck while I explain what I want him to do. It's an easy lift; in fact it's typically the first one they teach little kids when they are learning to pair skate. The guy bends his knees and elbows while the girl locks hers, and then he powers up, keeping his elbows bent while she extends her legs apart. Easy, except, not at all.

The actual mechanics of the lift are straightforward enough, and Heath lifts me without any obvious effort, but once he's holding me in the air with our joined hands at his shoulders and his chin resting low against my stomach, it feels anything but simple.

"Now what?" Heath asks, his breath warm against my belly even through the fabric of my fitted blue tank. It causes a tremor to pulse through my body that I know he can feel.

"Now nothing. This is the lift."

"That's it?" Another tremor.

"You can turn in a circle if you feel—yeah, slow like that. That's what we'd do if we were on the ice."

"Shouldn't I be pushing you up higher? Like a barbell?" He's already extending his arms as he speaks, lifting me above his head.

I squeak and my elbows buckle, sending my weight crashing onto his face and then both of us tumbling to the ground.

Heath lets out an *oof* as his back hits the grass and I make a similar sound when I slam into him. His hands fly to my thighs on either side of his as he lifts his head.

"Are you okay?" Before I can answer, he swears under his breath. "You're bleeding."

"I am?" I push up to a sitting position on his chest and then slide off, one hand lifting to my eyebrow and coming away wet. One glance at the tiny smear of red and my vision starts to shrink in on itself. Something warm presses hard against the cut and Heath's steady voice begins to penetrate the darkness.

"—you still with me? Brooke, look at me."

I focus on his face a few inches in front of me until the blackness begins to recede.

"There you are." He sits back and lets out a long exhale, his thumb still pressed against my eyebrow. "Your eyes started to roll back into your head for a second. It's only a little cut." He lifts his thumb. "Yeah, it's almost stopped bleeding already. Look."

I feel myself start to turn the color of the grass and I squeeze my eyes shut, hanging my head between my bent knees.

"Brooke?"

I wave off his concern. "Just give me a minute." I breathe deeply, in and out.

"Is it the blood?"

I nod. Deep breath in.

"Even that little bit?"

I nod again. Deep breath out.

"Wow. I've never seen anyone react like that before to the sight of blood."

"It's pretty much my whole family," I say, still focused on my breathing. "One time when I was like eight, my mom cut her finger while chopping tomatoes or something and Jason and I ran into the kitchen when she cried out. He passed out midrun, ended up slicing his chin completely open, and when I slid in a second behind him, I gashed my head on the corner of the island when I went down too. My dad had to take all three of us to the emergency room for stitches." It's only after I finish the story that I hear the sharp breathing coming from Heath. I glance up at him. He looks ready to pass out himself.

At first my eyes scan him for an injury I might have overlooked, but there's nothing to indicate he's hurt. And then I remember what I just said. The way my family freaks out around blood, relaying the story of Jason passing out from the sight of a mere cut finger. All I can do is stare at Heath with wide eyes.

Jason always reacted poorly to the sight of blood, and yet, somehow he stayed conscious long enough to stab Cal to death. I don't know how he could have done that, what would have overridden his mind so much to let him. Questions without answers keep me limp on the ground, but not Heath.

Wordlessly, he gets to his feet and starts walking back to his truck.

"Heath, wait! I didn't mean—"

He stops but waves his hand to cut me off without looking at me. "Look, it's late anyway. I need to be done for the day." He runs his hand through his hair and glances down before meeting my gaze again, and when he does he can't hold it for more than a second or two. "I told you before that I'd try to remember I'm not angry at you. I'm trying really hard right now, and I'm not gonna feel great later about what comes out of my mouth if I stay, okay?"

I wrap one hand around my opposite elbow and nod quickly, as though I completely understand and am not hurt at all by his needing to get away from me. I get it, I do, but my lungs still feel too tight when I breathe in. We keep trying not to hurt each other.

But I did and he did.

We are.

I don't even know how to say sorry except to let him go.

"Yeah, I guess it is late." I have time before my shift

starts but I can see how much his composure is costing him with every second that passes. I hate leaving things like this though, especially when I can't tell if he means he needs to leave now, or he needs to leave for good. "Will you...tomorrow?"

"I don't know right now. I gotta..." He gestures to his truck, and when he starts walking this time I don't try to stop him.

It's late that night, so late that it's technically not even the same day when I get his text.

I'll be there tomorrow.

CHAPTER 24

My second practice with Heath starts a lot better than the first, mostly because we don't talk about anything. We get the half press lift down—and by down I mean up—and with a lot of courage on my part, move on to the full press.

"I got you," Heath says, as we get into position.

"I know." I'm not worried he's going to drop me; I'm worried that I'll freak out being that high off the ground.

Remembering our previous failed attempt, Heath chooses one of the denser patches of grass for us to practice on. It'll still hurt if I fall, but hopefully we can avoid bloodshed this time.

He squeezes both my hands before squatting, and then I'm up, dizzyingly up. He doesn't pause at the halfway mark, lifting me above his head. High. Too high. My arms start to wobble as the horizon appears to toss like the waves of the ocean in my vision.

"Don't you break," Heath says, stepping slightly to the left to counterbalance us. "I'll drop you right on your ass."

My eyes snap down to meet his, my arms locking automatically at the threat.

"I'm dead serious. I'm not letting you take me out again."

I've never seen it before so it takes me a second to register the teasing gleam in his eyes.

"There you go. See? Not so bad, right?"

Looking at his upturned face and the one-sided smile he's giving me, I nod, but the second I glance forward, the vertigo charges back. Heath's reflexes are fast enough to keep us from hitting the ground when I fall this time, but I still solidly bang his nose against my sternum on the way down. Both his hands rush to his face the second he unceremoniously sets me on my feet.

"Oh, I'm sorry. Heath, I'm so sorry,"

He turns his back to me and his words are muffled. "Get away. I'm trying to tell if it's bleeding."

I take a huge step back, twisting my hands in the hem of my tank at I stare at his back. "It didn't feel like I hit you that hard this time. It's not broken is it?"

He turns to face me again and I can see his reddened but thankfully blood-free face. "No it's not broken." His eyes are watering a little, but otherwise he seems intact.

I bite both my lips. "I really am sorry."

He prods his nose. "Tell me again why we're not doing this in the water?"

"Because I have to go straight to work from here and wet hair and ice rinks aren't a good mix."

"Well then did you ever think that maybe ice-skating

isn't the best sport for someone who is afraid of blood and heights?" There's no animosity in his tone, but I must have hit him harder than I thought for him to even semi-serious ask that question.

"Why do you think I've always been a solo skater?"

He grumbles a response that I can't make out. "Can we stick to lower lifts for now until we can figure out the fear-of-heights thing?"

I refrain from saying that my fear-of-heights thing isn't something we can just "figure out," because I've dealt with it my whole life, and because I'm not exactly eager to be up that high again either. A little compassion would be nice though. "Aren't you afraid of anything?"

I'm looking for a basic phobia like mine—fear of enclosed spaces, fear of the dark etc.—but I can tell nothing like that is on his mind as he lets his hand fall from his face.

I feel an echo of the emotions from the first day, the trepidation and unease as he stands and walks farther under the shade of the tree. But I also feel something else, a longing that I can't quite put my finger on.

He moves farther away from me than I expect, as if he's remembering our first meeting under this tree too. "That's a question," he says.

"I only meant—"

"I know what you meant." He comes closer then, and after hesitating so briefly that I wouldn't have noticed it even a week ago, he brushes my fingers with his. There's that jolting thrill I feel whenever he touches me, but there's more than that awareness this time. I answer with my own fingers, and he takes my hand. That's where he keeps his gaze—our hands and not my face—when he answers.

"Cal was on a full scholarship to U of T. Maybe you knew that." He shrugs.

I did know that. It was one of those details that made my brother's crime all the more abhorrent to the people reporting it. Calvin Gaines wasn't your run-of-the-mill college kid. He was brilliant and driven and bursting with so much potential. *The world will never know what it lost* was a phrase I heard repeated over and over. My heart constricts, then constricts again because I can't think about Cal without thinking of Jason and hurting for him too. The guilt from that involuntary reaction nearly smothers me, but I can't pull my hand from Heath's without explaining. And I can't explain that to Heath. I can't even explain it to myself.

"My whole life he was always that guy." A smile tugs at the corner of Heath's mouth. "My first day of high school, the teachers were all giddy when they heard my last name. Calvin Gaines's little brother. They were thinking if I were half the genius he was then they'd be set. I don't think it took a week for them to realize the only thing we shared was a last name. I wasn't the academic or the athlete. Worse, in their eyes—teachers, Cal, my mom—it wasn't because I couldn't be, it was because I didn't care." He squeezes my hand then lets go, backing up a step and taking a breath. "I never cared, I don't think, about anything. I did just enough to get by. I let Cal be the golden son because for him, he didn't have to try. He was just that good at everything."

"Heath," I say, drawing his gaze to mine. "You did more than skate by." Even though I was a year behind him and we'd moved in different circles, I'd known who he was. And he wasn't what he was making himself out to be. Maybe he felt that way compared to Cal, but Heath wasn't a bad student that I know of.

"No, actually, skating by is exactly what I did. And it was okay. Because of Cal. He was going to be the one who did great things with his life—the one who did things period." His jaw locks, and I can tell he's trying to direct his anger at something other than me. "I didn't care about college so I didn't apply. I told my mom I'd look into community college but that I wanted to work for a while and save up. And the thing of it is—" his jaw clenches harder and I sense that he can't bring himself to meet my eyes "—the thing of it is, is that I was fine with that. No plans, no goals. I was going to work and live and die all in the same town without ever feeling like I missed a thing."

Was. That's what he said. He *was* going to do those things.

Heath's gaze lifts to mine, only the anger I expect to see pulling at his features isn't there. And I understand.

That life that he thought he was fine with, the life without any real highs or lows, without markers or accomplishments, it's not enough anymore. It's not enough because his brother is gone and he can't live his life watching a ghost from the sidelines.

And it's terrifying.

"What do you care about?" I ask Heath sometime later when we're sitting in the shade sharing a water bottle.

"Care about how?"

"The way I care about skating." I nod toward the tree

trunk with my chin. "Is it wood carving?" Heath has
shown me photos of a few pieces he worked on with his
granddad, and he's really good. I know my dad would love
to get his hands on someone with Heath's talent. If Heath
were anyone else, I'd have already introduced them.

Heath's throat moves as he drinks deeply before offering
the water back to me. "No, that's more about my granddad."

I take the water bottle. "What then?"

He shrugs. "I don't know."

"You're telling me there's nothing that—that, I don't
know, makes you feel like you're awake when everything
else feels like a dream?"

"Is that what ice-skating is for you?"

I nod.

He takes the water from my unprotesting fingers. "Must
be nice."

It's more than nice; it's vital. Skating is a part of me,
even if now it has to be a smaller part. It's kind of heartbreaking to think of Heath without that. "Did you have
anything before?"

"Before Cal died?" He waits for my nod. "I can't even
remember before Cal died. Does that make sense?"

It does. "I could help you find it, you know?"

He smiles at me, but it feels far-off somehow. "Something to make me feel awake?"

I feel my smile trying to compensate for the lack in his.
"Yeah."

He sighs, but it doesn't feel heavy, more like he's letting

go of something. "I don't feel asleep now. Up for trying one more?"

I don't think he means it that way, but it feels like the best compliment I've ever gotten. When he reaches for me, I know that I'm going to do everything I can to make sure he stays awake.

CHAPTER 25

Laura is sitting cross-legged on her bed and Ducky is in his cage whistling at her in a failed attempt to get her attention when I bound into her room the next morning, and I do mean bound. I have to overdo it if I'm going to have any hope of enlisting her in what I have planned for the day.

For as much time as she spends in her room, it's as slovenly kept as the rest of her. I shift a little so I'm not sitting directly on what looks like an old chocolate milk stain on her bedspread. There are similar stains on her clothes, both the ones she's wearing and the few that are scattered across the floor. The drawers to her dresser are hanging half-open and there's trash everywhere except in the wastebasket. It's not that she was any kind of a neat freak before—she was always in too much of a hurry to do something to care if her room was a mess—but she wasn't an open slob. Mom was too aware of her own harsh upbringing to force any of us to clean our rooms, and she never really had to with

Jason and me. Laura would eventually get frustrated when she couldn't find a favorite T-shirt and she'd beg me to help her clean her room. She'd keep things semi-neat for about a month then the mess would take over and the cycle would start again. But this… I don't think she's touched a thing since Jason was arrested. It doesn't smell like she has.

The only clean thing in the entire room—including Laura—is Ducky's cage.

Taking a deep breath through my mouth, I do my best to ignore all that and focus only on Laura's face.

"I'm busy," she says, without taking her eyes from the open laptop she's staring at.

I lean over and close it.

"Hey." It's a half-hearted protest at best, but still a good sign. I wait for her gaze to shift from the computer to me.

"I need you to come to a carnival with me."

My sister stares at me.

I spin her laptop toward me, open it and start typing. "There's one a couple hours away and I need you to come with me." I turn the screen back to her so she can see the site detailing all the rides and guaranteed fun for the whole family. I make sure the largest image clearly shows the Salt & Pepper Shaker ride that she used to love even though the sight of it makes me queasy. She glances at it then at me.

"Just go with Maggie."

I shake my head. "Her mom is making them repaint all the bedrooms in their house together. I want to go with you, and…I might lose my nerve if I wait too long."

The apathetic mask my sister always wears slips. "Nerve for what? Why do you need to go to this carnival?"

I take a deep breath. "Because it's the closest Ferris wheel I could find and I'm tired of being afraid of heights."

The mask stays down. "You're serious?"

She can see that I am.

"Why now?"

The fact that my sister is actually engaging with me is the deciding factor in telling her the truth—or at least most of it.

"Don't say anything to Mom, but the audition deadline for *Stories on Ice* is coming up next month. Maggie has been bugging me about it, so I figured it wouldn't hurt to at least film something. Anton already agreed to partner with me, but I'm having a hard time even being that little bit off the ground."

I tense as the oddest expression overtakes Laura's face. I'd almost swear it's relief, but that doesn't make any sense, and anyway it's gone too quickly for me to decide.

"You haven't mentioned it in so long," she says. "I thought you weren't going to try anymore."

"I'm not," I say, wondering that she's not more panicked the way Mom had been. I have to tread carefully here. If I bring up Jason directly, I'll lose her like I did last time, and yet I can't leave him out entirely either. "I don't know that I want to leave everyone here, at least not right now."

Laura turns to look at Ducky in his cage. "I think you should."

I'm sure I don't hear her right. "Audition?"

She nods. "I know they'll pick you. You should do it."

I reach to brush her knee with two fingers so that she'll

look at me. "They tour year-round," I say softly. "I'd be gone more than I'd be home."

She pulls her knee away from my outstretched hand so that I can't touch her even that tiny bit. "I know."

Slowly, I straighten. I want it not to sting, but the fact that she cares so little about seeing me regularly feels like a slap. "It would just be you, Mom and Dad for the next few years until you left for college. You'd be fine with that?"

She shrugs, and even that small gesture is half-hearted.

I know I wanted Mom to be sad that I was giving up on auditioning. I didn't want Laura to be sad exactly, but I wanted to see something that showed she'd miss me, not more of her indifference. That hurts worse than anything.

Laura clicks something on her computer and closes out the carnival page. "You don't need a Ferris wheel. Just go stand on the porch railing."

I slam her laptop shut. "Why don't you care? About anything! I could stand on anything or I could wait for Maggie. Instead I found a stupid carnival with one of those stupid Salt & Pepper Shaker rides that you love in a stupid town far enough away that no one will recognize us. I wanted to do something *with you*, spend time *with you*, face this thing that genuinely frightens me *with you*." I suck in a deep breath, waiting for her response, for her to say or do anything, but she doesn't. And it breaks my heart. "I'm trying so hard and you act like just being in the same room with me bothers you. What did I do, huh?" I stab my fingers against my chest. "What did *I* do?"

"Nothing!" she screams and I flinch back. "You did nothing! I told you something was wrong when he came home from college, but you didn't listen. We should have talked to him—we shouldn't have let him go out that night. I could have gone after him…" The heat in her voice vanishes as quickly as it ignites, and for a second I think she's going to cry, but she just presses her lips together until the rest of her face smooths and her shoulders lower back down.

She may have wrestled her control back but I haven't. My breath hitches as I stare at her. "You're saying—you think it's *my* fault? That I—we could have stopped him?" My eyes blur when she refuses to look at me. "Laur—you can't believe that anyone could have known what was going to happen. Jason didn't even know."

Her gaze snaps to mine, hard and glaring for one heart-stopping instant. "It doesn't matter now, does it?" She draws her laptop back and opens it, her finger gliding over the track pad like the last few minutes never happened.

I'm near tears and she looks like she could fall asleep.

"Laura," I say, trying to keep my voice steady. "Please come with me. We can talk and figure some of this out. I didn't know you felt this way, but I need to."

Without looking up she says, "You can go. I don't feel like going to a carnival."

I know Heath won't be there, but I go to our tree anyway. The early-morning mist hovering over the grass hasn't fully dissipated. It almost swirls as I walk through it. When I reach the trunk, I let my fingers linger over the scarred remains of Jason's initials.

I don't know what to do about Laura. I feel like every time I try, I make our relationship worse. Jason would have known what to say to her. If I were where he is and he were home, the two of them would be on their way to that carnival right now. I turn, sliding my back down the trunk until I'm sitting on the dew-damp grass. I don't know if she just can't deal with Jason's confession or if she blames me somehow or resents the fact that her favorite sibling is gone and she's stuck with me. We're so different. She'd always been the wild, impetuous one, leaping off bridges, whereas I start to panic when I'm a few feet off the ground.

I doubt I would have been able to set foot on that Ferris wheel no matter how determined I'd sounded earlier. It was one of those fleeting thoughts that I'd grabbed on to because I wanted it. Me and Laura, taking a mini road trip, eating fried everything and maybe, just maybe, helping me try something a little less extreme than a Ferris wheel, like a merry-go-round. I laugh to myself thinking about it, because Laura and I would have laughed too.

The sound trails off. It could have been a nice day. It could have been the start of a lot of nice days. I'm trying and she's not. I keep looking for ways to show her that I care, and she keeps showing me over and over again that she doesn't, that she won't. Nothing I say or do seems to change anything. I reach out and she pulls back, literally. I really thought it would be different this time, that she wouldn't be able to deny me asking for help, but she did. She more than did. She was worse than indifferent. And for the first time since Jason left, it doesn't make me feel sorry for her.

Filling my lungs with resolve as much as air, I push to

my feet and, without letting myself think about it, climb onto the waist-high branch in front of me.

Okay. This is fine. I can do three feet off the ground.

I step up on a higher branch, wrapping my arms around the trunk like a human koala bear.

Four feet off the ground. Still okay. Five…dizzier, dizzier. *Don't fall, don't fall.*

I flatten my belly on the branch I was standing on, sucking in air until my vision is steady and the ringing in my ears has stopped. Then, instead of climbing down, I stand back up again.

CHAPTER 26

"Why do you hate my face?"

"I don't hate your face," I tell Heath. It's nearing sunset the following day and even though I never made it above seven feet off the ground the day before when I was practicing on my own, I'm done with letting my fear of heights ground me. I need to acclimate to ten feet off the ground—not just getting my head ten feet off the ground, it's being that high while balancing on my stomach Superman style. I feel like I'm ready for more, which is why I just told Heath I want to start practicing overhead lifts.

"What happened to sticking with the low lifts? The ones that don't end up nearly breaking my nose?"

"The low lifts aren't good enough. It's the high ones that I need to be able to do." Then in a quieter voice, I add, "It's the high ones I'm afraid of."

Heath huffs a little. "Yeah, me too."

My nerves still feel somewhat frayed from the day before, what with Laura and the fact that I nearly fell out of that stupid tree more times than I can count. I'm annoyed and I don't care if Heath knows it. "Look, I have to learn this, okay? If you're not going to help me then say something now so I can start looking for someone who will."

Rather than draw back at my combativeness, Heath leans forward. "When did I say I wasn't going to help you?"

"You're complaining."

"Yeah, so? You've smashed into my face a bunch trying this stuff." He shrugs. "I'm going to complain about that and I'm not exactly psyched by the prospect of it happening again."

"That's my point," I say, a little too loudly.

"No," Heath says, keeping his voice steady if a little patronizing. "It's mine. You're afraid of heights—"

"I'm working on that."

"—and," he says without acknowledging that I said anything, "you're asking me to put you in a position where you're afraid and where that fear tends to cause me a decent amount of pain. I'm just stating the facts."

And I'm just grinding my teeth. "I have to film my audition video in five weeks. I have to do lifts—and not little beginner lifts—in that video. I have to do them on the ice, which means I really can't afford to fall. Falls are inevitable when learning lifts. I'd rather fall now, on the grass, with—" I'd been about to say *with you*, because unlike Anton, Heath's proved himself strong enough and quick enough to keep both of us from suffering any serious injuries, but something keeps me from admitting that "—enough time to get them right."

Heath doesn't act like he noticed the amended statement. "And I get that, I do, but how are you going to learn anything when you nearly pass out every time your feet leave the ground?"

I narrow my eyes at him. "I am not that bad."

He narrows his eyes back at me. "You're not that good either."

"I seriously want to scream at you right now."

"Yeah? Go ahead."

I don't scream at him. I let my nails dig into my palms until the urge passes. "I tried, okay? Yesterday I asked my sister to come ride a Ferris wheel with me."

Heath raises his eyebrows, and I can't tell if he's impressed or thinks I'm an idiot for even considering being up that high off the ground.

"And?" is all he says.

"And nothing, we didn't go. I asked, she told me to go stand on our porch railing instead. So I came here, and I climbed this tree." I turn my head to the live oak and look at the highest branch I reached. It feels pathetically close to the ground when I look at it. My shoulders sag and I sigh. "I sort of climbed this tree. I tried anyway." I gasp a little when I face Heath again because he's moved right in front of me. I have to tilt my head back to meet his gaze.

"You came here yesterday and climbed this tree?"

"Tried," I say, swallowing at how close we are.

"Did you fall?"

"I'm not going to answer that."

One corner of his mouth lifts. His eyes make a sweep of my body, head to toe and back again, and I feel dizzy even with both my feet firmly planted on the ground. "You don't seem hurt."

"That's because I only sort of climbed the tree."

The other side of Heath's mouth lifts to join the first. "Sort of is still something. I'm not a big fan of your sister for blowing you off, but I'm pretty impressed that you tried to aim as high as you did. Where's the nearest Ferris wheel?"

"There's a pop-up carnival happening right now in Lubbock."

Heath laughs out loud and I smile. "Would you really have gone?"

"To the carnival? Yes. On the Ferris wheel? I guess I'll never know." Considering that the mental image alone makes me feel like I have food poisoning, I have a pretty good idea.

"Kind of extreme though, isn't it?"

It is. If it were only about my fear of heights, the porch railing would have been more than equal to the task. But it was about Laura too, or I tried to make it about Laura. It's not easy talking about how things are between my sister and me, not just because I never have before, but because I can't fully suppress the twinge of guilt I feel complaining about anything related to this situation with Heath. But he encourages me to go on once I've started, and soon we're sitting together on the ground and the whole situation between me and Laura is out, her withdrawal from everything and everyone, including me, and my continued missteps every time I try to connect to her the way we used to.

Heath leans back against the tree trunk and watches the

fireflies blink off and on around the bank of the pond in the distance. Finally he turns to me. "That sucks."

"It does," I say, shifting my weight so I'm leaning more fully against the trunk too. It's plenty large enough for us to share, but I'd been worried about accidentally brushing shoulders with him while I was talking and had kept myself stiff and leaning slightly away. Now, when our shoulders touch, I don't feel the need to pull away. It's nice, feeling him there beside me. It's even nicer that he understands and knows that there isn't an easy fix to what's broken between my sister and me.

"Tell me about your sister," I say, wanting to give him what he's given me if I can.

Heath draws a knee up and drapes an arm over it. "Gwen and I were never close, but I guess we're further away now. The difference between us and you with your sister is that neither of us is trying." He looks at me, catches my gaze briefly before looking away again. "My mom had Gwen when she was really young, they made it work, my mom and dad, but they waited to have me and Cal until nearly ten years later. Gwen always felt more like a third parent than a sibling, and now that my dad is basically gone, she really tries to act like a parent. It's not great for any of us. She thinks she's helping by telling everyone what to do, but a lot of the time I'll turn my truck around when I see that she's home."

"Where do you go?" I ask.

"Nowhere. Work, if I can." He looks at me. "Here."

I hold his gaze. It feels naked and safe, and at the same

time, *I* feel naked and safe. And I feel warm—too warm, like I should look away but I can't.

"That sucks," I say.

Heath laughs, hanging his head a little as he looks away again. "Yes and no." He sobers. "I don't know what to do about my sister, but it's good…here."

"Hmm," I say, not wanting to probe into that last statement. I think I know what he means, and I know it's a lot safer to leave anything more unsaid.

"Tell me why you're doing this."

I frown. "What do you mean?"

"You're doing all this for an audition that you don't even plan to send in."

"I told Maggie that I'd—"

He waves his hands, cutting me off. "No, you said you'd audition to get her off your back. Why all the rest? Why do you care about adding lifts and working this hard on something no one else is going to see?"

Taken aback by the question, I falter. "I don't know. It's important to me to do a good job."

He leans into my personal space. "Yeah, but why? Is it so you can change your mind about auditioning?"

"No." The answer is automatic and loud even to my ears. Heath's expression says he doesn't believe me, and I feel my dimple as I clench my chin. "I don't do things halfway. That's not who I am. And this—" I gesture around our practice area "—this was my dream for a really long time." My throat tries to tighten but I keep going. "It's not—" I almost say it's not anyone's fault that I have to let it go, but that's not true, so I shift and hope Heath doesn't notice.

"It's my choice to let it go, but that doesn't mean it's easy. I still wish I could skate, and I still want to film the best audition video I can, even if it's just for me."

Heath stares at me for what feels like a very long time but in reality is probably only a few seconds. "And it has to be," he says. "Just for you?"

I don't have to list the reasons I mentally give myself. More than anyone else he'll understand my one word answer. "Yes."

Maybe I imagine the sadness in his eyes when he nods, or maybe I only imagine it's for me. Either way I don't know what to do with it, so I look away when I push to my feet. "Anyway, Maggie wouldn't let me get away with doing less than my best. She'd be suspicious and might even insist on being there when I submit my audition. If it's good, she won't have any reason to question me. I don't want to lie to her."

Heath makes a sound and rolls his head.

"What?" I ask a little sharply.

"It's just…you know you're still lying to her."

"I never agreed to use the audition. It's not a lie if—"

He holds up both hands. "Look, I don't want to argue with you. Send it in, don't send it in, that's up to you. But don't kid yourself about what you're doing." He gets to his own feet.

"I'm not kidding myself, I'm just trying not to hurt anyone."

"And how's that going for you?"

I suck in a breath but clamp my teeth to keep from saying anything that I might later regret.

"Seriously? No comment?"

I fight the urge to cross my arms. "I don't have anything nice to say right now."

"So? That never stops me."

"Maybe it should," I say with a little more heat than I intend.

One side of his mouth lifts, then the other. "That wasn't very nice, Brooke."

"Stop goading me."

"Stop being so goadable. What do you care what I say or think anyway?"

I gape at him. "Of course I care what you think. You're my—"

His smile slips along with my frown.

It doesn't feel safe to label anything between us, but considering he just called me out for being dishonest, I can't exactly take it back now. "You're my friend," I finish.

He tries to look away, but I catch something pained flit across his face before he can.

"Please don't let that be a bad thing," I say, looking at the sadness he always holds so tightly around himself, even when he tries to mask it in anger. "I don't think it has to be. You're the only person in my life that I don't have to hide things from. I talk to you about my family and my feelings. I even tell you about my nightmares." As much of them as I can anyway. "I know we can't change the past, but having you in my life helps. It helps me feel less alone. Isn't that…isn't that what I do for you?"

His gaze lifts to mine but he doesn't answer my question, he asks one of his own. "Would it help? If you knew everything about that night?"

My whole body jerks. "Do you know—"

His hand brushes my arm and he shakes his head, cutting me off. "No, I'm just talking. I have them too, you know. I guess I always just thought the truth might be worse than the nightmares. At least those we can wake up from."

"Not when they follow you from your bed," I say.

He falls silent, and something heavy forms in the pit of my stomach. "I don't mean that mine are worse than yours. I know they're not—"

"Brooke. It's okay." He doesn't reach out for me again, but his words are so gentle that I feel comforted all the same. "Friends, huh?"

"I mean, I know we can't exactly tell anyone, but..." I lift one shoulder, feeling suddenly and unaccountably shy.

He shakes his head and steps into me, causing my breath to catch when his hands mold around my hips. "Just try to be the kind of friend who doesn't break my nose this time, okay?"

When he flexes his knees preparing to lift me, a smile blooms on my face and I swear he draws in a breath seeing it.

CHAPTER 27

It's Friday night and I'm staring up at the tree alone and worrying my bottom lip between my teeth while trying to convince myself that the full moon overhead is a good thing. Being able to more clearly see each branch I grab or step on is a plus, but that also means I'll have a moonlit visual of those same branches if I fall past them on my way back down. I've actually been getting dizzy a lot less lately, both when Heath lifts me and when I'm climbing on my own. The former is because he talks to me constantly when I'm in the air, keeping me tethered to the ground by his voice even when I feel miles from it.

I glance up at the straight line carved on the trunk for the ten-foot mark—and I imagine I hear Heath urging me on as I suck in a breath and reach for the first branch.

There you go, that part's easy, right?

No. It's not easy, but I step up anyway.

Don't look down; you've been higher than this before.

My knees wobble a little as I stand on the waist-high branch, keeping my eyes up as if Heath is there talking to me instead of it just being his voice in my head.

See the line? Two more branches and you're there.

I keep my chin level, but my eyes glance down and it's like the ground starts to tip sideways.

Come on, Brooke. You're so close. How bad do you want this?

I press my cheek against the rough bark and force my eyes back up to the goal, to the line that means I'd be higher off the ground than Heath could ever have to lift me.

Hey. You can do this. I know you can.

And suddenly, I know I can too. Not just because Heath's been telling me for two weeks that I can, but because I know I'm more afraid staying on the ground than I'll ever be of falling.

I don't need anyone else's voice to grab the branch above me or pull myself another couple feet. I don't make it all the way to the line, but I come closer than I have before and I don't feel like I'm giving up when I climb back down. I know I'll reach it, I realize as my foot touches on the ground, just not tonight.

"Look at you not falling."

My hand flies to my heart. "Oh my goodness you scared me."

"You didn't hear me pull up?"

I shake my head, wondering if it's possible to have a heart attack at seventeen. My heart was already beating wildly from being up so high, and it kicked into hyper-drive when Heath startled me. Still, I can't help but smile seeing him. "What are you doing here? I thought you had to work."

"I gave away my shift. I had something I needed to do and I thought you might want the extra day to practice." He says this lightly, but the way he's looking at everything but me makes me think he's not being completely honest. My smile dims.

"You gave away your shift?" I know his family relies on his paycheck. If anything, he picks up extra shifts; he doesn't give away the ones he has. And not for this, for me. I start to ask him another question, but then I notice there's a sheen to his skin that I don't think the summer heat alone is responsible for. "Is something wrong?"

He shakes his head but he won't meet my gaze.

"Heath, you can talk to me…about anything." He's still shaking his head a little, and unease is starting to raise the hairs on the back of my neck. "What did you need to do?"

"I just needed to see somebody."

"Who?" I say, breathing the word. I could swear he almost looks guilty.

His gaze holds me bound when it lifts to mine, all his nervous energy gone in a flash. "Did you have a nightmare last night?"

I blink at the non sequitur. "I— Yes. Did you? Is that why…"

Heath frowns, and his unblinking stare makes my heart race faster. Finally, he says, "It was just one of those days, okay? I knew you'd be here so I came, but I don't feel like making a big deal out of it. Can we just…?"

I nod, longing to press for more but understanding that

he's not ready to give it. I can't help but feel like he's not telling me everything. He hasn't told me about what happens in his nightmares, but I've felt sick from mine more often than not and I can only imagine how much worse his must be. Still, I'm glad he sought me out, whatever the reason. Glad enough that I force the rest away.

He looks up at the tree. "How high did you get this time?"

"Almost nine. Eight and a half at least."

"Brooke, that's great." He hesitates but only for a moment before stepping forward and pulling me into a hug that I return. I've gotten very used to touching Heath over these past weeks, but it's usually in the guise of practice or the occasional conciliatory gesture when we are talking about our families. We don't touch each other just because, and I feel the difference this time when we do. I feel Heath with nothing else to distract me. I feel his strength and his warmth the same way I felt his voice when I was climbing. I feel his heartbeat and his breath exhaling over my neck and it's like the ground is moving again even though my feet are firmly planted on it.

He lets go before I would have and seems not the least bit affected by our embrace. "So eight and a half, huh? Does that mean we can try the *Dirty Dancing* lift?"

"It's called a swan lift."

Heath gives me a look.

"It was a swan lift long before that movie came out."

Heath continues to look at me.

"And my leg position is slightly different."

"Brooke."

"Fine. Yes, I think I'm ready to try it," I say. "Maybe."

"That's the kind of rock-solid confidence I'm looking for. Let's do this!"

Heath jogs back to his truck to turn his headlights on and give us some much-needed light. Watching Heath's silhouetted form walk back toward me has my heart galloping in my chest.

He stops in front of me, and I have to look up a little to meet his gaze. I hear myself swallow.

He looks at me expectantly. "So are you going to run at me?"

"No, I'll step into you, grab your wrists and, once I'm up and I have my balance, I'll let go."

"Sounds easy enough."

I give Heath a look.

"I'm serious."

I continue to give Heath a look until his smile infects my own.

"I told you I won't let you fall, and if I feel it starting to happen, I promise you'll fall on me and not the ground." He says it so seriously that my pulse kicks impossibly higher.

"I believe you."

Heath closes the remaining distance between us. "Where do I put my hands? Here?" His hands settle low on my hips. Since I was planning only on climbing a tree tonight, I opted for cutoffs and a loose tank top instead of the yoga pants and fitted racerback tank I normally wear when practicing. The cutoffs are low and the tank top barely skims the waistband, so his hands touch that thin stretch of exposed skin and I almost jump.

"Um, no. Here." I shift his hands so his palms are touching my hip bones and only the tips of his fingers reach the around the sides.

We practice me stepping into him and him finding the correct hand placement several times before moving on to the beginning of the lift, just a small hop off the ground so he can get used to holding my weight in that position.

I never get used to his hands on my bare skin, however small the contact is.

We move on to Heath lifting me higher—not over his head, but even with it. We work on this longer than we need to, more so for me to acclimate to the height than anything else. It does feel high, but so much of me is focused on my skin touching his that I don't cross that line of being scared. Not of falling anyway.

I step back and meet Heath's gaze. "All the way this time?"

He nods and I move.

I feel a zing when his hands touch me, another when my feet leave the ground and a third when I surge up over his head. I feel myself wanting to rush it, to hit the pose as quickly as possible so that Heath can lower me back down again. But I focus on his hands and the sound of his voice urging me on and when I feel steady, I release his wrists and extend my arms.

And down I go.

Heath is as good as his word. Somehow he surges backward as I'm tipping, and he keeps me from face-planting on the ground. Possibly even more impressive—not a single part of my body comes into contact with his nose.

Settling me back on my feet, Heath says, "Okay, that was not bad for a first go."

I have to agree. I was expecting it to go so much worse.

"How'd you do with the height?"

"Fine," I say, surprised that I actually mean it. "I think it was okay, it was just a balance issue." But even as I say that, my cheeks heat, because the truth is it was more a him-and-me issue.

"Okay like you're ready to go again?"

I start to nod then stop myself. "Your shoulders have to be getting tired." We've been working on this for close to an hour, which means he's probably lifted me a hundred times already.

He rolls each shoulder. "I'm good."

Still I hesitate.

Heath sighs, but he half smiles as he does it. "Come here."

I feel warmer all over as I step closer to him, a normal step not the kind that precedes a lift.

He reaches for me, his hands sliding up either side of my rib cage and then slowly, oh so slowly, he bends his elbows, lifting me until we are eye level. "My shoulders are fine."

My heart is not. As steady as his arms are, my heart is beating wildly. And he just keeps holding me in the air like that, like I weigh nothing and he can go on holding me forever.

The fading smile he started with is the only sign that

he's exerting any effort. It slips while I remain steady. And when his eyes dip to my mouth, I know. I know what he's going to do even before he lowers my feet to the ground without releasing me. And I know as I lift my face, that he's as afraid as I am.

The second his lips touch mine I feel like I'm off the ground again, only this time it feels like when I leap off the ice; it's that same exhilarating freedom and sense of rightness, that same fear-enhanced euphoria that tells me even if I fall, it's worth it. For a second, I don't think about anything except leaning into this kiss, into Heath, my hands rising up his biceps when he squeezes my ribs, sending goose bumps on top of goose bumps over my skin. His lips fit mine like they were made for me, and I feel myself getting lost in the mix of softness and strength I find in his kiss, in him. In something so perfect it aches.

But a second is all I get before reality tears my mouth from his with a soft cry I don't have to explain. Already that perfect moment is twisting in my memory, guilt tugging on my limbs and leaching away all the warmth I felt in his arms.

"We can't do this," I say, looking up at his moonlit eyes and hoping mine don't look half as tortured. I know what's going through his mind, because the same thoughts are accusing me inside mine.

My brother killed his brother.

He can't be with me without betraying Cal.

Even if he doesn't yet, he'll come to hate himself for kissing me.

And he'll hate me too for making him forget, however briefly, that he's not allowed to care about me.

But he's not letting me go. His hands flex on my ribs like he's seconds away from pulling me to him again, and I know with sickening certainty that I can't ever let him kiss me again.

"I have to go." I feel like I have to pry myself free from his hands. "Heath, you know I have to go." My voice cracks.

"I know, but…" He's frowning, not at me but in my direction like he can't fully understand what we just did or why he's not hurling himself away from me. But I do, and it's oozing around inside me like I'm balancing on the edge of a cliff.

"I don't think we can do this anymore," I say, staring at the ground in front of us.

"See each other, or touch each other?"

I meet his gaze. "Both."

There's a flicker of anger that moves across his features. "Because I kissed you?"

I shake my head, the slight movement and the admission that follows taking all my strength. "Because I liked kissing you."

His chest heaves as he lets out a breath, and I can't believe any part of him could be relieved hearing that from me, but then he says, "Just come back tomorrow, okay? I'll get someone to take my day shift and I'll meet you and we'll talk—"

I'm shaking my head to cut him off, stunned that I have to do that much. There is nothing that either one of us can say that we haven't already said to ourselves a million times. The difference is that now we have to listen. And if he can't, then I have to say the one thing he can't ignore.

"Tomorrow's Saturday," I say. "That's when I visit my brother."

CHAPTER 28

I'm already awake when Mom's whisper-soft tap sounds on my bedroom door the following morning. I hardly slept at all, and when I did doze off it felt like only minutes before my nightmares would hurl me back awake.

I'd be in the woods watching Jason and Cal fighting, and then suddenly Heath would be there, right in front of me. I'd start scrambling to get past him, to see what was happening with our brothers, or worse, I'd try to get him to look so we could stop them together, but he kept blocking me until I was pushing him, screaming at him to let me by because I could hear Cal dying...

My skin is clammy when I get out of bed, and it stays prickly and sticky even after my quick shower.

Heath didn't say anything harsh to me after our kiss and my revelation about visiting Jason today. I wanted to remind him that there were things much bigger than the two of us, things we couldn't let ourselves forget even though for the briefest of moments, when his lips touched mine, I had.

I'd paid for it with nightmares that I could still see whenever I closed my eyes.

When I find Mom in the kitchen, I try to smile warmly at her, guilt making me feel like I need to overcompensate. Until I take in her appearance.

She's still in her robe.

"Mom?"

She glances at me over her shoulder just as two slices of toast pop up in the toaster. "Brooke, oh good." She adds the toast to the tray I'm just now noticing, laden with ginger ale, saltine crackers and a big empty bowl. "Laura has been throwing up all night. I thought she might be feeling better, but she was just sick again."

"Oh, I'm sorry," I say. "I can stay home with her if—if you're okay going by yourself." I'm trying to ignore the way my belly twists with fresh guilt over how badly I want her to say yes, to let me escape from seeing Jason just this once.

Mom is shaking her head as she picks up the tray. "Dad's with her but she didn't even want me to come downstairs. I can't leave her." She halts at the doorway and the tray shakes ever so slightly in her hands. "I can't bear the thought of Jason going another week without seeing someone who loves him." She lifts her gaze to mine. "Will you still go?"

She's not looking at me; I don't think she wants to chance seeing an expression on my face that contradicts the words we both know I have to say. "Of course I'll still go."

Mom's relief is palpable. She sets the tray down again and crosses to me to press a kiss against my temple. "Tell your

brother I promise I'll be there next week. And tell him—"
she cuts off at the retching sound we hear from upstairs
followed by a pitifully weak call for Mom.

"I'll tell Jason you love him," I say, lifting the tray and
handing it back to Mom. "Go."

I've never been to see Jason by myself before. I talk to
him on the phone for a few minutes each time he calls,
but Mom is always hovering nearby, anxious to reclaim
the phone, so it doesn't ever feel private. This will be the
first time I get to talk to him one-on-one—excluding the
room full of other inmates, visitors and prison guards—
since before he was arrested.

I'm trying not to be nervous as I go through security, but
I'm so jumpy and twitchy that I'm amazed no one questions
me beyond normal. But they don't. And it feels faster than
ever when Jason is led into the visitor's room.

I stand to hug him, and for once he doesn't act like a
trained dog jumping back and checking for approval from
the guards. Instead he releases me and takes his seat, his
eyes wide with panic.

"Where's Mom?"

Mom never misses visitations. We were in a car accident
while driving to the prison one time. She swore she was
fine and didn't need to go to the hospital. Our car was still
drivable so we kept going. It was only after visiting Jason
that she admitted to feeling some pain in her left side from
where the other driver T-boned us. Turned out she had a
broken collarbone and a dislocated shoulder. Dad was livid
when he learned about it, but Mom would have endured

any amount of personal pain to see Jason. It took someone else's to keep her away.

I slide back into my own seat across the table. "Laura was up sick all night and still this morning, and Mom didn't think she could leave her."

Jason's expression alters from wide-eyed to pinched brows in concern for Laura, then back to wide-eyed again when the reality of the empty chair next to me settles in. Mom has always been the buffer when things get uncomfortable, the one who changes the subject when I tread too near topics better left alone. But she's not here to keep things safe and neutral, and we both know it.

And after yesterday with Heath, I feel anything but safe and neutral.

There've been times when I didn't want to come with Mom, but this is the first time *I* feel partially responsible for that feeling.

Jason leans back in his seat as far as he can go, his knee bouncing under the table so rapidly that the sound of his heel tapping the concrete floor is almost like a buzzing noise. He's eyeing me like I've got a bomb strapped to my chest and a twitchy trigger finger on the detonator. My strong, brave older brother has never looked so small or so frightened. If I didn't know better, watching him I'd think I'd suddenly caught whatever bug Laura has. The contents of my stomach are churning around like they don't intend to stay inside me for long. So I open my mouth while I still can, but all the questions I should be asking—the ones that torment me at night and keep me half-asleep during the day—refuse to come.

"The car's going well."

Jason's darting gaze stills on my face.

"Yeah," I go on, like his expression is an invitation to say more instead of a wary, painfully hesitant scrutiny. I want that hunted look gone from his face more than I want anything in that moment, even the truth. "I can stop halfway up the hill on Hackman's Road without stalling. Not bad huh?"

The whites of his eyes are still visible around his irises, but he looks slightly less like he might vomit before I do. "That's good. I knew you'd get the hang of it."

"The tips you gave me were really helpful," I say. "And my friend Maggie took me driving to practice. I actually think I prefer driving stick over automatic now."

Jason tries to laugh, but the sound is so strangled that I can't help wincing.

I find myself filling Mom's shoes without even trying. I keep making small talk after that, barely aware of half the things I'm saying or the guarded responses Jason gives in return. I just watch him, waiting for his knee to still, for his shoulders to lower and relax instead of looking like he's trying to push himself through the back of his chair. His eyes take the longest. Even when Mom is there, they never fully lose that tight, overly alert quality, like he has to be aware of everything around him at all times. I see his eyes like that sometimes when I try to sleep at night and it's all I can do not to cry thinking of him alone in his cell.

I've been glancing at the caged clock on the wall as often as I thought I could without Jason noticing, but his eyes don't miss much.

"You don't have to stay the whole time," he says quietly after my last check. "Just drive home slow. Mom won't know."

"No." I lean forward in my chair, barely checking myself so I don't reach for my brother's hand in reassurance. There's no touching of any kind allowed once we sit. "It's not— I don't want to leave early." It wasn't that at all, not anymore. I'm checking the clock because the time is passing too quickly, not the other way around. Short of Laura getting mono or something, I don't know when I'll get another private visit with Jason. I wanted to wait until he was at ease as possible, and the weary yet resolved way he just spoke to me is as close as I'm going to get.

I let my mask slip, the one that smiles too much and pretends everything is normal and fine so I don't risk making anyone feel worse, because maybe this one time he needs to.

"Jase—I really miss you." My voice breaks and I don't care. "I miss you so much, all the time."

His jaw does that thing where it flexes and I know he's trying not to show emotion, which only stokes mine higher.

"It's hard at home, harder than I ever thought it would be."

"Mom said you guys are doing okay."

Mom did say that. Every time we visit she makes sure to tell Jason just how well we're all doing. That's supposed be my job this time, but I can't do it.

Jason's jaw flexes again. "It can't be all bad. I mean you're still skating, and you must be getting ready to go out for the ice show pretty soon. When is it?"

"Next month," I say softly. "But—"

"Wow. That's fast. But you're ready, right?" He tries to smile. "Of course you're ready. You've been waiting for this your whole life."

I cover my mouth to stop the sound that slips through my mouth, the one that sounds perilously close to a sob.

"Brooke—"

I shake my head and draw my free hand under the table so he can't try to reach for me the way he was starting to. The guards are always watching. When I have myself under control I lower my other hand. "I'm not auditioning."

"What do you mean you're not auditioning? Does Mom know?"

"She knows." My tone doesn't leave any room for him to doubt how she feels about it. And it's like I've started speaking a different language, one that he never knew existed.

I tell him about Laura talking so little and leaving the house even less. I tell him about Dad's bursts of anger, not so much at Laura, Mom or me, but just these unrestrained displays of rage the drive him into his workshop sometimes for days at a time.

Telling him about Mom is the hardest, because while I knew Jason didn't fully accept the cheery picture she always tries to paint of Dad and Laura at home, she's been much more convincing about herself. Jason doesn't know about her crying at home, or the tears she takes with her to the shower after his phone calls.

I'm not telling him all this to make him feel bad, I'm telling him so that he'll understand that not knowing is destroying all of us. I'm asking him because I have to know.

"What really happened the night Cal was killed?"

CHAPTER 29

I couldn't have asked my brother anything more horrifying. It's the question I'm not supposed to ask, the question no one is supposed to ask. When Jason confessed, he explained that he and Cal got into a stupid, drunken fight and he made the worst mistake of his life. Everyone accepted the story, but I know there has to be more. There has to be a reason.

My eyes are swimming with tears, and I think it's the first time I've let my brother see me cry since this all began.

"Don't, Brooke." Jason's jaw is clenched tight, but I can see a faint tremor in his chin.

"I have to know," I say, as the first tear slips down my cheek. "I know something happened to make you—do what you did."

He holds my gaze, hard. "There's nothing else to tell."

Another tear falls. Not because I believe him, but because he'd never have had to try so hard to convince me if it were the truth. "I know you wouldn't have hurt him because of a stupid fight," I say again, not blinking under his stare. "I know you. I know you're capable of getting mad and losing your temper. But you get sick at the sight of blood just like me." I'm not even trying to wipe my cheeks dry. "So tell *me* what happened. Tell me why this time was different. Give me something, Jase."

Jason's chin is quivering nonstop at this point. He's trying so hard to hide it, but he can't from me. "We fought. I killed him."

I'm shaking my head.

"Yes, damn it!" Jason hisses at me through clenched teeth, making me jump with his vehemence. He presses the advantage. "I had a knife and when he turned around I stabbed him." He looks sick just saying it. He's still facing me, but I know he's not here anymore. He's back in the woods near the high school. I can see it too, the way it would have looked the summer night Cal died, empty and quiet. Jason keeps talking, slipping into the rehearsed words I remember from his confession.

"He died." His blank eyes have shifted to my right. In the visitation room, there is nothing there, but Jason's face contorts like his very heart is being ripped from his body. I don't say anything; I try not to even breathe as he goes on, telling me things he never has before. "He was just lying there on the ground and his eyes were open, you know? But he didn't look dead, he looked like…Cal." The voice breaking this time is my brother's. "But he wasn't. He was gone. He was dead and I ran after h—" Jason sits up straighter, but not before flinching. "I ran."

My hands clench the edge of the table so hard I expect pieces to snap off. "You ran after someone. That's what you were going to say." I watch awareness trickle back into Jason's eyes. His chin stops quivering but his jaw stays locked. It's almost scary, watching the broken version of my brother transform into the hardened prisoner he's showing me now. "Who did you run after?"

"No one." But that's not what he started to say, and I'm sitting up straighter too. The look in Jason's eyes puts his previously frightened expression to shame. My heart is beating faster and faster.

"Jason, was someone else there?"

He's trying to remain impassive, but it's a losing battle. "No."

"I don't believe you." I whisper it like it's a prayer. "You never mentioned anyone else. Not to the cops or the judge. You never talked about a third person that night."

"There wasn't anyone else."

But I'm only half listening. Fear and hope start entwining together inside me, and he can't kill it with the retractions that start tumbling from his mouth. It's too late. "You have to tell me."

"I already did."

"You have to tell me all of it."

"I told you. You won't listen."

"I'm listening now." My eyes and ears are wide-open. "Why are you lying?"

"I'm not."

He has no reason to lie. If someone else was there then maybe they could explain and I wouldn't have to wake up screaming into my pillow anymore. "Is that why you pleaded guilty?" There. He winces again. I lean across the table. "Are you protecting someone? Or are you scared of someone?"

The blood drains from Jason's face and for a second I think he might pass out, that's how pale he goes.

"You weren't drinking that night."

He says nothing.

"And you can't handle the sight of blood."

He still says nothing.

"Cal was your best friend. I still don't understand how you could have hurt him. Why won't you tell me?"

"It won't change anything." He's drawing in on himself, shrinking before my eyes. Shutting down. I keep repeating his name, louder and more forcefully, but he doesn't hear me. All around us people are starting to turn in our direction. Guards are leaving their posts by the door and heading toward us. And Jason keeps repeating the same three words.

"I killed him."

"Who else was there?"

"I killed him." Jason rises from his seat.

"Who else was there?"

The guards are at his sides, asking questions, but I ignore everything but my brother.

"Who else was there?"

"I'm done," Jason tells the guards.

I'm on my feet now too. "Why won't you tell me?"

"Now?" Jason is half pleading with the guards. "Can I go now?"

I call out again and again as he's led away. "Who else was there?"

My brother doesn't look back.

CHAPTER 30

Only one person can answer all the questions swirling through my head and he's the one person I'm physically barred from asking. So I sit in the prison parking lot watching all the other visitors trickle out, some crying, some angry, others hurrying to escape a reality they can only confront for a couple hours a week. I feel prone to all three and yet I don't start Daphne's engine. I don't even reach for my keys.

I've always had the same questions. What drove my brother to murder someone? How did he overcome a lifetime abhorrence of blood to stab someone to death? Why did he flee the crime scene and come home covered in blood repeating the same thing over and over: *I killed him but I didn't know, I swear I didn't know.*

After the first time in a year I've been alone with my brother, not only do I not have any answers, I have more questions. Who did he run after? Why hide the fact that he and Cal weren't alone that night unless he was scared of something worse than spending half his life in prison?

I glance out the window at the looming gray building with its armed guard towers and coiled barbed wire wrapped around the top of twenty-foot-high chain-link fences. It's not difficult at all to remember the first time Mom and I came here or the way I clutched her hand hard enough to bruise when we went inside. I gasp, sitting alone in my car thinking about seeing Jason trudging toward us, not wanting him to look up, and then feeling my knees start to buckle when he did.

His lip had been split and just barely scabbed over. One eyebrow was sliced open, and his left eye was so swollen that he couldn't see out of it. Mom's hands flew to her mouth but before she could say anything Jason told her in a low, raspy whisper that if she so much as thought about saying anything to anyone he would refuse to see her again. He'd glanced at me through his remaining good eye to make sure I understood that his threat was meant for me too.

He'd said it was nothing, a misunderstanding. But it was months before I saw my brother without fresh bruises on his face and longer still not to flinch each visit expecting them.

As I stare at the prison where Jason is locked inside, the windows start to bead with raindrops, but I can't see them through the tears in my eyes.

I make the drive back to Telford faster than Mom and I ever have. For once, I don't have to pretend not to notice the stares as I walk across the parking lot of Porter's Gro-

cery and through the automatic doors. I make a beeline
for the first person I see with a nametag, a plump woman
with fuchsia-painted lips that turn down as I approach.

"Excuse me, but could you please tell me where Heath
Gaines is?"

"Heath is working right now."

I ignore the frown she gives me as she takes in my face
and the evidence of the tears I tried to wipe away. "I know
he's working right now." I'm so flustered I fail to address
her as ma'am. "I just need to see him. Please."

She purses her lips and rests a hand on her hip, then her
voice softens unexpectedly as she looks at me. "I don't think
you're doing anyone any favors right now. Why don't you
go on home and think about whether or not seeing him—"
him seeing me is what she really means "—is the best idea."

I know I shouldn't be here—I shouldn't be anywhere—
but when I finally left the prison this was where I came.

I glance past her and see the entrance to the back next to
the butcher counter at the end of the aisle and I start walking, ignoring her calls to come back. Heath is a stock clerk,
so that's where he'll be. I brush past the hanging plastic
streamers in the doorway, barely glancing at the Employees
Only sign as I do.

Boxes line hulking industrial rows of shelving that extend nearly to the ceiling. There are a few guys who turn
in my direction when I enter, but I see only one.

Heath's brows draw together as I approach. For the first
time since I left the prison, I falter. How many people saw
me outside? How many more heard me ask for Heath by
name before charging back here? All these people watching

us now are his coworkers, the people he has to see day in and day out, the ones who are going to expect him to act a certain way toward me—a way he's not reacting.

"Is that—" one guy says. "It *is*. That's the sister of the guy who…"

"Brooke? What's wrong?" Heath walks toward me, ignoring all the heads swiveling back and forth between us like they aren't there. He reaches for my arm and searches my face in concern, oblivious or uncaring about the attention we've garnered.

"I should have called," I say, looking up at him. "You could have met me outside or somewhere private." In response, his hand gently rubs my arm, comforting me when I've maybe never needed it more despite knowing he's the last person I should accept comfort from.

"Tell me what's going on."

I open my mouth, but before I can say anything, the plastic rustles behind me and the woman I'd spoken to comes through. Her eyes lock on mine.

"Upset or not, you can't just go walking through any door you please. Come on now." She moves to the side and gestures for me to precede her back through the curtain. "I'm sorry, Heath, I tried to stop her."

"It's fine, Irene," Heath says. "She's my—" He cuts off, glancing at me as if I know how to finish that sentence. I don't, especially not with the rapt audience we've amassed.

I recognize two guys I used to go to school with, including Eddie Leonard, one of Jason's self-proclaimed former best friends who traded in on my family's suffering to stretch out his fifteen minutes of fame with every reporter who came knocking. He was the one who started the rumor about Jason bashing in the car of some guy for asking out a girl he liked when they were seniors. The way he's eyeing me now has me shifting to hide behind Heath, only to realize that only fuels the speculation of everyone around us.

Irene takes in Heath's hand on my arm and the way he's subtly placed himself in front of me, and she sighs loudly. The look she gives him is almost motherly. The one she gives me isn't exactly harsh, but it's disapproving all the same. I realize then that by turning me away, she was trying to spare Heath from exactly this situation rather than outright shun me. And whether or not he's aware of the repercussions that are going to rain down on him from my appearance here today, she has no doubt. "She shouldn't be here."

"It's okay," Heath says. Irene nods, not in agreement, in resignation.

"You can use my office." She spares one last look at me, reproof clear in every inch of her face, before clapping everyone around us back to work.

Heath's hand sliding into mine startles me and pulls my attention back to him as he leads us to a door marked Irene Willis, General Manager. As soon as we're inside and the rest of the world is shut out behind that closed door, I wrap my arms around myself and move away from his touch.

"I'm so sorry for that." I nod at the door and all the people on the other side of it. "I should have thought about what would happen if I showed up here where people know you." *And know who my brother is,* I add silently.

"Irene'll understand, and I don't care about the rest of them." He moves toward me, his brow furrowing when I retreat farther.

"I don't even know why I came," I say. "You're the last person I should be coming to about—about—"

A tendon in Heath's neck jumps, but his gaze on me stays steady. "This is about your brother?"

Looking into Heath's gray eyes, warmth beyond anything I've ever felt before suffuses my body, only to leave me cold and numb the second I lower my gaze. "It's always about my brother, isn't it?" I force my arms down, to release even that small gesture of protection. "What we're doing, what we've been doing... Heath, what are we doing?"

"I never made you show up at that tree." I see his booted feet come into view and I look up. He's close enough to touch me again if he wants, and with Irene's desk behind me, there's no more room for me to back away. His voice is like a caress when he speaks again. "You came 'cause you wanted something from me, same as I wanted something from you. Brooke, I—"

"It is about my brother," I say, stopping the hand he's started to lift to my face the only way I know how. "I told you I was going to visit him today. It's usually my mom and me, but Laura was sick, so Mom stayed home. It was the first time I got to see Jason and talk to him by myself since...since the beginning."

Heath is still holding my gaze, but he's tense now, like he's preparing for a bomb to drop. He's not wrong.

"I asked him about the night, to help me understand."

"Brooke." My name on his lips has never sounded so

loaded, so sad. He's warning me and pleading with me at the same time, and it makes me want to cry as I keep going. I have to tell him.

"It's all I think about. I have the same recurring nightmare of Jason and Cal fighting, only I can't ever make out what they're saying. I can't ever see that moment where my brother—"

"Stop!" I flinch as Heath barks the word out and squeezes his eyes shut. "You have to stop. He murdered my brother. That's all there is, and if you keep pushing for more—" he sucks in a deep breath through his nose and lets it out "—trust me when I tell you it won't help. Nothing helps."

"What does that mean?" He's never spoken to me like this before, like he knows something I don't, and every part of me feels alert waiting for him to explain.

His eyes open and lock on mine. "It means that we have to stop trying to let the past control our future. It means we don't need to keep finding excuses to see each other if that's what we want." He reaches for my hands. "It's what *I* want."

Inside I'm screaming at him. He *can't* want this, me, us. We would be a plague on each other, and if he needs any proof of that all I have to do is open the door and show him all the appalled faces waiting outside. Or better yet, I can take him home, introduce him to my parents and Laura and watch them recoil and flee, but not before they shatter into a million tiny pieces before our eyes.

Will he take me to prom? Ask his mom to help him pick out a corsage for me? Will our families have barbecues together and sit side by side at Friday night football games?

Will Laura want to tag along on our dates like she used to with Jason and Allison? Will he want me within a mile of him when the anniversary of Cal's death comes around, or will the mere thought of me make him gag?

It's making me gag now, because I know there can be only one answer, and it has nothing to do with what I want. I slip my hands free from Heath's. "Jason told me something today. He tried to take it back and say I was twisting his words, but he made it sound like there was somebody else there in the woods that night."

Heath recoils so fast that I start to reach out to catch him. The look in his eyes, the rapid rise and fall of his chest, and the fists clenching at his sides all but beg me to stop, but I can't.

"I can't let it go, I've tried and I can't. Not until I know if—"

"If what, Brooke? If the real murderer is still out there while your innocent brother rots in prison?"

"*No*, I'm not saying he's innocent. I know he's not, but if it's true that they weren't alone—"

"It doesn't change anything!" He all but yells. "I don't care if there were ten people who saw him do it. He still did it!" Heath grits his teeth. He's trying to calm down, but it has little effect on the temper he has barely leashed. "Do you want to know why the cops never mentioned a third person? Because there wasn't one. Your brother lured my brother to the woods that night—"

I start shaking my head as my eyes well up. "I know what happened. I don't need to hear—"

"—got him drunk, and then, when Cal stumbled or turned around for some reason—"

I shut my eyes, wishing I could shut my ears too.

"—your brother drove a knife into my brother's back, severing his spinal cord so that he couldn't even try to get away!"

My eyes snap open when Heath grabs my arm, not hard enough to hurt, but enough to force my attention where I don't want it. It's the same place he put his hand before, when he was trying to reassure me about showing up at his work. There is nothing comforting about his touch now.

"Look at me! You think I like saying this, picturing my brother dying? He was on the ground, couldn't even crawl away, but he was alive. They found gouge marks in the ground and dirt under his nails from his trying. Your brother is the only one who knows what Cal's last words were. I bet they were *help*, and *stop*, and *please God*, and—"

I jerk free from Heath, my eyes flashing at him. "Why are you doing this?"

Heath's eyes are shining. "Because it was your brother's prints. Your brother's knife. His—" He bites off a word and shakes his head as he tries to keep from losing it in front of me. Heath steps toward me, his voice soft now as his eyes swim with unshed tears. "That's all I need to know. If that's not enough for you…" He takes a step back again, and I can feel the disgust and anger he's so long held for my brother seeping into the space between us.

I suck in a shaky breath, wishing I could tell him whatever he needs to hear to take me back in his arms, but I can't. Every time I blink, I picture Cal's lifeless body, lying on the moonlit grass.

I blink again and see my brother's bloodied hands desperately reaching for the sink as Dad restrains him.

I see my sister crying into a plate of cold spaghetti.

I see Mom sobbing against the white tiles in her shower.

I see Jason in his orange jumpsuit and the lines that fear have etched into his face.

I see that fear swell into outright terror when I pounced on his slipup earlier.

I see Heath's unshed tears and the tight pull of his lips as he looks at me, except he no longer sees *me*—he sees all he'll ever see: the sister of his brother's murderer.

When I leave Irene's office I hold my head high even as I'm breaking inside with every step. I don't make eye contact with any of the employees or the staring customers as I exit the grocery store. It's clear that Heath's voice carried, and when it reached its limit, the people nearest the office were only too glad to pass along the highlights from our conversation. The news will spread faster than a brush fire. I can't outrun it as I head toward Daphne, chased by whispers on all sides.

CHAPTER 31

Mom knows exactly when visiting hours end at the prison and exactly how long it takes to get home. My phone has been ringing nonstop for the past forty-five minutes. Forty-five minutes where I neither called nor answered my phone. Forty-five minutes during which time I know she's been vividly imagining Jason's crushing sense of abandonment because she didn't visit him. Forty-five minutes where his breakdown was so cataclysmic that I can't bring myself to come home and tell her about it. Forty-five minutes where anything could have happened—and in her mind most definitely did happen—to me. Forty-five minutes where I never visited Jason at all but abandoned him and the whole family.

I come to a gradual stop at the yellow light in front of me. My phone is ringing incessantly as she punches redial the second my voice mail picks up. I glance at it each time the shrill, old-fashioned rotary ringtone I set floods the car, but my fingers don't even twitch in its direction. I don't know what I'd say to her or if I could hide the tears still choking my throat. I can't look at the phone when I finally reach one shaking hand out to switch it off. I have to stop thinking about Heath. Then I have to stop thinking about what Jason said. Then I have to think of an excuse to give Mom for being late and not calling or answering my phone.

Then I can retreat to my room and curl into my bed, and if I'm quiet, I can cry without anyone ever knowing.

It's worse than I imagined when I turn past our fence and up the long, red dirt driveway to our house. Mom flings herself free from Dad's arms and sprints down the porch steps, phone clutched in a white-knuckle grip in her hand. I can see the tears streaming down her cheeks while she's still thirty yards away. Dad moves to the top step but no farther, eyes on me, waiting.

I can hear Mom's gasping sobs, and I start hurrying to meet her. I don't have to feign the sick guilt and remorse I feel for having put her—and Dad and Laura—through this. "Mom, I'm so sorry. The screen on my phone shattered and I couldn't answer—" The painfully tight embrace I'm expecting from her raised arm turns into an ear-ringing slap.

"Carol!" Dad calls from the porch as my whole body half turns from the impact.

My hand flies to my cheek, hot and pulsing under my palm as I turn back to Mom. The shock of being struck is blocking out the pain. I've never been hit before, not by anyone. My parents never spanked me as a child and biting was the worst Jason and Laura and I ever did to each other. For a moment it doesn't feel real until I meet Mom's tear-filled eyes.

Every inch of her is shaking. She opens her trembling mouth but no words come out. I'm just as incapable of speech, but I lift my phone and show her the screen, shattered by my heel stomping and grinding into it minutes ago barely a mile from the house. Her eyes dart to it and she sucks in a shuddering breath. I can't help but flinch when she reaches for me, but this time her arms wrap around me and her hand moves to cradle my head to hers. She's saying something, but I can't make out the words through her tears. I hug her back though, and I say I'm sorry over and over again, and promise her that Jason is fine, but I don't cry.

Dad pries her arms from me some minutes later, she lets him, but only because he transfers her grip to him. Once inside, Dad suggests that Mom go wash her face and she nods in agreement, glancing at me so that I see her tearstained face one last time. As she goes upstairs, I move into the living room, wishing the ground would open up and swallow me. I watch Dad's eyes follow his broken wife; I can't keep my chin from dropping to my chest.

The floorboards creak as he walks around the couch toward me until his scuffed workboots come into my view.

Mom may have struck me, but I'm expecting Dad's words to level me for what I've done. Instead I find myself wrapped in his strong arms and held just a little too tightly.

"You want to tell me where you've been?"

"At the prison," I say, trying not to think about how long it's been since Dad held me.

"You want to tell me where else you've been?"

I turn my face into his faded chambray shirt to muffle my voice. "No."

"Brooklyn Grace."

I can feel the rumble of my name in his chest. He hasn't let me go, not one inch, but he will if I don't answer. "I didn't feel up to driving after, so I sat in the prison parking lot for a good while." If my face weren't pressed up against his chest, I'd have missed the sharp inhalation he made. As it is, I feel it like it's the closest thing to a broken heart another person can feel.

"You can't be doing this again. Not to your mom. Not to me."

I nod against his chest and I feel his hand come to rest on my head before he finally releases me.

"Let me see your phone."

I'm still holding it from when I showed Mom, so I just have to lift my arm. His work-scarred, calloused hands, so much larger and capable than mine, carefully take the phone. He raises it beyond where my still lowered eyes can see.

"Looks broken."

"Yes, sir." If his next question is to ask me whether I intentionally broke it myself, my answer will be the same.

"I'll get you a new screen and we'll see if that fixes it."

My eyes lift slowly, until I meet his, the same rich brown as Laura's.

His free hand rises partway, hesitates and then moves the rest of the way to gently brush my throbbing cheek with his thumb. "She shouldn't have hit you."

My chin trembles. "She was worried," I say. "About Jason. And me."

Dad shakes his head once. "No excuse."

Maybe not, but I still understand why she did it. I knew that from the second I walked out of the house to the second I came back, she wouldn't be able to think of anything else besides me and Jason and the fact that she wasn't with us. It would eat at her even while she took care of Laura. She'd probably held the phone in her hands for a long time before she gave in and called me, and then blind panic would have set in shortly after the first missed call, escalating beyond anything Dad or Laura could calm.

There were a million things I could have done to make sure this didn't happen, even if my phone had really been broken the whole time instead of for just the last few minutes. I could have come straight home or stopped anywhere along the way and called. Dad isn't saying it, because my face is bright red from Mom's hand, but he knows same as I do.

Dad's hand returns to his side. "Come on."

I follow him to the kitchen and lean against the island while he gets me a bag of frozen peas from the freezer. The first touch of cold on my overheated cheek makes me pull the bag away, but Dad gently presses my hand to rest it against my face again.

"Your brother all right?"

I hesitate, startled more by the question than the shock of frozen peas. I know he and Mom talk about Jason together, but never with me or Laura. I know it's hard for him, and yet, I can't begin to fathom what it must be like to watch your firstborn child be arrested, ultimately confess to something so unimaginably horrible and then know you might not live long enough to see that child released from prison. The guilt and grief and anger and helplessness must be overwhelming. On top of that he now has to watch Laura pull away from life more and more each day while Mom's forced smile grows equally more fragile. It might be easier to shut Jason out of his heart too, and all this time I thought he had.

It's such a small question, four little words, *Your brother all right?* But I don't miss the way Dad holds his breath waiting for me to answer.

I nod, and with a breath, so does Dad.

"Will you tell her? Not now but—"

"I'll tell her," I say, lowering the peas to the counter, but Dad stops me before I can turn toward the stairs with his hand over mine and eyes my cheek. It feels hot, which I know means it's still red. Mom will be feeling horrible enough without having to see the evidence of her slapping me. I bring the peas back to my cheek. "Tomorrow," I say. "I'll tell her tomorrow."

He nods, his eyes resting on the frozen peas before smiling. "I remember this." His smile grows. "Frozen vegetables on your knees or your ankles. You used to go on when you fell skating. Never saw such a little thing cry so much. But you never did want to quit, did you?"

"No, I never did," I say, wanting to smile and cry at the memories of me and Dad driving home from practice with ice packs or frozen whatever-was-closest-to-checkout-at-the-first-store-he-spotted-on-the-way-home vegetables.

He'd let me cry the whole drive if I wanted to, but he always had me stop before Mom saw me, saying that mommas don't like seeing their babies cry. It hurts their hearts in a way they can't ever forget.

"I miss seeing you skate," he says when I lower the frozen peas from my face. "Loveliest thing I ever saw was you on that ice."

"I still skate," I say, but it's not the same and we both know it. My lungs swell and I have to look away because I'm afraid that I'll see my father cry if I don't.

I'm in bed but awake much later that night when I hear footsteps outside my door, light and soft, and I know they're Mom's. I pull the quilt higher under my chin and wait. There's no tap on the door, no whispered words. There is just silence, long and aching, from her and me, and then the footsteps retreat.

CHAPTER 32

I drive Bertha's ancient rusted form to the edge of the rink, ready to give the ice its first smoothing pass of the day to remove any moisture and impurities that the low humidity air in the rink would have drawn out overnight. Even though my feet won't be touching the ice, my heart, so heavy since the events of yesterday and the quiet empty kitchen I left this morning, lifts a little as it always does. Then it lifts even more when I look up and see Maggie coming through the entrance. Shattering my phone the day before had deprived me of my one last lifeline, and I felt like I wouldn't make it another minute without seeing my friend.

If Bertha's top speed were anything above a snail's pace, I would have skidded with how quickly I stop her. I hop down, waving as I call Maggie's name, though I know she already saw me. We aren't officially open yet, so there's no music pumping through the speakers. If there weren't already a few people milling about I might have sprinted to her and worried about explaining myself later, but there are, so I walk. I round one end of the rink and expect to see Maggie rounding the other so we can meet halfway like normal, but the long walkway in front of the benches and rows of bleachers is empty before me. Then I see that Jeff has waylaid her and my desire to reach her intensifies, for my good and now hers too. Whatever he said to her must have been brief, because he's walking away when I finally reach her.

"I'm so glad you're here," I say, closing the last few steps between us and throwing my arms around her. "I had a really bad day yesterday. And a really bad night. And until now a really awful morning."

Maggie doesn't say anything.

And she doesn't hug me back.

I never feel the chill from the ice when I'm at the rink, but I do now. I pull away and look at her. She removes her aviators to reveal eyes that are red and puffy, like she's been crying all night. And she doesn't have a stitch of makeup on. Maggie would sooner leave her house without pants than set foot outside without doing her eyebrows, but they're bare. All of her is. Something is very, very wrong.

I reach for her hands, concern chasing away—at least for the moment—my own issues. "Maggie, what—"

"My mom was at Porter's Grocery store yesterday," she says, flatly, drawing her hands back before I can grasp them.

My insides start to freeze. Frost seems to lick its way up my legs and arms, converging in my chest and finally encasing my heart in a solid block of ice. All those eyes, all those whispers. I don't know what Maggie's mom heard, but an internet search would have filled in anything she missed. All the gory, seedy details splashed in vivid color on her screen.

I can barely meet Maggie's gaze, and when I do I want to look away. It's more than the fact that she's not wearing makeup; Maggie doesn't look like herself when she's not smiling. I feel the first crack splinter through my frozen heart when her lip trembles.

"All this time you lied to me. Why, Brooke?"

"I couldn't lose you."

"Your brother killed someone."

I start to shake my head, a reflex not a denial, but Maggie makes a choked sound.

"Don't lie to me anymore." Her breath comes in small, sucking sounds, like she's trying not to cry. Or not to start crying again. "You told me he was messed up with drugs." Her voice grows quieter. "All the people in town, Jeff, Elena and everyone here—that's why you don't want me talking to any of them. Not because they're all horrible people who took the wrong side in a breakup, but because your brother killed someone."

I wince, her words ripping into my heart.

"I thought you were helping me, protecting me in real life like you do with commenters on my videos, but you weren't. I didn't know anyone when I met you, and I thought I was lucky to have found the one good person in this town to be my friend."

"I *am* your frie—"

The reproach in her tear-filled eyes stops my mouth.

"You were my best friend, and you've lied to me over and over again since the day I met you."

"How could I tell you the truth? How?"

She shakes her head at me. "You just do."

"I'm sorry." But those are only words, and they mean less than nothing compared to all the lies.

"Would you ever have told me the truth?"

She can see the answer in my face; I don't try to hide it. "I couldn't stand to have you look at me the way everyone else does."

"You didn't give me a choice. Instead you told me who to stay away from and when to keep my mouth shut. You always had reasons too. So-and-so hates me because...or what's-his-face is a jerk because... Maybe it wasn't all lies, but *all* of them? Every single one? I believed you and because of you, I've treated everyone here like scum." She straightens her shoulders even as her eyes fill with more tears. "There are people here that I've literally turned my back on when they tried to introduce themselves. I thought I was being loyal to you. I even felt good about it, but the reality is you made me act like a complete jerk to people who didn't deserve it."

"I'm sorry."

"Sorry you got caught. You just admitted you weren't ever going to tell me the truth, which means that list of people I was expected to write off on your say-so was just going to get longer. Do you get that? You say I was your only friend, but you made sure that I didn't have anyone else either."

"I'm sorry," I whisper, again and again as she goes on. I

can't defend myself, because she's right. I paint everyone in this town with the same brush. A lot of them have earned my low opinion, but not all, and none of them have earned Maggie's. I didn't set out to isolate her the way I isolated myself, but hearing her spell it all out like this...that's exactly what I've done. I don't know which is worse—all the lies, or all the manipulation.

"Stop saying you're sorry." She brushes first one cheek dry and then the other. "I don't want to hear that you're sorry."

But I am, and I don't know how else to tell her. "When I met you I had never been lower in my life. I had no friends, no future, and no hope for ever seeing my family happy again. Everyone in this town knows me by name if not by sight, but *you* didn't. I got to be who I used to be with you, before everyone knew me as the sister of a murderer. I should have told you then, but every time I tried, I couldn't get the words out. It was so nice to be able to spend time with someone who didn't treat me like Jeff, or Mark, or my old friends, but someone who just treated me like *me*. I got so scared that someone would say something to you that I did warn you off people. I didn't lie about anyone though. I did have a bad breakup with my ex-boyfriend after he sold pictures from my diary to a news outlet. And I don't talk to Elena because she set me up to be ambushed by reporters the day Jason pleaded guilty. The people I used to trust and care about...so many of them turned on me that I didn't give the rest a chance to do the same."

Maggie looks sick, and I don't know if she's listening to me anymore as she hugs her arms around herself.

"But you're right, it wasn't everyone." Most days it had just felt like everyone. "And even if it was, I had no right to try to tell you who you could be friends with, indirectly or not." I lift a shoulder. "The truth is I barely know who would give me a smile if I gave them a chance. It's so easy to read hostility in someone's expression when you're looking for it."

Maggie stands there when I finish. She looks ready to cry again. Like I hurt her irrevocably. She takes one shaky breath.

"You really hurt me."

"I know."

She shakes her head. "I don't think you do." Then she turns and walks away. It's only when I finish my shift and get ready to leave myself that Jeff tells me Maggie put in her two weeks.

CHAPTER 33

My family members are scattered when I get home from work, Dad in the basement, Laura in her room. I don't know where Mom is, and I don't feel ready to look for her just yet to give her the blow-by-blow from my visit with Jason.

I trudge up the stairs. Laura's door is shut and so is mine, but farther down the hall, Jason's is cracked just a sliver. It looks like someone meant to shut it and didn't make sure the latch caught before walking away.

Mom is the only one I know who goes in there, and it's not like her to leave the door open even a little. My brows draw together as I head to the room.

For me, Jason's room has never been the shrine it is to Mom, the closed door to be ignored to Dad, or the land mine to be avoided at all costs by Laura. It's my brother's room. I haven't tried to avoid it or seek it out, to keep it from being a space that lets me deny reality or succumb to it.

But it's been a long time since I've gone inside, months, and as I reach for the knob my hesitating hand says I'm not as unaffected by it as I thought.

I push open the door. It doesn't creak—not that I would have expected Mom to let it—and the room is just as it's always been, though neater and better-smelling than when Jason lived there. It's also empty. I wasn't expecting Dad or Laura to be sitting on the bed in the throes of an unguarded emotional breakdown, but disappointment slows my steps as I enter the room. Navy bedspread, white walls, the desk and headboard Dad made. Mom had hung a couple pictures of sailboats on the walls, more to keep with the color scheme than any nautical obsession on Jason's part. He never complained. The only real time he spent in this room was when he was sleeping. Jason was always the type who struggled to sit still. He was always moving, surging from one activity to the next, unable to stay in the same place for too long. I push that thought from my mind knowing that's exactly what he's being forced to do right now.

I trail my fingers over the silky smooth surface of the desk. I can feel the hours upon hours Dad spent planing and sanding the rough wood, the days of layering coats of wax onto the walnut until it gleamed. It looks as pristine as the day Dad finished it, because the only thing Jason ever used it for was holding his book bag. He and Laura were alike in that they preferred to do homework outside on the porch when they could.

Unlike my siblings, I need the quiet, distraction-free

solitude of four walls to focus. From my window, I used to watch the two of them rocking on the porch swing—Jason's long legs propped against the porch railing and Laura's folded underneath her, their matching honey-brown heads bent over books or laptops. They wouldn't talk, just enjoy the quiet company until Jason would slam his book shut and silently declare he was done with a grin. He was always the smartest of us and could breeze through assignments that I later learned took me sometimes twice as long. Laura struggled more, but Jason, when he finished with his homework would, without fail, move down the porch swing and slide whatever papers she was hunched over halfway onto his lap so they could finish hers together. After so many years of him figuring out ways to help her learn, she's better now with schoolwork, but when she does struggle, watching her makes me miss Jason so much I can't breathe.

The bedsprings squeak ever so slightly when I sit. I suck in the stale air, trying not to miss Jason, trying not to feel that sharp pain in my chest, the one that throbs endlessly like nothing will ever be good so long as he's gone. A year ago, I thought I'd lost everything, but in the span of two days I've lost Heath and Maggie too—the one person who had started to give me hope for the now, and the other who had relentlessly given me hope for the future since the day I met her.

I try to smother the sob that slips through my lips, but it reaches my ears anyway, and a second later, footsteps in the hall precede Laura's appearance in Jason's doorway. My sob cuts off before it can take hold of me the way it's promising to. If I've learned anything about my sister since Jason went away, it's not to cry in front of her. She breaks down completely, worse even than Mom.

Laura clutches at one side of the doorframe; the toes of her bare feet almost curl back from the threshold so that not even the tiniest part of her enters Jason's room. I wonder not for the first time how she can dismiss him so easily, decide that a lifetime of love means nothing. I know it hurts that Jason is gone, that we're all of us suffering because of what he did, but we still have a brother. We're still a family who should love each other, strengthen each other, not forsake each other even when everything else is telling us to.

"Why don't you ever come visit him?" I ask her, traces of the sob staining my voice. "He misses you. So much," I say. "You have to miss him too, Laur, I know you do."

She doesn't say anything, but her eyes blink faster.

"He knows what he did was unforgivable, that's why we have to forgive him. He's not—he's not doing great."

Laura's blinking stops and I can see that her eyes are glossy wet. Barely more audible than a whisper, she says, "Mom said…"

I don't have to tell her that Mom sees what she wants to see.

It's a huge ask, wanting Laura to visit Jason, but maybe just coming into his room? That can't be too much, it can't.

I reach a hand toward her. "Sit with me?"

Laura's eyes, which had softened, go wide and frightened now; her fingers dig into the doorframe.

The ache in my chest sharpens. "Please?"

But she won't. He loved her—loves her—so much, and she won't set foot in his bedroom.

"He'd come for you, you know he would. It wouldn't matter what you did. He'd camp outside your cell if they let him, find a way to get himself thrown inside if he could, just so you wouldn't be alone. Remember when he got you Ducky? He worked for Mr. Zellner at the pet shop cleaning cages for weeks, getting up at four every morning before school after we had to give the kitten back because you were allergic. Or what about that outer space diorama in third grade that you dropped and broke the night before it was due? He stayed up all night redoing it with you. He gave you his shirt when you fell and split your pants on the church hiking trip. Do you even remember how sunburned he got? He couldn't go to school for a few days afterward."

My heart is breaking saying these words, every one of them true. They should be breaking hers too, but they aren't. She doesn't let go of the doorframe, and her toes don't slide even an inch forward. "How can you turn your back on him like this?" My head swings down and away, unable to watch her deny him even so small a thing when he would gladly give his life for her, or me, or anyone he loved. And he loved so much.

My gaze catches on the collage of photos tacked above Jason's desk, his one nod to decorating. There are a lot of him with his friends, one of him and Dad fishing, one of him and Laura on the porch swing that Mom took unawares. He's smiling down at her, and you can tell from the lift in her shoulders that she's smiling too. I'm on my feet then, moving to pull it free to show it to her, but when I get closer, my eyes drift to another photo, one that had been blocked by a lamp from my angle on the bed.

I've seen it countless times. Before his arrest it was his profile picture on all his social media accounts and the wallpaper on his phone. It's of him and his then-girlfriend, Allison. She's on his back in the photo, laughing with her arms loosely wrapped around his bare shoulders, and they are both dripping wet from swimming. Jason's face is in profile as he looks back at her, smiling. Seeing that photo the first time, I believed my brother when he said he'd marry that girl. I used to believe Allison felt the same way, and not just about Jason, about all of us.

My hands go to the edge of Jason's desk, supporting my weight that suddenly feels like too much for my legs. Jason said she wasn't in town that night, but would he have told us if she were? Or would he have lied to protect her from the accusations and implications that would have assaulted her if anyone thought she was a witness?

"Brooke?"

I turn to my sister, the photo of Jason and Allison in my shaking hand, but I don't say anything. My thoughts are coming faster than I can sort them. Something happened to make him lose control that night, I know it did. I glance at the photo, at the lovesick boy and the girl who was never far from his side. If someone else was there, there's only one person it could be.

CHAPTER 34

Despite having heard nothing from her for a year, it takes me only a few hours to track down Jason's ex-girlfriend. According to her old college roommate's Facebook page, she's currently working nights to put herself through nursing school just outside Austin. I learned from the same former roommate that she doesn't go by Allison or Ali anymore either, and that her famous waist-length blond hair is long gone too. Knowing all this still doesn't prepare me for the first sight of her through the window of Rosanne's Diner the next morning.

Unlike Allison, *Lissa's* hair barely reaches the shoulders of her cream-and-tan waitress uniform. It isn't golden like I remembered it either; it's duller and a little darker too, like it hasn't seen the sun for a good long while. None of her looks like it's seen the sun in a good long while. She isn't as pale as Jason, but there's a wanness to her complexion that is unsettling all the same.

I watch her for a few minutes, trying to see the girl I knew in the waitress listlessly taking orders and delivering food. She smiles easily enough at customers and coworkers, if with less abandon than she used to.

I can still remember the first time Jason officially brought her home to meet us during their freshman year at the University of Texas. They'd been dating only a few weeks, but it was already clear that my brother was walk-into-walls, forget-his-own-name in love with her. It was harder to tell just how much she liked him in return, but being with Allison made him happier than I'd ever seen him, and a big selling point for me was that she didn't try to pull him away from his family like a few other girls had in the past.

Whenever she came home to visit with him, she was often the one who invited me and Laura to come to the movies or out to eat with them, and it rarely felt like an afterthought. She would even bake with me and Mom while Jason helped Laura with her homework, and afterward seemed perfectly content to watch TV with all of us squished onto the couch rather than slip off alone with her boyfriend—even when he not-so-subtly hinted that he could use a break from his sisters.

Allison loved spending time with us and made no attempt to hide how much she liked being a part of a family. Her own was tragically splintered. She'd been raised by a declining grandmother and had only a much older half sister to otherwise claim as family.

I liked having Allison around and I really liked how happy she made my brother. She and I were very different people, and while we probably wouldn't have been best friends without Jason to connect us, it wasn't long before my brother wasn't the only one imagining a future where she'd become my sister.

Which was why she was the first person I'd called when Jason was arrested.

I never heard back from the frantic message I'd left on her phone that night, or any of the others I left afterward. I know Mom called her too. Allison never contacted any of us, never came to see us. Jason had no explanation beyond that he'd broken up with her and told her to get as far away from Calvin's death as possible. I understood his wish, but I couldn't fathom her leaving then any more than I can fathom it now. They'd been together nearly a year, and yet she vanished without the barest of goodbyes for any of us. She deserted Jason without a backward glance when he needed her the most. I know it would have been hard and I'm not saying she wouldn't have ended up walking away in the end, but she left while there was still hope. I don't know that I can ever forgive her for that. That's all I can think of now as I watch her wave and smile to her coworkers before leaving the diner.

I push open my car door and cross the parking lot toward her. Focusing on the back of her head, I wait until I'm about ten feet away before I call out the name she tried to leave behind. "Allison."

She stops, almost skidding on the asphalt. When she turns there's not so much as a trace of a smile on her face. She shed her expression along with her nametag the closer she got to her car, like it was part her uniform as much as the clothes she wore. The second our eyes meet she freezes.

This close to her, I see more differences. The change in her goes beyond a tired girl finishing the graveyard shift at a busy diner. She looks…she looks how I feel most days. Bereft. I almost wouldn't know her as the carefree girl who stole my brother's heart. This girl looks like someone who's lost something, who still suffers dearly from it. The trudge of her steps, the droop of her head. The girl in front of me looks like she's never been truly happy a day in her life.

"Brooke?" Allison says my name and edges toward me the way someone might when entering a dark house they fear is occupied. She's afraid of me; so afraid her voice is shaking. Then she goes still and deathly pale, her hands jerking closed around the strap of her bag. "Is it Jason? Did he—is he—?"

I stare at her, trying to decide if she's afraid something happened to my brother or afraid for herself. I hate that I can't tell. The former would soften my words while that latter would sharpen them in to spikes; it's the uncertainty that keeps them flat. "Jason's fine." I almost choke on the word, as if he could ever be fine where he is, but I'm watching for her reaction too intently to get hung up on anything more than the straight facts.

Allison's eyes drift shut and she draws in a breath so full it strains the buttons on her uniform. Her grip loosens on her purse strap before she opens her eyes again to find me frowning at her with a lump in my throat so big, it can't be swallowed for all I try. She doesn't move toward me, but it feels as though a part of her is reaching out to me. "I should have called you," she says. "I should have been there. Your mom and Laura— I didn't mean to leave like that, but I just couldn't stay. I—I think about Jason every day. Sometimes he's all I can think about." A tear slips down one of her cheeks. The sight of that one, lone tear now when she couldn't offer any when he needed them clears my throat.

"Then why didn't you? I know Cal was your friend too, but you loved Jason, and you left before he confessed. You left while there was still a chance he was innocent."

Allison sucks in a breath. It's an insignificant sound when compared to the early-morning traffic buzzing by on the road behind us, but I hear it. I see what I've never seen from anyone else after making that proclamation: guilt. I take a step toward her, feeling the strength of conviction in my voice and willing it to still my shaking hands.

"Were you there the night Calvin was killed?"

I could have pulled out a knife and charged her and I don't think Allison would have reacted more strongly. She lurches backward into her car, shaking her head in denial as tears stream down her face.

"No, I wasn't. I wouldn't have—I wouldn't have—" A full, body-racking sob brings her almost to her knees.

I move forward automatically to catch her, and she clutches at my forearms, relying so heavily on me to support her weight that I stumble and nearly go down with her.

"I told him I should have been there." She forces my gaze to hers and brings me much too close to the genuine anguish bleeding from her. Her eyes are so wide that I can count the bloodshot veins.

"Told who—Jason? When did you talk to Jason?" But she can't hear me over the words and tears choking her.

"I should have been there. I could have stopped him, stopped everything. I should have—I should have—"

I have to pry her hands from my arms to get away, staggering back a few steps when I finally break free. She sags against her car, the only thing keeping her from crumbling to the asphalt. "He said someone else was there. It had to be you, it had to," I say before sucking in a choppy breath. "Please, just tell me what happened. They were fighting but something more must have happened, something to make Jason..."

Her mouth continues to gape open and closed, but only sobs come out.

"He won't tell me or anyone, but I know he's trying to protect you. Maybe there was an accident and maybe he didn't mean to hurt Cal and maybe—"

"No," she says, and it's like a million blades slicing up my heart. "He meant to kill him, I know he did. I should have been there. I should—"

"I don't believe you," I whisper in a voice just barely louder than her crying. I move farther away from Allison, and her tears seem to increase with every backward step I take. I believe her tears, I even believe her regret, but I don't believe anything else.

"I loved him," she whispers, not even to me. "I did. I loved him so much. Tell him—" But she can't get any more words out, and I wouldn't ferry them to my brother if she could. She should have been the one telling him she loved him, she should have showed him from the beginning, but she didn't.

It's only when I'm back in my own car, trying for the third time to put the key in the ignition, that I realize my own cheeks are streaked with tears.

CHAPTER 35

The drive home seems much longer. I replay the scene with Allison over and over and I feel just as empty when I get back to Telford. It has to have been Allison who was there, it has to. But if she won't talk to me either... I don't know what to do, and fortunately—or unfortunately—I don't have the luxury or torment of time to spend trying to decide.

I'm a few minutes late for my shift—a first in all the time I've been working at Polar Ice Rink, but Jeff acts like I'm strolling up after a week of dereliction. I thought I was finally starting to win him over after Maggie got hired, but now that she's quitting he's worse than ever. I haven't been able to do a single thing right all day, and he's been only too eager to point out my shortcomings.

The sparkling clean toilet bowls aren't as clean as they usually are.

"I'll clean them again."

The spotlessly scrubbed floors aren't as pristine as when the tiles were laid. Ten years ago.

"I'll scrub them again."

I missed a gum wrapper stuck to one of the trash cans I emptied.

"I'll go back and get it."

I don't give him any attitude. I don't give anyone anything beyond flat, emotionless responses as I trudge to the next task and the next task, all the while listening to Jeff remind me I need to care about my job enough to show up for shifts on time because, in case I've forgotten, I'm easily replaced. This last line is delivered as I rub my aching knees after spending a good hour kneeling to scrape crusted nacho cheese product from where it's been sun-baking on the brick wall outside. Jeff waited until the hottest part of the day to tell me about it.

"Yes, sir," I say. I should be snarling, at least inwardly, but I feel lost and the kind of bone-deep sorrow for my brother that makes just standing exhausting. Outside, the bricks are still warm from the sun I usually complain about beating down on my skin, the same sun that he gets to feel for only an hour a day in the prison yard. My tears feel closer to the surface than ever. Seeing my too shiny eyes, Jeff finally gives me a moment's peace and goes back inside.

I gather my trash and the discarded nacho cartons from the ground and throw them all in the Dumpster. I can tell I'm not alone even before I turn back. I'm expecting to see Jeff stalking back having found yet more fault with my work thus far that day.

I'm not expecting Maggie.

She looks half-surprised herself to be standing there. She's not scheduled to work that day; I know because it was the first thing I checked after Jeff finished initially berating me about being two minutes late. She knows I'm working though, and even if she somehow forgot and was stopping by to grab her paycheck or something, she could have easily come and gone without me knowing.

That's when I notice the black, padded camera bag slung over her shoulder. She watches me take in the bag and lets confusion ripple over my face before she speaks.

"This isn't me forgiving you or saying I'm over what you did. I don't and I'm not. I made a promise," she says, shifting the bag in front of her and checking one of the compartments. "And so did you." There's an unmistakable challenge in the lift of her chin, like she's daring me to back out.

Like Jeff, she's close enough to see my eyes, but unlike Jeff, she doesn't let my barely checked emotions send her scurrying away. If anything, her chin lifts higher.

Mine trembles. I did have that split-second hope that she's here because she forgives me, or at least because she's willing to talk. That hope crashes to the ground, barely limping. "You don't have to film anything. I'm not auditioning."

"I already promised Jeff we would close so he could leave early, since I'm sure he has a date."

I almost want to smile at how neatly Maggie backed him into a corner. "I'm still not auditioning."

Maggie carefully lowers her bag to the sidewalk and shrugs at me. "Why not?"

"You know why not," I say, because finally, she does.

Maggie nods to herself. "Because of your brother."

"Yes," I say, kneeling in front of the brick wall again to continue scraping off dried cheese.

"Because you can't leave him."

"Because I can't leave any of them." Now more than ever, the thought of deserting my family is unthinkable to me. I can't do it. I won't do it. My hand stills. "They need me."

"So you get to love them but they don't get to love you?"

I turn toward her, frowning.

Sighing, she squats down to join me on the ground and picks up a wire brush to start scrubbing another section of the wall. She's attacking it with more aggression than it deserves, and I know most of that is her redirecting that emotion away from me. "Does he even know, Brooke? Did you tell him what you're giving up because of him?"

My scrubbing slows while hers intensifies. I didn't tell him it was because of him.

Huffing, she goes on. "I don't know a thing about your brother." She side-eyes me without stopping her scrubbing. "I looked at one story online, and one was enough."

My ears start to burn thinking of all the stories I read before Dad banned us all from looking at any more. Reading each one had felt like being stripped and publicly flogged. And those were just the ones that reported the facts. The ones full of wild speculation and expert analysis into the mind of a teenage murderer could cause me to break out into a cold sweat just from the memory. I'm too much of a coward to ask which one she read.

"But," she continues, "where is the logic? How does it help him or your family to deny yourself something that you've spent most of your life working toward? You're passing up the chance to skate professionally so you can stay near your family. Are you going to do that with every choice you make for the next thirty years, give or take depending on good behavior?" The air rushes out of me like I've been punched, but Maggie doesn't stop. She tosses her brush down and twists to face me. "Not so nice to think about, is it? Maybe you need to." Finally her voice softens, but with that softness comes the pain threaded through her voice. "Look what you've done since he went to jail. You've cut yourself off from almost everything. Skating was the one thing you held on to, and now you're letting it go too."

"I'm not—"

"You *are*. And worse, you think you're being noble." She brushes one angry tear away with a slap of her hand. "You're not. I bet your brother would hate this."

My heart twists in pain, but Maggie gives me no chance to say anything.

"You say you love your brother—does he love you? Does he? Would it make him happy, seeing you out here like this when we all know you belong in there on the ice?" She lowers the arm she pointed with. "Would your parents be proud of you for this? Would your sister look up to you?"

I want to close my eyes, to block out the fierce expression on Maggie's face. "My mom knows I have to stay here. I may want to skate, but she's right." I start to shake in the humid afternoon air. "Jason wouldn't survive in that place without me and my mom visiting him. My mom would be a mess if she had to go by herself. My dad might never leave the basement, and Laura would find a cage just big enough for her and throw away the key."

Maggie doesn't say any more until we finish the wall and go inside. "Brooke. Do me a favor and skate. Try."

I glance from her to the ice and back again. "It doesn't matter anyway. My friend Anton, the guy who was supposed to skate with me, I told him I don't need him anymore." It was the first thing I did after I left Allison.

"You never needed a partner. Audition on your own. Partner stuff is nice but you don't need it. You know you don't." She sighs. "I can't make you audition. I think you should. I think you're wrong about the people who love you. I hope your brother is one of them. If he is, then I bet he'd love to think about you on the ice, that it would make him happy even if it meant seeing you less."

But she's wrong. Nothing will make my brother happy again, me leaving least of all.

At home I stop midway to the kitchen when I hear Mom's voice. Only it's not Mom's real voice, it's the falsely bright one she reserves for only one person.

"—much better. I don't know if it was the flu or food poisoning, but she's fine and no one else got sick." Pause. "I'll tell her you're glad she's feeling better."

I linger at the foot of the stairs, listening for a few moments from around the corner and wishing that the happy, carefree reality Mom relays to Jason on the phone were the true one.

Mom and I haven't really talked since Saturday, but fresh

off the heels of a phone call with my brother is not the time to do that. When I can tell the conversation is winding down, I tiptoe quietly up the stairs as quickly as I can and into the office to grab the handset before retreating to my room.

I press the button to enter into the call when I hear Mom laughing, hoping it'll cover the sound from the phone.

"Good, Mom. That's good," Jason says. "I just wanted to make sure everyone is okay." It sounds like he swallows. "And Brooke?"

Mom doesn't miss a beat; she never does when she's talking to Jason. "Of course she is." And then, it's so faint I'm not sure I hear the tremor of uncertainty weave into her voice. "Why wouldn't she be?"

Jason passes off this question with an aplomb he could have only inherited from Mom. There are no more pauses and no more wavering words, my heart tries to break in two different directions as they say goodbye.

"I'll see you next week."

"You will." Mom's vow is steel. "I love you, Jason."

"You too. Bye."

"Bye."

I say his name as soon as I hear the click from Mom hanging up. "Jason?" There's a pause, and I think I've waited too long.

"Brooke?"

A sigh of relief slips past my lips. "It's me. I thought you already hung up."

Another pause. "I'm still here." But by the sound of it, he's ready not to be if I say the wrong thing.

"I just—I heard Mom on the phone with you and I wanted..." *Deep breath, don't cry.* "I wanted to say I'm sorry." I bite my lips, hard, as soon as I say the words. I'm not as good as Mom at hiding my emotions from him and the last thing I want him to hear is the anguish clawing at my throat.

"Sorry?"

"For Saturday," I say. "I don't know why I jumped all over you the way I did. I know—I know it's hard for you to deal with me pressing you for answers and explanations that you won't give me. I wanted there to be something you could tell me that would help me understand." My voice cracks a little, but I go on. "I hope you'll tell me one day, but I won't... I'm not going to push you or anyone else anymore." My eyes roam sightlessly around my room, seeing nothing as I wait for Jason's response. It takes a while, and I can't tell what he's feeling from his voice when it does.

"Yeah, okay— Wait, what do you mean anyone else?"

My hand tightens on the phone. "You. I'm not gonna push you anymore."

"Brooke." There a low, alien current in my brother's voice, a warning to tread carefully here. My heart stops and starts in the pause before he says, "What did you do?"

"I couldn't get it out of my head," I say, rushing to get it out and over as quickly as possible. "You said you ran after someone."

There's a sound from Jason's end of the phone, a strangled word that might have been my name again.

"And—and I suddenly realized there was only one per-

son who'd have been there with the two of you, so... I
went to see Allison."

I think he hangs up. I don't hear the phone slam down
or a dial tone, but he's so silent... "Jason? *Jason?*"

Then a breath, a harsh and ragged one fills my ear. "You.
Stay. Away. From. Allison."

My lungs seal shut, not letting a breath in or out.

"Do you hear me?" my brother says, and I can tell that
his lips are barely moving.

I nod, though he can't see me, and then flinch when I
hear something bang from his side of the call.

"DO YOU HEAR ME? YOU STAY AWAY FROM
HER!"

I recoil from the roar that comes through the phone,
dropping the handset in the process, then scrambling to
pick it up again as soon as it crashes to the floor. As though
from a distance, I hear a squabble and inaudible commands
shouting in the background, a grunt that sounds like Jason.

"Get off me! I said get your hands—"

And a dial tone.

I sit on the edge of my bed with the phone lying limply
in my shaking hands, the dial tone still wailing dimly up
at me. *That* wasn't my brother. Denial rings over and over
again in my head. *That wasn't my brother.* I couldn't see his
face; I can't even imagine what it would have looked like
in those last few minutes. My brother's sweet, smiling features wouldn't know how to contort and scream at me. He's
never—he'd never— I half convince myself that another
inmate must have taken the phone from him, because Jason
would never act like he hated me. Like he would hurt me.

My thumb moves to end the call and silence fills my room. I slide down the side of my unmade bed until my back rests against it and my knees are tucked to my chest. The phone weighs my hand down to the wood floor.

Every time my brain starts to turn in one direction, the gears grind to a halt. I try another and again they refuse to turn. Nothing makes sense. Nothing.

CHAPTER 36

I slip out my front door and into Daphne the next afternoon. I know where I'm going—there's only one house at
the end of Mulberry Street, but I don't know what I plan
to do once I get there. I just need to see his face. Maybe I
won't even get out of the car.

But, of course, I do.

I'm smarter about it this time than I was before. I call
him first instead of just bursting inside.

"Hello?"

"I'm outside," I say when he answers his phone.

A moment later, his front door opens and Heath steps
out onto his porch. I feel my heart lurch toward him a second before my feet follow suit. I slow as I reach the bottom
steps, not because my longing to be near him has lessened
any, but because he hasn't taken even a single step to meet
me. His hand is still resting on his screen door.

I thought no one else would be home. He told me before that he usually has the house to himself for an hour or two in the afternoons, and I made sure there weren't any other cars parked out front beside the truck when I called, but now I'm not so certain. I want there to be a reason he's keeping his distance besides the one I gave him last time we were together.

I stop before ascending the steps, looking at the house behind him with uncertainty. It's a nice ranch house, the kind that looks so much a part of the surrounding landscape that one could imagine it growing from the earth alongside the honey locust trees heavily shading either side of the porch. The shingles on the roof are lifting and the stone-gray paint on the siding is cracked and faded in places. There's space though, enough land that the nearest neighbor is little more than a smudge in the distance.

I've never been here before. I had no reason to come before I met Heath, and after...

It suddenly strikes me as every kind of foolish I've ever been to come to his house like this, worse even than bombarding him unannounced at his work. Then, at least, he'd still had reason to want to see me. I may need him now, but that doesn't mean a thing has changed for him.

And this is his house. The home his brother lived in.

"I wanted to see you," I say, feeling the need to at least try to explain myself, though it's as plain as the expression on his face that he doesn't feel the same way. I stand still, my heart high in my chest as though awaiting a pardon or an execution.

Heath's eyes never leave my upturned face. His brows

are drawn together, as unmoving as the rest of him, but then they relax. Just a little, but I see it.

"Come on." He steps back, holding the door open for me to follow.

There's a TV on somewhere in the distance. Heath leaves my side and disappears down the hall to shut it off. I start to follow, but stop when I see all the photos. So many I can barely make out the paint color of the wall behind them. They span floor to ceiling, photos that look to stretch back generations, many of which appear to have been taken in front of this very house. My eyes scan faces that must belong to Heath's great-great-grandparents all the way down the hall to Calvin in his cap and gown at his high school graduation.

"My family is big on photos," Heath says, making me jump. I don't look away though, I can't. I remember Cal, but distantly, the way you remember a face you saw only a few times and didn't realize at the time it was important. And it was impossible not to see his face plastered online and on TV, but it was usually the same one or two photos. I never watched long enough to see more. I don't have the option to look away now, and I don't think I'd take it if I did.

Instead, I look my fill, and Heath lets me, offering commentary when I stare longer at one photo or another. He speaks stiffly at first, then with greater ease the longer he talks, as though warming up a muscle long out of use. The more comfortable he becomes, the more uneasy I grow.

Heath doesn't act embarrassed when his voice cracks, and he doesn't turn away. It's the most naked I've ever seen a person and it's hard to watch, hard to hear. Cal has always been a person to me. I never tried to pretend him away for the sake of my brother. I know he had a family, parents, plans for his life that were cruelly cut short. But that knowledge has always been in the background, deeply and profoundly sad, and yet, hard to focus on when Jason occupied so much of the foreground. The perspective is changing now.

Heath and I are standing at the end of the hall now. I can see that the pictures continue around the corner, but these are the last ones of Calvin. High school graduation, one of him standing in front of his red truck, loaded for bear on his way to college. As with many of the photos, Heath and their older sister are in it with him.

"That's the last one of the three of us. My mom was certain we had some from Christmas and her birthday, but—" Heath shakes his head and taps one finger against the glass "—there's just this one."

I turn, watching him watch his brother as he recounts that day, smiling a little here, voice catching a little there. He doesn't jerk away or even start when I slip my hand into his. His thumb grazes over the back of my hand and he keeps going. The story ends, not when it's over, but when Heath is too choked up to go on. His face is a blur in my tear-filled eyes when I tug him toward me, rise up and brush my trembling lips to his.

It's only meant to be a small kiss, a light gesture of the heart when neither of us has words left. But when I would have dropped back down on my heels, Heath's arms encircle me, holding me to his chest while his mouth presses more insistently against mine and I taste our mingled tears.

All the hours I've spent held in Heath's arms practicing lifts, and even the first kiss we shared pale in comparison to this. This kiss is still forbidden, but unlike the hesitancy that accompanied our first kiss, this one is bold, reckless. All the pent-up desire and longing we've both been feeling is unleashed and poured into each other. It's almost frightening how tightly he's holding me, or it would be if my grip on him were any less fierce.

I give in to this kiss and the tears that won't seem to stop. I taste them on his lips. I hear them in the soft sounds of my breathing and his. The rise and fall of my chest and his is the only movement between us as we break apart and our eyes meet.

We're still pressed against each other and every breath I take comes from air leaving his lips. Heath's hands slide up my sides, ghosting over my rib cage, and trigger endless tremors to pulse through my body.

"I'm sorry I hurt you," I say.

"I hate that I hurt you. I'll never do it again." One of his hands breaks free to trail over my shoulder and leave goose bumps along the supersensitive skin at my neck. It takes almost no urging to lift my chin and meet his lips again. To taste, not tears this time, but something infinitely sweeter.

I lose all awareness of time and myself in this kiss, in Heath, in the way I feel in his arms. It goes on forever, flaring up then burning low, but never dying out.

My first sense that something is wrong doesn't come from anything I hear but from something I feel. Heath jerks in my arms as though whipped. His head lifts from mine, and my emotion-fogged vision clears as panic shoots wide in his eyes. I have just enough time to crank my neck around to see two women striding in the front door. One in her early fifties and the other in her early thirties. Heath's name dies on the younger one's lips as she sees us.

"What on earth? Heath Christopher Gaines, who in—" His mother's words end in a strangled choke as Heath drops his arms from me. He doesn't look at me, and an icy cold sensation eats the last trace of our heat away.

Heath doesn't look at me, but his mom and sister do.

I thought I knew that look, the one that curls lips and ensures a wide berth. What I see in Mrs. Gaines's eyes and that of her daughter, Gwen, is filled with so much more than distaste and anger. Mrs. Gaines's arm shoots out to clutch her daughter's when I shift my feet. I thought it was to steady her from the shock at finding me in her house with her son, but I quickly realize my mistake. She's not holding herself up; she's holding her daughter back.

"Her? You're with *her*?" Gwen is looking at her brother like she just walked in on him making a bomb instead of making out with a girl. And she's looking at me as though she could detonate me herself and not blink an eye. *"Her brother murdered Cal!"* Cal's name tears out of her, a twisted, pained screech, the sound almost makes me cover my ears.

Beside me, Heath says nothing, does nothing. He holds his mother's gaze and I can practically feel the shame seeping from his pores.

"Allison wasn't enough for you? First it's your brother's

girlfriend, and now the sister of his murderer!" Gwen chokes. "In our house, in Cal's *house!*"

"Gwen—"

Gwen slaps away her mother's whispered word along with the hand restraining her and starts toward her brother. "Get her out. Get that fu—" the rest of her words are muffled with the wild blows she rains down on her brother when he walks forward to intercept her and I back away. He barely tries to block them, letting her hit him as she screams.

I can't think and I can't look at Heath. I flatten myself against one wall as Mrs. Gaines moves to the other. Our gazes meet. She doesn't scream profanities at me, but there's no hiding that she wants me out of her house just as desperately as her daughter.

I run out the front door, chased by the sounds of a broken family and nothing else.

CHAPTER 37

Clouds of rich red-brown dust billow around Daphne's tires as I hit the brakes harder than normal and throw the car into Park in front of my house. Laura is on the front porch and she stands as soon as she sees me. For once, I barely notice her as I hurry to get inside, numbness keeping all but one thought at bay.

Allison was…Cal's girlfriend?

But I stop on the top step at a sight that I haven't seen in I don't know how long. Laura on the porch swing is common enough, but Laura without her earbuds, without her phone?

"What's wrong?" I ask, my brain skidding to a halt along with the rest of me. "Did something happen?"

"No, nothing. I just—" Without her phone to hold, Laura doesn't know what to do with her hands. She wrings them to the point that I half expect her to draw blood. "I wanted to talk. We never talk anymore."

I blink at my sister. *I'm* not the reason we never talk. I'm the one who has tried over and over again to restore some semblance of the relationship we used to have, and she's shut me down every time. It didn't matter how I cried or pleaded, she always turned away.

And right now, with my stomach churning in sickening knots, I'm the one turning away.

I say something to her as I pull open the door. *Not now,* or *We'll talk later,* I don't even know the words that come out of my mouth and as I hurry up the stairs, I don't look back to see if my dismissal wounded her half as much as all of hers wounded me. I can't think about my sister right now. I can barely think at all.

My urgency to flee and hide deserts me when I reach the hall. *She can't be right about Allison and Cal.* My steps grow slower, heavy as fresh dread hits me from inside and out as I approach the door to Jason's room, fully shut this time. I reach for the knob then flex my fingers before grabbing it and opening the door. My mind has been showing me what I'll see since I left Heath's house, I know it, yet I need to look at it again before I let the final piece lock into place.

Not wanting Mom to notice it missing, I'd returned the photo of Jason with a laughing Allison on his back to its proper place the other day. It's tacked up over the desk, both of them seeming to smile at me as I approach.

Jason adored this photo even though the top of Allison's head is out of frame and there's some random guy photo-bombing in the background. But I never asked him why. It was something in her smile, in the way her hands curled around his shoulders and the tilt of her head against his. A stranger could have looked at that photo and known with complete certainty that she was in love.

Only, she's not looking at my brother, she's looking at the person taking the photo. My eyes start scanning the other photos, searching for   something that itches at the back of my mind. Not quite a memory, more like a space where a memory should be.

There.

It's a tiny corner peeking up from behind his desk. I inch the desk forward then bend down to pick up the fallen photo.

It's the same day. Allison is wearing the same sky blue bikini, and the same white-and-yellow daisy is threaded through the braid in her hair. She has one arm over Jason's shoulder as he holds the phone out in front of them and the other around Cal.

She's not looking at my brother.

Her expression is the same. It's exactly the same.

And the picture's been ripped in half, severing Cal from Allison.

I start shaking all over.

"Brooke?"

I don't answer my sister; I don't even turn to look at her. I can't look at anything save for the two photos in front of me, photos that might finally explain what seemed impossible to me.

"He said there was someone else there that night." I free the first photo from Jason's wall. "He didn't mean to, but he said it. I knew it had to be Allison, but I didn't understand why she'd stay silent." Laura is standing in the doorway when I turn, outside Jason's room, never in. She's shaking too, and that's before I lift the photos.

The words start off slow, testing to make sure Laura doesn't run screaming from the house, then grow faster, surer when she stays. I tell my sister everything about my last visit with Jason, everything about seeing Allison, everything I couldn't tell Heath.

Everything that is starting to make a horrible kind of sense.

Jason loved Allison with every fiber of his being. I saw too much proof of that love for nearly a year while they were dating to ever doubt it. He would have died for her.

He had, I was sure now, killed for her. She was the reason he and Cal fought. And if she'd been there, maybe come upon them right...before. Maybe she ran. Jason said he'd run after someone. That would explain her guilt. Maybe if she hadn't run, she could have stopped it. Maybe if Jason hadn't run after her he might have stayed...there might have been time for him to regret his actions in time to get help for Cal...maybe... I can't think too long about this, or it'll all collapse like a house of cards.

The more I talk, the wider Laura's eyes get, bugging out completely when I start toward the hall. "I have to talk to Allison again."

"No!" It's not the cry that leaves my sister's lips that arrests me; it's her charging into Jason's room and clutching my arm. "Please, you can't go. You can't go. Not you too. Not—" She buries her face in my shoulder, sobs and pleas alternating from her.

The photos flutter to the floor as my arms come up to

hold my little sister, each rack of her body calling a tear to pool unshed in my eyes. Laura's terror is palpable, and with crystal clarity, I understand it. My arms tighten. Laura has already lost one sibling, and I've just told her I'm planning to confront the person who may have driven him to commit murder.

I have to go though, have to know what truly happened that night, but every time I try to release her and explain, Laura redoubles her grip and tears. I've never seen her like this. It's so alarming, and loud, that I'm worried Mom will hear from downstairs.

"Okay, okay," I say, rubbing her back. "I'm not going anywhere. Laura, I promise I'm not leaving."

Her small, tearstained face lifts. "You can't go."

"I won't. Come on, let's go to my room, okay?"

Laura clutches at me all the way down the hall to my room where we awkwardly crawl onto my bed, holding each other the way we used to when we were little and Jason would pressure us into watching a scary movie.

We don't watch any scary movies that night. We watch *Some Like It Hot* and with my sister's head on my shoulder and her silky soft hair under my chin, I almost forget the two photos on the floor of Jason's room.

Marilyn Monroe's Sugar Kane is singing "Runnin' Wild" on the train for the second time that night when I'm at last able to slip out from beside Laura's sleeping form and tiptoe down the hall to Jason's room.

The pictures are right where they fell.

It's after midnight, but instead of going quietly back to my room, I grab my keys and move whisper-quiet downstairs and out the front door.

CHAPTER 38

I don't register a single car, a solitary landmark, not one single person on my way to see Allison, though for all the miles I drive I must pass countless people and vehicles.

The first thing I see is the neon red-and-gold sign from Rosanne's Diner glowing in the night. It's late, after 2:00 a.m. so the diner is even emptier than my previous early-morning visit. But Allison is there. I see her through the windows when I approach.

And she sees me.

Allison wasn't enough for you? First it's your brother's girlfriend and now the sister of his murderer.

That's what Gwen said to Heath. Nausea churns my stomach. He never mentioned her, not once in all the conversations we had, in all the times I confessed how desperately I just needed to understand. Is she the reason he shut me down so completely at his work? Did he know that she'd been there that night? Was he protecting her too? And why? For his brother's sake or his own?

Could I have been this stupid? Everyone I trusted betrayed me. Why did I think Heath would be any different?

Because he was supposed to know what it felt like. We were supposed to be the same.

I physically try to shake these thoughts from my head, though the gut-twisting sickness stays slick inside me as I watch Allison jerkily shove a notepad into another waitress's hands before pushing open the glass door to join me in the parking lot. She never takes her eyes off me, not once.

"I know about you and Calvin," I say. I'm expecting the revelation to send Allison reeling, collapsing to the ground again. I'm not expecting her to slowly close her eyes and let out a breath it feels like she's been holding for years.

"How?" she asks, her eyes still shut.

"I found a photo of you with him." I swallow. "And from Heath."

Allison's eyes fly open as the implications hit her. They hit me too as the memory of being in Heath's arms when his mom and sister walk in crashes over me like a bucket of ice water. And then Laura, shaking and seeming so small in my arms.

Emboldened, I cut off Allison as questions begin to fly from her.

"When?" I say, not needing to elaborate further.

She pleads with me silently, but I don't so much as blink. At last she lowers her eyes to a thin gold bracelet on her wrist. "We didn't mean to fall in love, and we tried to deny it for so long because we both loved Jason too. But it didn't stop, even when we stayed away from each other."

"You didn't try very hard." I pull out the torn photo of her with Jason and Cal, the one where she isn't gazing longingly at her then-boyfriend. Allison can barely bring herself to look at the two halves when I hold them together.

"That's why we knew that we had to tell Jason the truth before—before anything happened. We owed him that much. I wanted to do it by myself, but Cal insisted we face him together. So we did...and..." Allison's lips tremble. "It was awful. He didn't believe us...and then..." Her voice goes hollow. "It was worse when he did."

My eyes squeeze shut thinking how destroyed Jason must have been, not just over losing the girl he loved, but losing her to his best friend, just like Uncle Mike lost Mom. And I never knew. None of us did. He never said a word. I open my eyes and a single tear trails down my cheek as Allison goes on.

"He was so angry. He—he drove his fist through the window of Cal's truck. He started to get sick, you know, because of the blood, but when we tried to help him...he broke the other window."

I feel cold, listening to her recount Jason's violent outburst, remembering the way he screamed at me on the phone. The rumors of his temper back in high school.

"That was a week before Cal died, and he was so upset about what happened with Jason that he broke it off. He said that we were a mistake, and if we'd given it more time apart we would have realized it before we hurt Jason." Her fingers twist tight around the bracelet. "The day before he

died he even told me he was going to look into transfer-
ring to another school out of state. That was the last time
I saw him. I wasn't there, Brooke, but I know..." Her eyes
well with fresh tears. "They met up that night so Cal could
tell Jason he was leaving. The last thing he tried to do was
make it right between them."

It's my turn to stagger this time, shaking my head and
acutely trying to block out Allison's words. "And you were
just going to go back to my brother like nothing ever happened?"

"No," she whispers. "If I couldn't be with Cal I didn't
want to be with anyone."

"You told Cal's brother this?" I ask, even though it
shouldn't matter anymore, even though nothing matters
anymore.

She hesitates, and then nods. "A month ago, maybe. I
was at his house and..."

I almost double over. The day he kissed me. I knew there
was something he wasn't telling me. Why does that hurt?
Why do I care if my heart is breaking when it was already
broken beyond repair?

"I'm sorry, I'm so, so sorry." Allison, openly crying now,
takes a desperate step toward me but I instantly retreat. "I
did love Jason. I did. God help me, I did." She collapses.
Not physically, she keeps her feet, but emotionally she
shreds before my eyes. Her voice is so choked with tears
that I can only make out every other word and have to fill
in the ones I miss.

She had to disappear after Cal died. She blamed herself
for what Jason did that night and she was afraid that if she

came forward and talked to anyone about her relationship with both Jason and Cal, then they might have grounds to add premeditation to the charge. That would have meant life in prison at the very least, and more than likely the death penalty.

She couldn't let the only two people she'd ever loved both die because of her.

Unbidden, pieces from Jason's arrest and arraignment come back to me. Evidence that fits Allison's narrative, things I ignored, things that my happy-in-love brother couldn't possibly have done...but a blindsided and betrayed one?

"I'm sorry...sorry..."

I check the impulse to wrap my arms around her. How can I offer her comfort when she's taken all hope from me? But I can't just stand there watching her cry either. People inside the diner have taken notice of us, of the keening noises coming from Allison; a few have even started to approach the door.

"What can I do?" she asks, tears still spilling down her face.

I shake my head. "I don't know." I don't know what any of us can do. Pushing away the thoughts of her with Heath and the agony Jason must have felt when she chose Cal over him, I look at the broken girl in front of me. "I wanted it to be your fault," I say softly. "But it's not."

She lets out one more sob, one so deep and gasping that it sounds like she's been holding on to it since Cal died.

Mine stays firmly lodged in my throat.

Reaching Daphne, I rest my palms on the cool metal side, gazing at my faint reflection in the glass window, trying to imaging hitting it hard enough to shatter, not once but twice even as I fought nausea over the sight of my own blood.

Then realizing that hitting a window wasn't enough.

My shoulders straighten as I pull open the door and slide behind the steering wheel. I no longer believe Allison was there the night Cal was killed, but someone was.

Someone who actually saw what happened.

CHAPTER 39

I don't know how I survive until Saturday. I work. I skate. I miss Maggie. I can't think about my brother, so I think about Heath until ice fills my veins. And then I do it all over again.

Mom's sitting on my bed when I get home from work Friday night. I know she's been crying. Her eyes are red, but her cheeks are dry and her makeup has been touched up. I don't like that I hesitate in my doorway. I knew we'd have to talk—it's been nearly a week since we've said anything meaningful to each other, and I'm not afraid of her, but still, I hesitate. She sees it and awkwardly stands. She takes a step toward me, pauses, then takes another, and then quicker ones until she's close enough to wrap her arms around me.

For the first time in my life, my arms don't automatically encircle her back. They stay limp at my sides while my eyes prick. I know she can feel how stiffly I'm standing but she doesn't pull away; she strokes the back of my hair.

"Sweetie, I'm sorry. I'm so sorry."

And the thing is I know she's sorry. I knew it the second she slapped me, even before her eyes went wide in horror. All week I've known she was sorry and ashamed. All week I've known I should go to her and tell her it's okay, that I love and forgive her, because I do. I did lie to her. I knew my actions would send her into a panic and that she'd be terrified and angry when I didn't come straight home after seeing Jason. I knew all that, and I didn't even call. I shattered my own phone so I wouldn't have to.

And my arms remain at my sides while she hugs me just feet from where I've hidden her mother's quilt.

For how long, I don't know, but it becomes clear that she's not letting go until I respond. I hug my mother like a stranger and it splinters my heart when I do. "It's okay, Mom."

At last she lets me go. Her eye makeup has started to run, but I've kept my eyes dry by sheer will. She strokes my cheek, my arms, my hands, seemingly unwilling to let go of me entirely after so many days of complete emotional and, in large part, physical separation as well. She sits us both down on my bed and tells me things I already know, things her own mother never said to her.

She'll never raise a hand to me in anger again.

She'll never react without giving me a chance to explain again.

She loves me.

She's so sorry.

So, so sorry.

She can't bear feeling so much distance between us.

Will I forgive her?

I answer truthfully. I believe her and I forgive her, but she's the one who hugs me again and I have to force myself to respond in kind.

It feels like a lie, but I don't understand why.

"Mom," I say, pulling away. "I need to ask you for something tomorrow."

Her hand is immediately cupping my cheek. "Anything."

I take a deep breath. "I want to visit Jason again by myself."

Her hand on my cheek stills then lowers in jerky motions to her lap.

I know what I'm asking, the impossibility of it in her eyes. She'd sooner cut off her own arm than miss seeing her son another week. The fact that I'm asking such a thing, fresh off the heels of her desperate attempted reconciliation no less, it feels cruel. We both know it.

I still ask though.

I have to see Jason alone, and she can't be sitting quietly at another table or even waiting for her turn in the parking lot. It has to be my brother and me, just us.

Mom's eyes are swimming as she looks at me. I'm making her choose, and I've never felt more disgust for myself.

She doesn't say anything.

"We had a fight last time," I tell her, thinking that if I give her a reason, something good and sibling-unifying to think her absence will help bring about, it might devastate her less. "It was stupid, but I need to see him, alone, and make it right."

I can see how tortured she is thinking about my request. Inwardly she must be writhing. I don't think she's going to be able to bring herself to agree, so I do something awful.

"I promise to call this time. Dad fixed my phone so I can call the whole drive back. You won't have to…be upset when I get home."

She makes a sound like her heart has torn in two, a soft whimpering gasp. I blink back tears waiting for her to say the only thing I've left her with.

"Okay, Brooke."

I put my grandmother's quilt back in the attic that night.

CHAPTER 40

Jason stops midstep when he enters the visitation room on Saturday morning and sees me alone at the table. From twenty feet away I see him swallow before the guards urge him to keep moving. After that he practically stalks to me. The first thing out of his mouth isn't about Mom.

"What did you say to Allison?"

I draw back against my seat as he leans across the table, almost glaring at me.

"Mom's fine," I say, finding my spine. "Laura and Dad too. Uncle Mike came for dinner the other night, and he's good too."

Jason's narrow-eyed expression falters, but only briefly. "What did you do, Brooke?"

"What did *I* do?" His continued anger throws a spark that kindles my own temper. "What do you think I did? You let slip about someone else being there the night Calvin was killed, someone you care enough about to protect by staying in this—" my lip curls "—place longer than maybe you have to. Who else is there besides Allison?"

Jason flinches when I say her name.

"I thought it was her because...because..." My anger is doused almost as quickly as it ignited. "I found out about her and Cal."

Jason screws up his face and shakes his head softly while flexing his hand, a hand that I can now see bears tiny white scars along the knuckles. The memory of finding out about his girlfriend and his best friend still visibly pains him, seemingly more so than the memory of smashing a window.

I suddenly feel eight years old again, pleading with my infinitely older brother for...something, anything. I was always asking him do things with me, go places, play games. He could have said no or put me off, but he almost never did, and more than that, he'd make it seem like he was having so much fun. With me.

My heart fractures seeing him now, in this place, fading before my eyes. Even anger isn't enough to rouse him for long.

"Jason, please. You have to tell me. I know it wasn't Allison, but it was someone, wasn't it? Why are you protecting them? Please." I let him hear my voice break, and it makes his face twist tighter, his head dropping to his chest. "You know it's not just you in this place. Mom and Laura, me and Dad, Jase, we're locked up too."

He remembers what I told him last time about Mom crying, Dad retreating and Laura withdrawing, I know he does. But he doesn't know about me.

"I don't sleep anymore," I tell him. "When I close my eyes at night I see Cal dying over and over again. It's never the same, because when my mind tries to fill in the details they don't fit. Nothing about Cal's death makes sense to me. I wake up gasping and crying and there's no one I can talk to, because Mom and Dad and Laura are hurting too much to hear." He looks away like he doesn't want to hear either, but he's the only one who has to. "You never asked why I'm not auditioning for *Stories on Ice*. Don't you care?"

"Brooke, don't." There's a choked quality to his request that normally would have silenced me, but I can't stay silent anymore.

"It's not just about Mom, Dad and Laura." The hand I'm resting on the table strays a few inches toward him. "I hate the thought of leaving them like this but I can't bear the thought of leaving you at all."

I know he's crying. His head is lowered and he's barely moving, aware even now of drawing that kind of attention to himself in this place, but I know my brother.

"Allison made it sound like—she thinks you planned it— I can't believe she's right, so you have to tell me. Please, Jason. Please."

Slowly, so slowly, Jason lifts his head. His eyes are glassy wet, but open. There's no scowl, no anger. There's something else, something that quivers in his chin as he holds my gaze, willing me to see a truth he can't bring himself to say.

"Jase—" I wait for him to say something, to blink or breathe in a way that means anything other than what his face is silently telling me, but he doesn't.

"I died when she told me, when *they* told me." His voice

is like broken glass, sharp and so cutting that I flinch. His hands flex again, drawing my eyes to the scars left from breaking the windows of Cal's truck. "I couldn't believe that she'd do that, that he'd do that. For days it was like living in a nightmare that I couldn't wake up from. Nothing I did helped. I even went to the tree, you know, and cut out our initials with a knife."

My heart pounds, remembering the brutal attack on that tree, the one I'd briefly thought Heath responsible for. It was so savage, full of so much hate, but not for my brother like I'd thought. For Allison's initials linked with his.

"That's where I was when Cal called. He was drunk and said he was leaving but wanted to see me first."

"No, Jase," I say, my lips trembling. He keeps looking at me, so I say it again, quieter. "No."

"I didn't think I'd do it, Brooke, I thought he'd fight back."

Tears run down my face. "You brought the knife, Jase. You could have left it in the car but you brought it with you."

Jason says nothing.

Sickened and destroyed, I stand to leave, but stop to ask the one question that has been plaguing me. "Who was it that you ran after that night?"

Jason's face goes white. "I didn't know she was there. I swear I didn't know." Tears are thick in his throat. "I didn't see her until after, until it was too late…"

I can't say her name and I silently beg Jason not to say it either.

"She hid in my car," he whispers.

I'm shaking my head now endlessly, feeling my heart break over and over as my brother continues his confession. Laura had followed him. She was always following him. Off bridges, on dates, everywhere.

She was there the whole time, she watched him. She ran when he saw her. All four miles home she ran, and he couldn't catch her, he kept slipping from all the blood.

I let out a sob and Jason reaches for my hand. Before he can touch me, the ever-present guards bark a warning. Fingers, just inches from mine, draw back.

Another sob slips from my lips.

"Please, Brooke, please."

I turn my back and all but run from my brother.

CHAPTER 41

I'm early getting home, so early that Mom isn't even expecting my call yet. I slip inside the house and go upstairs
without anyone noticing.

Straight to Laura's room.

When I open the door, she looks up from where she's
sitting on the bed with Ducky in his cage between her
outstretched legs. I don't give her a chance to react before
I'm sliding onto the bed in front of her. I cried myself out
on the drive home. All I feel now is broken. Laura moves
Ducky's cage to the floor.

"I didn't know," I say. "I'm sorry, I didn't know."

Laura stiffens when I reach for her hand.

"No, no, please don't," I whisper. "Not anymore."

I didn't think it was possible to hurt more than I did after
Jason's confession, but looking at Laura, thinking about
what it must have been like for her to have witnessed Jason
kill someone and then have to endure it all alone, I do.

"I'm so sorry, Laura. I didn't know." I just keep repeating the same words until with a full-bodied shudder, she goes limp, no longer holding herself rigid and away from me.

"Why didn't you tell me?" I reach for her hand again, and this time, she lets me take it.

She lowers her eyes, but we're not doing that anymore. I'm not letting us.

"Laura." I say her name softly, but firmly and she looks up.

"It wasn't like he said." Her eyes move between mine, measuring my response. "They didn't fight. Cal—he—" Her voice breaks and her chin trembles.

And then she tells me.

It was only a week into summer, so hot already that she'd been begging Jason to take her swimming every day since he came home from college. He'd told us that Allison had gone to visit a friend and would be coming down in a few days, so Laura knew her time to have her brother all to herself was limited. After putting her off for the third day in a row, never letting her come along wherever he went each night, she decided to go anyway.

It was easy to sneak into the back seat of his car before he came outside, and she was still small enough that she could curl herself into an undetectable little ball on the floor behind the driver's seat.

At first he'd just driven around. He'd pick up his phone as if to call someone then throw it down in the passenger seat. And he drove fast, fast enough that even her thrill-seeking heart grew worried. At last she felt him pull off the road, bumping along an uneven path until he slammed his brakes and threw open his door all in one motion, not even shutting it behind him when he got out.

She twisted enough to see from her hiding spot and recognized the tree by Hackman's Pond. She was about to call out and reveal herself, sure that he'd have to go swimming with her now that they were just feet from the water's edge, but something stopped her. It was more than the glint of the knife springing open in his hand—that was a common enough sight at that tree—it was the way he held it fisted tight as he stalked to the tree. And then she jerked as he made the first blow, not to carve but to destroy. She knew the place he focused his attack on and the names he hacked at again and again, even if she wasn't close enough to see them.

His and Allison's.

And she heard wretched sobs tear from his throat.

She started when his phone rang on the front seat, curling even tighter in on herself as he came back to the car and answered it. She didn't recognize the voice that came from him or the stream of hatred that spewed from his lips when he said Cal's name. She couldn't make out Cal's side of the conversation, only that her brother kept telling him to stop, that nothing Cal could say would ever be enough. But then his voice changed so suddenly that she chanced a small peek through to the front seat. She could see only the side of Jason's thigh and the knife in his hand as he slowly turned it over and agreed to meet Cal and talk in person.

She felt cold and sweaty when he started to drive again, not speeding this time, and he kept the knife open in his hand until he parked again. Rather than toss it back in the glove box, he slid it into his back pocket and kept his hand over it as he walked into the woods.

She didn't want to watch anymore, but as the minutes passed in silence, her fear of something she didn't even have a word for pulled her from the car and into the woods and the clearing she was too young to have ever been to yet.

The heated, raised voices she'd been expecting based on the earlier phone call weren't there. Instead, Cal and Jason stood just feet away, talking, not fighting. Cal was the one talking with real animation, repeating an apology that she could tell he'd already tried to make before. Jason didn't accept it right away, shaking his head and raising his empty hands whenever Cal took a step toward him. Only once did Jason lash out verbally.

"How could you take her from me like that? You always took everything else, but she was mine!"

Whatever Cal said in response was too quiet for her to hear, but the earnest way he placed his hand to his heart and kept his eyes locked on Jason made her think he was making some kind of promise. And after a minute, Jason nodded. His whole body remained stiff, but he raised one arm to clasp Cal's back when his friend moved in to hug him.

Jason was facing away from her, so she saw him slide his free hand into his pocket and pull the knife out. She claims she heard the sound it made when the blade sprang open, though Cal didn't jerk away, not until Jason plunged the knife into his back.

The details grew hazy after that. She remembers Cal stumbling as Jason pulled the knife free, then his whole lower body just gave out. She heard him gurgling as he collapsed facedown in the damp earth. Then she didn't hear anything except her own silent scream as her brother followed his friend down to the ground and drove the knife in again.

Cal's hands were digging into the earth, clawing, as Jason stabbed him a third time. Cal looked up then, caught her gaze and lifted one hand toward her before Jason's knife came down again.

Then she screamed.

Jason saw her.

And she ran.

CHAPTER 42

I want to throw up. I want to throw up. I want to throw up.

My skin has gone clammy and I can't swallow fast enough to keep splashes of bile from scalding my throat. Only it's nothing compared to the tremors racking Laura's slight body.

"I didn't say anything. I didn't say anything. Not when I saw the knife, not when—"

I half expect Laura to stiffen when I move to embrace her, the way I did yesterday with Mom, but she goes willingly into my arms, like she's been as starved for me all this time as I've been for her.

"It's not your fault," I tell her, my tears falling onto her unwashed hair as hers drip onto my shirt. "It was never your fault."

Over and over I repeat this to my sister, trying to hold still and be strong for her, to make her hear the conviction in my voice rather than the bleeding in my soul.

★ ★ ★

It could be an hour later when she stops crying, not, I'm sure, because she's done, but because she's too physically exhausted to shed more tears. For the past few minutes all she's done is tremble as I stroke her hair and murmur word-less comfort. When the shaking fades but I know she's still awake in my arms, I rest my cheek on her head and softly I say, "We need to talk to Mom and Dad."

"No!" Laura flinches away from me, shaking her head almost violently.

I reach for her, pulling her grief-weary body back into my side with only a little resistance. "Laura, you need help." My voice cracks on the last word. "We all need help." I'm so gut-sickeningly ashamed that I could be so blinded to one sibling's pain by the other's. That I tried to guilt her for staying away from Jason when she witnessed it all.

Not the fight or blind-to-reason fit of rage I'd always tried to imagine. Not the shock and horror that trickled back to him and sent him to his knees trying to staunch the blood. Not even him running home for help when he couldn't.

I shudder, and Laura lifts her head to look at me. "I'm afraid."

I want to pretend I don't understand, but I do. From the very instant I knew what Jason was being accused of, I recoiled against it, vehemently and vocally. My brother wasn't a murderer, and woe to anyone and everyone who dared say otherwise. I was terrifying back then, especially those first few weeks, I know I was. And even after he confessed, when not even I could deny that Cal's life had ended by Jason's hand, a part of me still sought to minimize it. I'd been trying ever since to imagine circumstances and provocations that could drive him to kill.

And I'd ignored and suppressed anything that might so much as hint otherwise.

It was true we rarely spoke about Jason at home, but at least with Mom and me, there'd been this undercurrent of denial and sense of injustice, however little we allowed ourselves to look closely at that belief. It had grown more difficult since Heath came into my life, since I was forced to think of the true victim and not just the one I imagined Jason to be.

It's excruciating to let go of something I clung to so fiercely for this long, but as I clutch Laura tighter to me, the pain shifts. It doesn't lessen, I don't know that it ever will, but it becomes distant and far removed from the flesh-and-bone girl in my arms.

"It'll be okay," I tell her.

Laura trails behind me like a wraith as we go downstairs and into the kitchen. She's so silent that I have to keep looking back to make sure it's her hand I'm holding and not just my imagination.

Mom is sitting on a stool at the island, her eyes unblinkingly focused on the rooster-shaped clock on the wall instead of the pot threatening to boil over on the stove. Uncle Mike is on the stool next her, his hand making circles on her lower back as he speaks softly to her. He stills his hand when she starts at seeing us—even after all the time I've spent with Laura, she isn't expecting me home from the prison yet—and Uncle Mike drops his hand like Mom's back suddenly caught fire. For a moment it's all I can do to stare at him.

He twists away and stands, putting a good six feet between him and Mom, as though the distance now will make anyone forget how close he'd just been to her. "Hey, kid. We weren't expecting you home for a spell yet. Your mom and I were watching the clock."

Mom was watching the clock, he means. We both know exactly what he was watching. And somehow, there's room for that to hurt too.

Laura shifts closer behind me as Mom starts firing questions at me. "Why did you leave early? Is Jason all right? Is he hurt or sick? Why didn't you call?"

Instead of answering, I turn my head to the stove. She follows my gaze and then leaps off her stool to turn off the burner and clean up the soup that started boiling over. Uncle Mike makes to help her, but I catch his eye and he wisely stays back. I grab a rag to help Mom and nod at Laura to go down and get Dad.

"Everything's gonna be fine," I tell her when she hesitates, and I see a flicker of her former strength spark in her eyes before she disappears downstairs.

"So," Uncle Mike says, and I can hear the effort behind the lightness in his voice. "Your mom is real anxious to hear about your brother."

"He's fine," I say, turning to put my rag in the sink so I can have a moment without seeing Mom's worried face. "I'll tell you everything when Laura and Dad come up."

"—I'm in the middle of something," I hear Dad say as

he thuds heavily upstairs. "What's so important that your mom needs me—"

"Not Mom," I say. "Me. Me and Laura."

Dad frowns, seeing me, not in anger or annoyance at having been interrupted, but in surprise. His gaze shifts to the clock too, noting the time and the fact that I'm home early. "Is it your brother?" His voice is even, but the muscles in his face twitch when he asks, telling me he's as inwardly afraid of the answer as I am.

Beneath Dad's calm exterior there's always been a despair that shakes me whenever I glimpse it. His only son, the boy he raised to be good and kind, brutally murdered his friend. Mom may have been the one crying in the shower, but Dad has been grieving no less deeply. And for him, feeling impotent to make it better for any of us when he felt it was his job to safeguard us had made it all the more acute for him.

I've always struggled more with Mom. I don't know why but I have. Dad's and Laura's behavior makes sense to me—their guilt and remorse caused them both to withdraw, because they didn't know what else to do. In contrast, Mom threw herself into the futile task of forcing us all together and ignoring our efforts to stay apart, even Jason's. For her it was like nothing changed when he admitted his crime and was locked up except his location. She acts like he's innocent, and I can't help but think I might have seen the truth, seen Laura's suffering for what it was sooner, if she hadn't.

I glance at Uncle Mike, who keeps glancing back and forth between my parents, between the one he so nakedly longs to comfort and the one who'll never let him. He sags when Dad does what he can't, moving to Mom's side and tucking her under one arm.

I've never felt sadder for Uncle Mike.

But then Laura is next to me, and I don't have any pity to spare for him.

My mouth opens and then closes and opens again. I don't know how to say any of this, to explain something that parts of my brain are still railing against.

And that's when Laura does it for me.

She tells them the story she told me about sneaking into Jason's car that night, following him into the woods and witnessing him kill Cal. She doesn't soften the details. She doesn't stop when Dad's knees buckle, not even when she has to raise her voice to be heard over Mom's sobbing.

Somehow it's worse, hearing it the second time, when I can anticipate her words and the blood-chilling horror they'll spawn. And this time I'm afraid, because even though the redness on my cheek has long vanished, I can remember Mom slapping me.

I promised Laura it would be okay, that they wouldn't blame her, but I know with sickening certainty that she'll carry their response from this day to her grave.

And I don't know if it'll be the right one until Dad falls to his knees in front of her, gathering her up like a doll and Mom is only a heartbeat behind him.

CHAPTER 43

The first week of August is hard. Despite the truth being unveiled within my family...we've spent a year strangling that truth about Jason's crime, even from ourselves. One tear-filled night doesn't make it go away.

Things are better with Laura though. We've started meeting with Pastor Hamilton, as a family and individually. Laura and I have been spending a lot of time together and talking late most every night, sometimes until dawn. Sometimes about Jason, but mostly not. There's a lot that has gone unsaid for too long. I don't know if she'll ever be able to do that, to reconcile the endless love she had for our brother with the way she feels about him now. I haven't begun to try myself.

What I have done is skate. Laura says I'm an addict and she's not wrong. I spend hours at the rink, as many as I can despite Jeff's ever watchful and disapproving stare. But Maggie's gone now—she finished her notice, and I haven't seen her since. She hasn't contacted me or shown up with her camera equipment in tow. It hurts to think I've truly lost her too. I know I could try to talk to her again, but I don't know what I'd say. I'm not sure there's anything I can say. I have no defense for my actions.

Jeff's still looking for someone to replace her, and in the meantime he's been filling in himself—driving Bertha, not cleaning bathrooms. But I don't even mind his presence that much, because I've been skating in a way I haven't since before Jason went away.

I work on choreography and jumps, on spins, footwork and combinations. I don't consciously put an audition routine together, but that's what I end up with all the same.

When Laura asks to see what I've been working on, I bring her to the rink one evening when it's not too busy and Jeff is off.

"It's just for fun," I tell Laura as I finish lacing up my skates. "So don't expect perfection here."

With a brisk nod Laura says, "I'm officially lowering my expectations."

I smile, and it feels beyond amazing to see her smile back. And then I'm on the ice where everything always feels amazing. I have to modify my routine a little to accommodate the other skaters, but I still get in some of the more impressive elements and I land my jumps so cleanly that a couple little girls clap. From there I enter into a layback spin bending my head as far back as I can while holding my free leg in an attitude position before grabbing my blade and pulling it up over my head to finish in a Biellmann spin. I didn't stretch as much as I should have before heading onto the ice, so my back protests the extreme bend when I try to hold the spin for more than five rotations. But if Laura notices me shortchanging the spin, she doesn't react; in fact she turns away almost as soon as I straighten.

"Laura?" I call from the ice, before skating to her. She doesn't face me again until I stop at the other side of the half wall.

Her eyes are swimming when she lifts her head. "When I told you before to send in your audition I just—I thought maybe you wouldn't be as good as you used to be."

My eyes dart back and forth between hers. "That's not why I brought you here," I say over the lump forming in my throat. "I wanted to show you that I don't need *Stories on Ice* to still skate." The lump swells. "I don't want it anymore."

She nods, blinking a little too fast. "The audition deadline is in a little over a week?"

"Yes, but—"

"You have to send one in."

For a second I think she's forgotten what that could mean. If they cast me, I'll be touring right after I graduate. Depending on the show, I could be away for six, even eight months of the year. That thought isn't any less painful now that I know the depths of Jason's guilt and that my family has begun the long and difficult journey of healing together. It might be more so. I know just how much Laura needs me, wants me, how much I need her.

"That doesn't matter anymore." I try to catch her eye but her gaze moves back to the ice and the people skating past me, and she sucks in a breath.

"You have to try so I won't feel like it's my fault that your life is over too."

"It is not your fault," I say with enough power behind my voice that she starts. "Any of it." I've been saying that to her nonstop since finding out she witnessed Jason's crime— we all have—but I know she still blames herself.

Her gaze slides back to mine. "But if you don't audition, that will be."

Saturday comes both slowly and quickly. A knock on my door wakes me in the morning, but it's not Mom's soft tap, it's Dad's loud double rap. I dash out of bed to open it, almost tripping when the sheet tangles around my ankle, and find Dad staring down at me.

"You visiting your brother today?"

My sleep-addled brain hasn't fully awoken, but I force my thoughts to clear. I've been trying not to think about Jason and instead focus on Mom, Dad and Laura, but I always knew I'd go back today. I have to see my brother again, to look him in the eye knowing full well what he did. "I— Yes, sir."

Dad nods and turns back down the hall. I call after him. "Is Mom coming?"

"Not this time." That's all he says before heading down the stairs, leaving me to turn my head and stare at their closed bedroom door at the far end of the hall.

I dress as quickly as I can and go in pursuit of Dad and answers, but Laura is the one I find in the kitchen, and the soft whir of power tools coming from the basement tells me Dad won't be joining us anytime soon.

My heart starts thudding in my chest seeing Laura. She's never in the kitchen on Saturday mornings. She knows what those are.

"Where's Mom?" I ask, moving slowly toward the island where Laura is sitting with a mostly untouched bowl of cereal. She jumps at the sound of my voice, kicking my pulse even higher. She can't mean...to come visit Jason too?

Laura reaches for her spoon like it's some alien tool she's never seen before. "Dad said he needed another pair of hands today." She stirs her cereal.

"He what?" I turn to look at the basement door. "When has Dad ever—" I break off when I turn back and see Laura staring at me.

"She's downstairs with him right now, so, you know, she can't go with you today. It's just you."

I join Laura at the island and look at the empty counter in front of me. "So I can see Jason alone."

"If that's what you want." Laura keeps stirring her cereal. "Is it?"

Is it? There aren't any more confessions to extract from him, but I'll admit, if only to myself, that I'm relieved Mom isn't coming. Laura isn't looking at me when I glance at her. I'm glad her only role this morning is that of messenger and not visitor. I can't bear the thought of having to sit by and watch Laura see him for the first time since his imprisonment, or him her.

But the answer is no, I'm dreading this, and the thought of going alone is torturous, regardless of it being the best—and only—of my available options. I move to slide off the stool, but Laura's hand on mine holds me in place.

"You don't have to go. If you don't want to. I think—I think that was one of the reasons Dad needed help today." So I wouldn't have to endure Mom's wounded reaction if I decided I was done visiting my brother, is what she means.

I hug Laura with my free arm. "It's okay. I need to go. I'll, um, see you when I get home, okay?" She's still holding my hand against the counter, and I have to exert a little pressure to slide it free. "It'll be okay."

And when I push open the front door, I find Maggie sitting on Daphne's hood, waiting for me.

"So you don't have to go alone," Laura says from behind me. She gives me a small smile when I glance at her over my shoulder, then shuts the front door.

Maggie has her pink aviators on, the ones that used to exactly match her hair before she dyed it again. The current shade is one I hadn't seen yet. It's a swirl of lavender and periwinkle that makes me think of unicorns. She keeps her sunglasses lowered as I approach, her weight supported by her arms outstretched behind her on Daphne's hood.

"Laura called you?"

"Well it wasn't you."

My neck warms. "I didn't know what else to say."

"So you say the same thing. Again. Until I hear it."

"I'm sorry, Maggie. I really messed up."

Maggie tilts her head down so she can peer at me over the edge of her sunglasses. "That's it?"

"I should have trusted you with the truth and I never should have manipulated you in order to keep it from you."

"You should have and you shouldn't have." She flicks her eyebrows up, indicating that I should keep going.

"And these past couple weeks have been horrible for a lot of reasons—which I will tell you—and not having you to talk to made it so much worse," I say, taking a step toward her. "I get that I deserve this, that it's my fault, all of it, but I really miss you."

Maggie slides forward until she's standing on the ground and takes off her sunglasses. "Laura, she kind of filled me in. I always thought she was a bit of a brat, you know? Barely saying anything when I tried to talk to her." One shoulder lifts. "But she's not so bad."

"She's amazing," I say, looking at Maggie, standing in front of my best friend because of my sister. "I can't believe she called you."

"*You* should have called me."

"I know. I'm just glad you're here. And I'll keep saying it this time. I'm sorry."

"—and you love me, and you miss me, and your world means nothing without me in it."

I smile, feeling my heart swell.

Maggie's expression, close to smiling back, goes flat. "It has to be different. It can't be us against the world anymore. I don't want that."

After this past week, I know I don't either. "I know."

"I'm not saying everyone without exception, but I get to decide who I want to be friends with. No more looking to you for a thumbs-up or -down, Caesar, okay?"

"It should never have been that way," I say past the lump in my throat. Even if Maggie forgives me, I won't be forgetting what my selfishness cost her anytime soon. "What else?"

"Well…"

"Anything," I say, meaning it.

Maggie glances down at her feet. "As much as I'll miss Bertha, I don't think I can go back to working for Jeff again. I can't believe I lasted as long as I did. Another day and I would have done something bad, end-up-on-my-permanent-record-and-affect-what-kind-of-college-I-get-into bad. I can't risk it."

"That's it?"

"What do you mean *that's it*? That's a big deal. I'm throwing you back to the wolves, alone. At least, I'm throwing you to one wolf, and he sucks out loud."

I smile at my best friend and my heart flutters when she smiles back. "I really missed you."

"I missed you too."

It feels like a missing piece of my heart has been given back to me when we hug. But then I make the mistake of opening my eyes and I see Daphne parked and waiting for me. Maggie feels the change in me and pulls back, turning so that we're both staring at my car.

"So you're going?"

I glance at her, unsure how much Laura told her.

"Everything," Maggie says. "She told me everything."

In a way I'm relieved. I don't want there to be any more secrets between me and Maggie, but the old part of me, the part that's been hiding things from her since the day we met, feels uncomfortable, exposed. And woefully unprepared for what lies ahead of me.

Maggie takes a deep breath then moves around to the passenger door. "Then let's go."

"Maggie," I say, loving her but knowing I have to tell her no. "You can't come with me. You're not on the approved visitor list and—and I have to see him on my own."

"I'm not going *in* with you, dummy. I'm staying in the car so I can make sure you go in and so that I can be there, waiting for you when you come back out." Her expression softens along with her voice. "However you come out."

CHAPTER 44

Details from the prison assail me when I walk inside. Acidic disinfectant smells, the soft clanging of keys from guards walking around me, and the squeaking sound of thick black rubber-soled boots on linoleum flooring. Hands and questions and metal detectors. Even the scratch of the pen as I sign in. My nerves are jangling and buzzing like live wires under my skin when I'm ushered into the visitation room. I'm never calm entering this room, but I've never felt so primed to bolt before. Counting cracks in the ceiling or eavesdropping on neighboring conversations, nothing distracts me from the lone door in front of me. When it finally opens, I nearly do run.

I'm not ready to see him, not ready to contend with this new horror, the sure knowledge that my brother committed cold-blooded murder. And yet, as repulsive as the reality is, when I finally see Jason's face, the orange of his jumpsuit bringing out the sallow green in his skin, the startled yet relief-filled look in his eyes, revulsion is not there. I don't feel it when he sits across from me and folds his trembling hands on the table. His chin quivers once before he starts talking.

"I thought maybe I'd never see you again."

I suck in a breath, not wanting to admit that I'd had the same thought. Even now I don't know what to say to him. It hurts. It hurts so bad that it makes me want to hurt him, even if it's only with my silence.

Jason's eyes well with tears as he looks at me. "I wouldn't have blamed you. I don't blame Dad or Laura." He chokes saying her name, and my heart clenches in response. "I can't give Cal back his life, not even by spending the rest of mine here. I can only tell you I'm sorry, I'm so sorry." Tear-filled apologies tumble from his lips and my chin starts quivering too. "I killed my best friend and I don't deserve forgiveness for that—" His voice cracks. "I wish I could take it back, Brooke. All of it. I wish Cal was alive and that I was d—"

"No," I whisper, squeezing my eyes shut as my heart threatens to stop. "Don't say that."

He tries to soften his voice if not his words. "He's not the one who should be in a grave."

A tear slips from the corner of my eye. I wish Cal were still alive too, but I'll never wish Jason dead.

Because he's my brother.

And I still love him.

I love him for all the reasons I tried to give Laura—for swimming at Hackman's Pond together, for waking me in the middle of the night to play outside the one winter it snowed in Telford, for putting a frog in my cereal box as a kid so that I nearly screamed the house down when it hopped into my bowl, for telling me I was beautiful when I got my braces, for telling me I was a brat when I refused to wear the scarf Laura knitted me for Christmas, for telling me Mark wasn't good enough for me and that no one ever would be.

The realization jolts me in my chair. It's almost as much of a shock as learning the truth about that night. The two facts don't easily reconcile, especially when I think about Cal's family. One has caused the other the single greatest pain they'll ever know. I feel sickness twist deep in my belly at my own clashing emotions, and a different kind of despair knowing that whatever I had with Heath is over too.

I try not to think about that as I sit with my brother, unable to reach him in every sense of the word as he tries to explain how he ended up standing in front of Cal with such hatred in his heart.

"It's my fault," he says, sniffling. "I'm not telling you this to change that. I'll regret what I did for the rest of my life. I just didn't want to become Uncle Mike."

I draw back. "You—what?" But I think I understand the answer even before he gives it.

"He's been in love with Mom since college, and he swears she loved him back, at first, before she met Dad."

"Jason." There's so much sadness in the way I say his name. "It's not the same. Mom barely dated Uncle Mike, and you and Allison were practically engaged."

"She still chose him."

I don't know if he means Mom chose Dad or Allison

chose Cal, but however much I love Uncle Mike, the future parallel is ludicrous to me. "But you'd have met someone else. You wouldn't have become like Uncle Mike and— and—"

But Jason just looks at me until I fall silent, remembering how he lost it with me on the phone for talking to her.

"I would have," he says it with such conviction that another tear slips down my cheek. "I'd have loved the same girl for the rest of my life, stood beside the man I wanted to be at her wedding, played godfather to her kids while cursing the fact that they weren't mine. I'd have probably become a drunk too when it all got to be too much. I'd have watched her and regretted her with every breath I took."

"You don't know any of that," I say, but the objection sounds weak even to my own ears.

Jason shifts his gaze past me, not focusing on any one thing. "When Uncle Mike used to get drunk and pass out on our couch, what did he always say was the single greatest mistake of his life?"

He doesn't make me say the answer even though I know it as well as he does.

"Letting the woman he loved go without a fight."

Tears are trickling down my face now. "He didn't mean— Jase, he never meant—"

In a voice barely above a whisper, Jason says, "Sometimes I don't know."

I press a hand to my mouth. He thinks Mike wishes he'd done to Dad what he did to Cal? Jason's gaze focuses on me again. The second it does, the tears he's been fighting to hold back start to break free. I'm the one fighting tears now. He can't cry here. I know he can't, even if he's some-how forgotten. And if I cry with him...

"Don't," I say, blinking my eyes dry. "Don't. Jason, you can't."

For a second I think I'm asking too much, that he's reached a breaking point and no longer cares what will happen to him once I'm gone. But then he sniffs again and wipes one eye with his shoulder, a gesture small enough not to attract undue attention.

I exhale.

"No," he says. "I know Uncle Mike never thought about doing what I did. I knew it even when the knife was in my hand." His head lowers so that no one in the room, not even I, can see his face. But I don't have to see him to hear the tears in his voice. "'Cause now I don't have either of them, and the girl I love is as gone as he is. If I'd thought about it even for another day, I'd have realized that I should have loved her enough to want her to be happy, even if it wasn't with me."

I bite the inside of my cheek, hoping the sudden, sharp pain will keep my eyes from welling up again. I want to say something to banish the sadness from him, but I can't do that for him anymore. I know now that I never can. My voice is thick when I finally find my words, and I don't know if they're the right ones but they're all I have. "What you did—Jase—" I swallow down a sob. "It was terrible. I understand now, but I can't—it's not my forgiveness you need. I know you know that. But I love you. You're my brother and I'll always love you."

It's another minute before he can look up at me, and I

need just as long to compose myself. He wipes his face as discreetly as he can, but when he meets my gaze and his fingers twitch on the table in my direction I'm grateful for whatever holds them back. "I want you to sleep at night, Brooke. Will you be able to sleep now...that you know?"

After a moment I nod, but the truth is everything he told me is wrong and sad and I ache so much to change the past for all of us that I don't know if the nightmares will ever leave me.

When visiting hours end, it's with heartbreaking uncertainty that Jason lifts his arms.

I don't have to hug him, we both know that. It's enough, more than enough, that I came to see him at all. I don't feel ready to embrace him, not when just looking at him has been so hard. I love my brother, I do, but he still did something unfathomably evil. He killed someone, someone he claimed to love, someone whose loss torments someone I care deeply for.

I'm not ready to hug my brother.

But I tell him I'll be back to visit him again next week.

CHAPTER 45

I all but collapse into Maggie's waiting arms when I reach the parking lot. She takes the keys to drive so I can continue to ugly cry most of the way home. She pulls over a few miles before we hit the Telford city line and performs all manner of witchcraft and sorcery on my face so it's mostly hard to tell that I've been crying for the past few hours.

"Thank you," I say, when she refills the makeup bag that she packed in advance with my shades. She apparently knew before I did that forgiving me had been a foregone conclusion.

"Figured you wouldn't want to go home looking like the girl who snot-cried her guts out halfway across the great state of Texas."

My laugh comes out a little more watery than I'd like. "No, I wouldn't."

Maggie shifts in her seat to face me. "I can't even imagine."

I sniff and nod. "It hurts that I could be so wrong about

him, and yet, in a lot of ways I still feel the same. I know he deserves to be in prison for what he did—he knows it too—but I…"

"You still wish he wasn't."

I lift my gaze to Maggie's and see that her eyes are shining. "I know I shouldn't want that, but I do."

"Why shouldn't you?"

That's when I tell her who Heath is to Jason, who he's become to me.

She falls utterly silent.

"I don't know if it would matter if I knew Cal's family or not. They would still deserve justice. I don't want to take that from them and I'll never try to, but I can't help feeling both things—love for my brother, and yet because I've seen Heath's grief firsthand, I feel that too. I feel it now more than ever, because I know exactly what Jason did."

Maggie still says nothing.

So I tell her what happened at Heath's house too.

She has to fix my makeup again when I'm done. And her own.

I think it helps to get it all out. Laura and I have talked endlessly over the past week, about everything except Heath. I'm not ashamed about Heath, but it all felt so impossible in my head that I could never let the words reach my lips. It doesn't feel any less impossible saying them to Maggie, but I don't feel as alone with them.

"What does that even mean Heath was with his brother's girlfriend?"

I drop my head an inch. "I don't know. I don't want to think they were *together*—not that we were, exactly—"

"Brooke."

I sigh. "It means he lied to me. At the very least it means that."

Maggie pauses, then says, "And at the worst?"

I shrug to deflect from answering. At the worst it means he didn't care about me the way I cared about him.

"Are you going to talk to him? Ask him?"

"He just let me leave, Maggie. He didn't try to explain or stop me. I don't think he even looked at me."

"I bet he was in shock."

"I was too."

She tilts her head sideways against her headrest. "What if you guys had been in your house? What if your parents and Laura had walked in and found the two of you? How much would you have been thinking about him and how much would you have been thinking about them?" She sets her hand on my arm. "Whatever the answer is, multiply it by a million, because he isn't the same thing to your family as you might be to his."

She makes me cry again. Everything makes me cry. I know she's right. I knew it even before she said it, but it was easier to focus on him lying to me than to think about what Heath must have be dealing with this past week. Definitely self-recrimination for bringing me into his house, maybe even for letting me into his life at all.

That thought pierces straight through me because, lie or not, I don't think I'll ever regret him.

"I think you should talk to him. If for no other reason than to let him explain. And maybe, tell him where you're at now."

I nod, though I stay silent. I can't imagine seeing him again, telling him anything about the reality I've lived this past week. Whether he can explain Allison or not, I don't think he'll ever be able to just see me again.

I don't know that he'll want to try.

Laura is on the porch waiting for us when Maggie and I pull up. I don't have to ask to know that Mom's absence can be explained by Dad still making sure she gives me some space.

Laura stands when we climb up the steps and I hug her.

"It's okay," I tell her. "It hurts but it's okay."

She nods and wipes the corner of one eye when she pulls away, then turns to Maggie. "Thanks for going with her."

"Thanks for letting me know she needed the company."

Seeing my best friend and my sister together is like a balm on my bruised and battered heart. It makes the decision I have to make crystal clear in my mind. I know Maggie will be all over it and I have to hope it will show Laura that neither of our lives are over.

"I think I want to film my *Stories on Ice* audition," I say. "Will you help me?"

Maggie repeatedly fist pumps the air, then slowly lowers it when she sees me watching Laura's face.

My sister smiles at me even as her eyes fill with tears. "You have to try, right? We all have to try."

CHAPTER 46

Laura lets Mom and Dad know where we're going, and we pile into Daphne as soon as I'm changed. The rink won't be empty at this time of day, and Jeff will likely be apoplectic seeing me show up with my sister—two Covingtons—during business hours, but if I don't do this now, I'm worried I'll lose my nerve.

Thankfully, the ice isn't too crowded when we get inside, and people give me plenty of space once they see Maggie with her camera. The music pumping through the rink's speakers isn't what I'd planned to skate to, but Maggie says she'll strip the audio and add the music in post when she edits the video.

I know my routine; I've practiced little else the past week, but there's a queasy clench in my stomach when I step out on the ice. Or there is until I see Laura's beaming face beside Maggie's. After that, I don't see or hear anything else.

I don't skate flawlessly the first time through my routine. I wobble on my sit spin and the landing on my double toe loop is far from clean. But as Maggie is quick to remind me, she's good for as many takes as I am. So we film the jump again, and I spin until the world seems to turn with me. I skate for the pure, simple joy it brings me. I skate knowing my sister is watching and is proud of me. I skate because my best friend never stopped believing I could. I skate because it's the only thing I've ever wanted to do, and because now, I don't have to feel like I'm trading one part of my soul for another. My family isn't going to wither away if I'm not there to stop it. For the first time in a year we've started growing again.

And I love my brother, but I know now that I don't have to sacrifice my future because of his past. I can show Laura that she doesn't have to either.

I hockey stop in front of Maggie and Laura when I'm done, and I don't need to see their faces to know I skated well. It never felt better, more hopeful. I felt free. I still do.

We're all three of us talking over one another as I sit to remove my skates and tie my sneakers back on, when Laura gasps beside me, followed almost immediately by a similar sound from Maggie. The hairs on the back of my neck rise as I straighten.

Maggie tugs a statue-still Laura to her feet, whispering frantically in her ear to get her to move as Heath walks slowly toward me. He glances down at my untied shoe, then drops to one knee to tie it while I'm too stunned to do anything but watch. He stays kneeling in front of me when he finishes and looks up.

"I never imagined you would look like that." He nods his head toward the ice without looking away from me. "It was beautiful. You were beautiful."

I don't feel beautiful. That gloriously soaring feeling that lifted me on the ice deserted me the second Heath knelt at my feet. "What are you doing here?" I ask, letting the pang in my chest color my voice.

"I found you here the first time and the second. Thought it couldn't hurt to try again." His smile, slight as it is, doesn't touch his eyes.

"Heath."

His gaze flicks back and forth between my eyes. "I didn't know what to say to you." I try to look away but he follows with his head to stay in my sight line. "You were there. It wasn't good."

No it wasn't good but it was real. There's always been this huge, gaping canyon between us, one where my brother and Cal would always reside. It was there under the live oak, back when we needed the rain as an excuse to see each other, and it's still there now. There's no way to reach each other, and the longer we keep ignoring or pretending otherwise, the more people—like his mom and sister—we risk hurting in the meantime.

To say nothing of each other.

His hands, which were resting on the top of my foot, slide up to the bench on either side of my hips, bringing him painfully close. His eyes are all over my face and I feel his gaze like a caress. "But I'm here because I missed you. Tell me you missed me too."

I can't. I can't even squirm away, because that would be

like denying I'd missed him too. "People are starting to notice us." My eyes dart to a woman slowly skating past, as though scrutinizing a car wreck on the side of the road.

"Brooke," Heath says.

I have to drag my gaze away from her even as I feel more and more eyes settle on us. He's staring at me, and only me, in a way that says, unlike me, he never looked away.

"I don't care who's looking. I haven't for a long time."

"You should," I say. "And you do care." I'm not judging him for that day at his house. He did the only thing he could do. I can tell from the way his expression softens that he knows what I'm referring to.

He draws back a little, just a little, his hands moving to the front edge of the bench. "I wish that could have been different. I'm not saying that introducing you to my family would have been easy, but it shouldn't have been like that. I should have done better by you. I tried to explain it to them, you and me, but…" He lets the word trail off. "It's a big ask."

"Bigger than you and Allison?" I expect the question to make me feel small and petty. What does it matter when his brother is dead and mine is gone? But as soon as the question passes my lips I know it's neither.

I'd let myself care about Heath—more than care about him. He was the first person who knew about my brother that I didn't push away. I have to know if I was wrong about him, even now that it's over.

His eyes leave mine for the first time. "It's not what you think."

"You—" I start, and then have to swallow before I can get out the rest. "You never told me about her and them.

And you." I'm glad he's not staring at me, because I can feel my chin quiver. "I told you about my nightmares and all the time you knew—"

"No." His head jerks up. "I never met her until after Cal died. I knew about Allison and my brother because he told me. I knew about his guilt and his love for this girl he thought he had to walk away from, was going to walk away from rather than hurt his friend." His eyes find my face again and the quiver I can't stop in my chin. "I also knew it was over, that Cal's killer was in jail and now I was the one with the girl that I was supposed to walk away from. I would break what was left of my family's hearts—my heart—if I didn't." My eyes prick because I see it, his heart breaking right there in front of me.

"I didn't know I was going to care about you when we met. I didn't know I was going to track down the girl my brother loved—something I hadn't been able to do when it was just my nightmares I was living with, but yours?" His face scrunches up like he's in pain. "I found her number in his phone and asked her to come to my house, told her there were some things of Cal's he'd have wanted her to have." He swallows as if remembering something he doesn't want to and I hold my breath. "She started crying the second she walked into his old room, and I talked to her, grieved with her until Gwen came home."

"Did she even recognize Allison?"

Heath nods. "There were pictures of her on his phone. Nothing bad," he's quick to add. "Just more pictures of her than anyone else. Gwen knew he must have cared about her and decided real quick that I had no business being with her, innocent or not. And it *was* innocent, Brooke."

I try not to flinch when he says my name. I do all the same. I actually believe him, which makes it worse. "You still didn't tell me. That day at your work. I was so—" I close my eyes "—broken, and instead of telling me what you knew—that there was more to know—you let me leave."

Heath shakes his head. "No. I found Allison because I thought she might know something that would help you, not hurt you more. I wanted that for you, and I didn't find it."

It's my turn to shake my head, not in denial but because for every second that passes without telling him about Laura, I'm doing the very thing that I'm accusing him of.

"Hey." Health lifts a hand to cup the underside of my jaw. "It's not us. It was never us, okay? However hard it may be for some people to accept, the crime wasn't yours." He glides his thumb along my cheek. "I was wrong. I was such an idiot to have ever treated you like it was."

Gently, even though I want to do the exact opposite, I tug his hand away, following it with my eyes so I don't have to see Heath's face.

"What if I did," I say, my throat so thick it's painful to speak. "What if I found something that would hurt you more, should I tell you? Should I protect you from the truth too?" I'm still holding his hand, so I feel his tendons tense even though his face is expressionless.

"There is nothing that can hurt me more."

But he's wrong. He's so wrong.

"My little sister...she was there hiding in the woods that night. She—" my voice cracks. "She saw everything. There was no fight. Cal... He was there to tell my brother he was leaving, that he was sorry. Jason led him on, made him think he was going to accept the apology so Cal would come close enough..." I can't say the rest. I don't have to say the rest.

Heath's other hand moves to his head and clutches it. "Did she—" There's almost more air than sound passing through Heath's lips. "Did she hear if he said anything before he died?"

"He didn't say anything." Tears are welling up in my eyes and his when our gazes meet. "I know all this, what he did, but he's still my brother and I'll always love him even while I hate what he did. And I know that means that you and me..." I shake my head. "Heath, I'm so—" I don't get the *sorry* out before Heath has me in his arms.

"No," he says and I feel his lips moving against the crook of my neck. "I don't need apologies from you. I just need you."

Maybe people watch us, maybe they whisper and gasp. Maybe they skate by without noticing us, or not caring if they do. The only thing I know is that Heath is still holding my hand when I introduce him to my sister.

And he never lets go.

CHAPTER 47

I'm the one who hesitates at our porch once Laura and I get home after dropping Maggie off and saying goodbye—however temporarily—to Heath. Laura halts at the top step, looking back to see I haven't even started the first.

"Brooke." My name isn't a question. She knows why I'm hesitating, but she's urging me on all the same. "No more secrets."

It's what we promised each other driving home. Heath was my last one, and she took it so much better than I expected her to. I owe a lot of that to Heath, for the kindness he showed her even after what I'd just told him. I also owed Maggie. She filled Laura in on how Heath and I fell into each other, how it was strange and not strange at all that we shifted from the connection our brothers foisted on us—one full of anger on his part and guilt on mine—to one of our own making; one we thought no one in our small town or smaller houses could ever condone. And how that blew up in our faces. Heath and I haven't talked about how our families are going to handle the idea of the two of us together, but I know he's right; the crime isn't ours and no one, let alone our families, should punish either of us as though it were.

I'm not expecting to win my parents over easily, and not just about Heath, but when Laura offers me her hand, I take it.

There's no machinery whirring in the basement when we walk inside. I guess that Dad's efforts to distract Mom have run their course, or else he's as anxious to hear what came from my meeting with Jason as she is.

They're together at the dining room table—the two of them, not Uncle Mike—and Dad stands when he sees us. I'm not entirely sure if Laura is up for participating in this conversation with me or not, and I can't force her. I let go of her hand and approach the table, more relieved than I can express when Laura matches my steps rather than retreating upstairs.

Mom is holding a mug, watching us. She doesn't say anything, but her grip on the mug is causing the muscles in her arms to flex to the point that I worry she might shatter the ceramic. Dad must have a similar concern, because he slides the mug free and replaces it with his own much less breakable hand and returns to his seat beside her.

Then there's no more delay.

"He's fine, Mom, Jason's fine."

Her grip on Dad's hand doesn't lessen, and her knuckles are still bone white.

"And so is Brooke," Laura says from my right.

Then, only then, does she loosen her hold. Watching it, I feel an invisible fist relax around my heart, one that I only just now realize has been slowly clenching tighter and tighter since Jason's arrest. I swallow to push down a sudden thickness in my throat. I've always known Mom loves me, and I understood that Jason's situation would demand more of her attention, consume her heart even as it filled it with pain. I never thought I resented or felt slighted by that, but I have. I've had to be the strong one, the one who holds on when everyone else is letting go. The one not allowed to fall, not allowed to falter or hide. The one who was expected to wake up every Saturday morning and visit a prison not always because I wanted to see my brother, but because I couldn't let Mom go alone. I came home today thinking that's all she'd be able to care about—whether or not Jason was okay, whether or not I was going to keep visiting him so that, in her mind, he'd stay okay.

I didn't think there'd be anything else left.

Mom pushes back her chair, rounding the table to my side. My face crumbles as she reaches me.

And I reach back, realizing that while her love and attention may have tipped disproportionately toward Jason, I've never lost it and I never will. Nobody can cry like my mom, but I give her a run for her money today. The truth is appalling—hide in the garage to cry, sob in the shower and weep with her spouse at night unbearable. And not just what Jason did. It's what we've all done this year as a result—hide and ignore and pretend. It feels good to be held by her though, to shore myself up for what comes next. Because things have to change. Laura and I have already started, and the pain is so much more bearable when we carry it together.

"There's something I want to tell you about," I say to Mom and Dad after she's reclaimed the seat next to him. "Someone I want to tell you about. And please hear me out before you react."

They both go painfully still and Laura nods at me to go on.

"I've been lying to you," I say, and the admission makes me want to shrink in my seat but I know I can't. "I've been seeing Heath Gaines."

Mom's hands jerk around Dad's and he seems to stop breathing. "Why?" she asks. "Why would you do that?"

"I didn't do it to hurt you." I shift my glance to include Dad too. "Any of you. I needed to talk to someone about what things are like now, and the last time I tried talking with you…you sat right in that chair and told me never to mention Calvin's family ever again." Mom winces, but I have to keep going. "I could never pretend the way you all needed me to." I focus on Mom. "That he was away for a little while." I shift to Dad. "Gone forever." And lastly I turn to Laura and squeeze her hand under the table. "Or never was. I know we were all doing the only thing we could, and I understand why, but I couldn't. And Heath…" Mom's wince is smaller when I say his name this time, but still there. "He was going through his own issues with his family, and we didn't start out knowing we'd end up help- ing each other at all, but we did."

"He—" Mom clears her throat and tries again. "He let you talk about your brother with him?"

"I didn't try at first. It was more that we talked about what things are like now." I'd briefly mentioned my nightmares during our last family session with Pastor Hamilton, but I didn't want to cause more of Mom's silent tears in this moment, so I say only that Heath has trouble sleeping too. "It's hard for him with people in town too, except it's pity in his case, not…" I don't want to give a word to the way I'm often treated in town. "Anyway it's different but it's also the same in a lot of ways."

It gets easier the longer I talk, not because Mom or Dad relax their rigid postures, but because Laura holds my hand the entire time. It also gets easier because talking about Heath, even to people who've long associated his name with pain, fills me with so much hope and happiness that I can't keep it in anymore. I don't want to.

I see the point in my story where Mom's expression changes from one of disbelief to dimly masked horror and I choke off before she can interrupt me.

"Brooke. No. You can't mean you—not with him— baby, you know you can't—" She casts her stricken expression toward Dad, but he hasn't looked away from me.

"You like this boy?"

When he holds me with his gaze like this, when it feels like my entire fate hangs in the balance, I feel like an animal caught in a trap. Not because he could forbid me from seeing Heath anymore, but because it would devastate me if he tried. "Yes, sir. I more than like him."

Beside Dad, Mom makes a whimpering sound.

"I like him too," Laura says in a quiet voice, drawing all eyes to her. "I met him today after—" She cuts off then, looking at me to know if she just revealed something she shouldn't have. It's not fair to hit them again so soon, but I have to consider it a small victory that no one has fled or stormed from the room yet. I'm not letting go of Heath. It will take time to show them that, to show everyone. But he's worth it. He's worth all of it. But he's not the only thing I'm not letting go of.

I nod my head a little at Laura to let her know it's okay and Mom notices the exchange.

"What?" she says. "What else?" I can see the familiar panic beginning to seep into the edge of her eyes, and I know I can't hold off any longer.

"Laura and I didn't just go skating this afternoon," I say. "She came to help me film my audition video for *Stories on Ice*. I know I said I decided on community college instead, but that was only because I thought—I thought I couldn't go and leave you all, not with everything the way it's been this year." Beside me I feel Laura press her leg against mine, offering silent support. "And with Jason where he is." Mom's lip trembles but she doesn't object. "Jason is where he has to be, but I'm not."

"You haven't seen her on the ice in so long," Laura says, capturing Mom's heart-heavy stare. "She has to try—I want her to try." She starts to lower her eyes, but instead holds them up. "I think Jason would too."

I think, maybe, this is the first time in a year that Laura's said his name out loud, and it has the effect of a tree suddenly sprouting full grown through the center of the dining table. Three sets of eyes turn to her in shock.

Two months ago, the four of us sat around this table and

she could barely look up from her plate, let alone speak even a single word. She's been little more than a shell of her former self since witnessing Cal's murder, and we've all been helpless to watch as she diminished day by day until barely anything was left. Now, her voice is still timid and her chin still wants to drop, but it's like watching someone fighting back from a long, life-threatening illness.

She wasn't fighting before.

It's impossible for Laura's support not to carry weight with our parents, with me too—and not just about auditioning, about Heath too. I haven't told Jason about my plans, but I will. And I think Laura's right. He'll be happy for me.

I stare at my sister in wonder even as I continue talking to Mom and Dad. "I'm still going to keep visiting Jason. It won't be every week like it is now if I join a tour, but I promised him I'd still come. I won't ever break that promise."

I hear Mom's relieved exhalation, and her eyes are shiny again as she reaches for my hand and I meet hers halfway.

"Do you have it with you?" Dad says. "Your audition?"

"No," I say. "Maggie's editing it for me, but I can show it to you when it's done."

Dad's beard twitches and I know he's smiling beneath all that hair. "I think we could all do with seeing you skate again."

CHAPTER 48

Four months later

The porch is empty when I get home from work. It's actually colder in December outside the rink than in it, so I've kept my jacket on driving home—Daphne's heater is… temperamental to say the least. Maggie has been watching endless videos online about how to fix it. I'm close to caving and agreeing to try to fix it ourselves before we both have to start school again—online for me, in person for her, but I might wait until there's actual frost crystallizing on the grass. I am loving the warming lip gloss she got me for my birthday the month before though.

I pull the collar of my jacket tighter against my chin when I get out of the car, expecting the wind to send a chill down my back. Instead, warm arms and even warmer breath envelope me from behind.

"I didn't see your truck," I say, turning in Heath's arms

and pressing my lips against his much colder ones. I shiver for a lot of reasons. He's supposed to be picking up Laura and me for a movie.

"It's in the shop." He finds the warmest spot beneath my ear to press his chilled nose against.

I half-heartedly try to leap away. "Again?" He doesn't let me. And truthfully I don't try very hard. "You're not cold enough to have walked here." I press closer to him to confirm that, and the heat radiating from his chest assures me I'm right.

He stops searching for especially warm parts of me to press the especially cold parts of him against and draws back just enough to capture my gaze. "Gwen dropped me off."

"Yeah?" I say, a strong breeze stealing most of the sound as it rushes past, but I can't blame the wind for the sting I feel in my eyes.

Apart from Laura, our families have been slow to thaw to the idea of us being together. Beyond our initial confessions, we haven't wanted to push the other in our respective families, more so his than mine, because of the pain it still causes. But neither have we withdrawn from each other, so inevitably his family sees some of me and my family sees some of him. Even if it's just looking out the front window when we drop off or pick each other up—usually me picking him up because his truck has broken down.

Maggie has started looking up videos for fixing that too. Heath told her it's never gonna happen.

But his sister driving him to my house... I have no words.

"She made me walk up the driveway, but—"

I kiss him again, smiling against his mouth. She could

have dropped him off a mile away and I still would have felt like cheering. Gwen voluntarily coming anywhere near me or my family is huge, and Heath knows it.

When I finally let Heath come up for air, he's grinning too, and not just from our kiss. I snake my arms higher around his neck. "I think I'm happy right now."

"Yeah?"

I nod. "You?"

"You always make me happy." Then he pulls me closer. "You want to be happier?"

I laugh and start to push him away, not expecting him to let me go so easily, but he does. When I give him a somewhat surprised look, his cheeks flush redder than the chill alone can account for.

"I just made the deadline. I'm now officially enrolled at Howard College. Classes start next week and— Hey, hey." His hands come up to cup my face and catch the tear that slips free. "It's just community college. They literally had to let me in."

"But you had to want in," I say, a laugh bubbling up out of me. "And you did, you do."

"I don't have a major. I still don't know what I want to do."

"But you're awake now, aren't you?" I say, thinking back to that conversation we had all those months ago by Hackman's Pond.

"Yeah," he says. "I think maybe I am."

I wrap my arms around him, and his hands slide to my waist, lifting me off the ground to kiss me. I feel dizzy in a way that has nothing to do with heights. It's too soon when he lowers me back down.

"I'm officially out of time." He nods at my house. "Laura's been checking the window for you for the past fifteen minutes. I think maybe you got something in the mail that you've been waiting for." My eyes widen. "Go on," Heath says, smiling and shoving his hands into his pockets. "Before she sends that bird out to get you."

I start to move toward the porch, then turn back. "Come with me?"

He looks at me, then my house. He has been on the porch before, and even inside once when Laura was the only one home. I think maybe my family is ready, but Heath has to be ready too.

He's not yet, but he will be.

And I know he'll be worth the wait, however long it is.

I give him Daphne's keys so he can enjoy what little heat she puts out and promise to return as soon as I can.

Inside, Laura is waiting for me as soon as I open the door. She shoves an envelope at me before I can even get my jacket off, Ducky swooping from her shoulder to the bookcase because she won't stop bouncing.

"Is it?"

"Yes." She fists her hands under her chin as I look down at the letter in my hands. It's hard to imagine something better than the true smile on Laura's face—one that I'm still getting used to seeing again, or the knowledge that Heath is right outside waiting for me. Behind Laura, our parents also enter the living room, their smiles more timid but no less genuine as they wait for me to open my future.

I'm smiling before I tear open the envelope.

★ ★ ★ ★ ★

ACKNOWLEDGMENTS

"Outside my window, past the blackberry bushes that glint silver in the moonlight, Jake is waiting for me under the sweeping bows of our weeping willow tree."

That was the first line of the short story that eventually became *Even If I Fall*. I wrote it back in 2015 based on the simplest of prompts from my two longtime critique partners, Sarah Guillory and Kate Goodwin: write a summer love story. That seven-hundred-word short story has grown and changed a lot since I first imagined Brooke and Heath, and it would never have become the book you just read without the help and encouragement of so many people.

I always have to start with my agent, Kim Lionetti. I think I sent you about a dozen story ideas when you started nudging me for "what's next" and I'm so, so glad that you saw the potential in this one even before I knew what it could become. Thank you for always steering me in the best possible direction. I can't wait to see where we go next!

To my editor, Natashya Wilson. I didn't hesitate for a second when I was given the chance to work on two more books with you—I would have done ten! You see the hearts of my books and characters and never let me "skate over" the hard emotions. Thank you for bringing out the best in my writing.

To the endlessly amazing team at Inkyard Press and HarperCollins Children's, including Shara Alexander, Laura Gianino, Linette Kim, Meredith Barnes, Emer Flounders, Andrea Pappenheimer and the Harper Children's Sales team, Gigi Lau (thank you for another beautiful cover!), and everyone who has had a role in supporting this book. I'm so glad to be part of this family.

To my critique partners, Sarah and Kate. This book literally wouldn't have happened without you two.

To my awesome friends from the AZYA author's group, including Steph, Kate, Kelly, Sara, Mallory, Traci, Nate, Dusti, Mary, Shonna, Paul, Ryan, Joanna and all the Amys. We're too big to name everyone but I love you guys!

I'll never get tired of thanking my parents, Gary and Suzanne Johnson. Mom, thank you for all the hours you spent teaching me to read when my second-grade teacher said I was failing. Dad, thank you for the endless boxes of books you brought me home every week once I read through everything in the house.

To my siblings, Sam, Mary and Rachel. I thought of you three endlessly while writing this book. Rachel, you're too young to remember, but I loved getting to revisit all those summer days we all spent fishing and swimming at Hackman's Pond.

To my family, Jill, Ross, Ken, Rick and Jeri, the whole Depew family, Nate—because you've been family for years—and the aunts, uncles and cousins I don't get to see nearly enough, especially Brooke this time for obvious reasons.

To all my nieces and nephews, Grady, Rory, Sadie, Gideon, Ainsley, Ivy, Dexter and Os. Being your aunt is my favorite thing in the world.

To my friend, former corrections officer Jill Porter, thanks for answering my many, many questions. Any mistakes are my own.

I don't know if you'll see this, but thanks to my high school woodworking teacher Mike "Mr. D." Drobitsky. I never made anything as beautiful as Brooke's dad in this book, but you could have.

And thanks to all the readers, bloggers (shout-out to Christy from BookCrushin and Nancy from *Tales of the Ravenous Reader*), bookstagramers and librarians who've shown my books so much love. From the bottom of my heart, thank you.